SEDUCED BY MURDER

AF541712

SEDUCED BY MURDER

SAURBH KATYAL

BLUEJAY

Bluejay Books Pvt. Ltd.
A-8/76, Ist Floor
Sector 16, Rohini
Delhi 110 085
info@bluejaybooksindia.com

First published by
Bluejay Books Pvt. Ltd. in 2014

Copyright © Saurbh Katyal, 2014

All characters in this book are fictitious, and any resemblance to real persons, living or dead, is coincidental.

The author asserts the moral right to be identified as the author of this work.

All rights reserved. No part of this publication may be reproduced, stored in a retrieval system, or transmitted, in any form or by any means, electronic, mechanical, photocopying, recording or otherwise, without the prior written permission of the Publishers.

Printed and bound in India

I was glad it was raining. Glad, because it gave me a reason for staring out of the window of my office and appear preoccupied, while the poor lady wept her heart out.

She was crying because I had just given her proof of her husband's affair – the photographs lying on the table, of her husband and her best friend, in various compromising positions. I prepared myself for the uncomfortable task of saying something reassuring.

I began with a feeble attempt to pacify her. "Mrs Singh, would you like some water?"

The hitherto inaudible sobs rose to an embarrassingly high pitch.

"That bitch Seema! I will kill her! We used to play tennis together. How could she do this to me?" she said in between sobs. To my mind, the answer was simple. Seema accomplished this by being twenty kilos lighter. Nevertheless, I maintained my silence and nodded sympathetically.

The rain ceased, forcing me to stop staring outside. I glanced at my watch and realised it had been over half an hour since I had shown her the pictures. It was time to bring up the subject of the remainder of my fee. As per the contract, seventy five percent of my fee would be payable on submitting conclusive evidence. This was my tenth extramarital affair case since I had become a detective, and each time I was confounded by the seemingly simple task of bringing up the subject of my fee with some poor lady who had just discovered the infidelity of her spouse.

At the same time, I had learned from previous experience that if the disturbed wife left the office without paying, I might as well kiss my fee goodbye. The actions of an emotional woman were only as predictable as the actions of the Indian cricket team during a series.

I got up from my chair and walked towards her. I stood behind her, whispered a few words of empathy, and placed my hands on her shoulder. The closing act was always crucial. If successful, it would get me an endorsement at her next kitty party or aerobics class. Nothing spectacular, but something modest like, "It was the most trying time of my life! Thank God for Vishal Bajaj, the detective I hired. I don't know what I would have done without him. He's the man for all jobs – discreet, charming, and cute too!" I used my fingers to massage her shoulders. Being hasty while discussing the fee was always a mistake from a repeat-business perspective. Cheating-husband jobs were my core competency. My jealous competitors had given me the sobriquet *toy boy*. The more crass ones called me a gigolo.

Last week, a lady had walked into Eagle Eye Detective Agency just across the street, and asked for me. They tried to inveigle her into appointing them but it was Vishal Bajaj whom she wanted (and whom she got). Such occurrences were common, and my competitors retaliated by spreading rumours about my promiscuity.

But they were just that – rumours. On principle, I never got cosy with any of my female clients. There were times when the ladies themselves tried to seduce me but I maintained a strict client-detective relationship. I saw my job as an honourable one. I was like an alchemist, transforming women with low self-esteem into beings filled with hope and optimism; counselling rich, middle aged, jilted wives to cope with the fact that they were no longer attractive to their husbands.

I felt her shoulders relax under my fingers. She had finally stopped sobbing. I said softly, "Mrs Singh, there is the subject of my pending fee."

I wished she would pay and leave. The post-mortem of a case usually involves a deluge of emotions and, as I often say to my second-in-command, Pranay, "Too many emotions give me loose motions."

Mrs Singh was silent for a few seconds.

Then she asked, "Do you think I am attractive, Vishal?"

Uh-oh.

"Of course, Mrs Singh! I find you quite attractive. Your husband is unfortunate not to cherish a lady like you."

"Let's go out somewhere and spend time together. I am very lonely."

The conviction with which she said that terrorised me. The expression on my face must have been evident because she started sobbing again.

"You don't like me, do you? I am old and ugly."

"No, no, Mrs Singh, you are definitely a very attractive lady," I mumbled. "But you are confused and hurt right now, and I would never take advantage of you in this state.

"You are a woman of character, and you will have to be strong and clear-headed to get through this. I know your husband is concerned about his social standing; I recommend that you confront him with the pictures and demand an explanation ....”

I was glad I had worn a clean shirt because Mrs Singh had started sobbing again, using my shirt as a tissue.

Mrs Singh had wrapped her arms around my waist. She had stopped sobbing, and I waited for her to release me. I was acutely aware of her ample breasts resting against my thighs. The heat from her breasts was transmitting to Junior’s territory. I panicked, and gently tried to unclasp her hands to break the embrace, but she held on. It was too late. Junior sprung up in interest. I felt Mrs Singh stiffen as she felt the movement in my trousers.

I tried to discourage Junior by thinking of something repulsive. Rats – big, thick jungle rats. I had seen that on Discovery Channel. But Junior extended to his full length. I pushed her shoulders back so that her breasts would stop ironing my trousers. She leaned back and looked up at me coyly.

I glanced down, and my eyes were drawn to her cleavage. I could see two milky globes clasped in a black brassiere. I tore my eyes away and smiled weakly. She smiled coquettishly, her big brown eyes reflecting her anticipation, her ripe-red lips opening slightly.

I was beet red with embarrassment, and said quickly, “You want to let go of me? I think I need a glass of water.”

She held on and asked, “You’re sure you don’t want to come with me for a drink?”

I feigned confusion at her words, and raised my eyebrows in a *what is going on* gesture. She responded by indicating *whatever Junior wants*. Junior interpreted the signal faster than my brain could, and threatened to disown me if I let this opportunity go away. I admonished him, reminding him of the golden principle of Hunt Detective Agency, *never breed with the feed.*

I forcibly unclasped her wrists, went and sat on my chair, and let a few awkward seconds pass.

She took the initiative. "I guess there is no use crying over spilt milk. We had ten years of a happy married life. And men and dogs will always go where the meat is."

I smiled to accentuate my dimples.

"I am glad you are taking this in the right spirit. Life goes on. Take him, or dump him. The power is within you, Mrs Singh."

"Call me Preeti, please."

She definitely didn't feel old and ugly now. It took me five minutes to cajole Preeti into leaving my office. I promised to keep in touch, and escorted her out of my cabin into the able hands of Aarti, my secretary. Aarti had been the victim of an abusive marriage, and had divorced her husband after two long, torturous years. I returned to my cabin with a sigh of relief.

It was only ten minutes after Mrs Singh had left that I realised I had not collected the balance fee. I was too insouciant to regret that. It was noon, and I decided to call it a day.

I went to my desk and took out a half empty bottle of Scotch from the drawer. All that stuff you read about detectives having microphones, guns, and other fancy gadgets in the drawers, is strictly for the cows. Just like the eyewash they show in the movies – detectives leading a life of action and adventure. The only action we ever get is killing mosquitoes during an all-night watch. Our preferred choice of weapon is a spray can of mosquito repellent, and a steel flask of whisky. Most detectives die young, not from gunshots, but because of a pickled liver, or malaria. It's a shitty life, but you get to be your own boss.

I poured a generous amount of Scotch into the coffee mug. I went to stand by the window, letting the ice melt in the Scotch. The phone rang. Credit card companies didn't call on Sunday afternoon. It had to be a potential client. I kept the glass on the window sill, and picked it up after a few rings and said sharply, "Hello, Hunt Detective Agency."

There was a pause. New clients often find themselves at a loss for words when they actually hear a detective's voice. Some of them hang up. I spoke encouragingly, "This is Vishal. You can talk to me. Confidentiality assured."

"Hello, Vishal?" she said.

Immediately, I knew it was her. Back from the past to haunt me.

When we had just broken up, or rather, when she had left me for another man, I used to often wonder what my reaction would be if life ever brought us together again. Now, three years later, I knew the answer. All that crap about time being a great healer is bullshit. Time heals nothing. Well, acne maybe.

"Hello? Vishal?" The urgency in her voice brought me back.

I composed myself and said calmly, "Yes, Aditi. This is Vishal."

"You recognised me!" she said, evidently pleased.

"Lucky guess. Everything okay?"

She sounded distressed.

"Something terrible has happened, and I didn't know whom to call."

"What happened?"

"Sunil's elder brother was found murdered at our farmhouse an hour ago. No one knows what to do."

Sunil was her husband, the man for whom she had dumped me. All three of us had been classmates in college.

"Have you informed the police?"

"Yes, Sunil has just called them."

"Okay. Everyone else safe?...Okay. Give me your address. I will be there as soon as possible."

The farmhouse was in the suburbs, about sixty kilometres from the city. The uphill road meandered dangerously, with a steep fall on one side and a rocky cliff on the other. Pranay winced when I overtook a police jeep in front of us, on a particularly narrow stretch of the road. I could feel my Honda City dangle in the air for a few heart-stopping seconds, before it screeched back to the road and zoomed ahead.

Pranay screamed, "Easy dude! You want the police to pull you over? That would delay us further!"

"Where do you think they are heading, Sherlock?"

One phone call from Aditi, and nostalgia was pulling my mind faster than quicksand dragging mating hippos.

I swerved the car at a sharp right angle, resulting in a four-wheel drift that made the tyres screech. Pranay made another attempt at conversation. He likes to talk when he gets nervous.

"She is the same dame, right?"

Pranay was twenty-nine years old, a year elder to me by birth, and several years younger to me personality-wise. He had joined me as a partner at Hunt Detective Agency. It was an arrangement in which I spent my time and money handling affairs of the office, he...well, spent it.

He used to be on my team when I worked in an American IT company. After my MBA, I had pursued the dollar dream, worked eighteen hours a day, over achieved my targets and became the youngest general manager in the history of the company. In the first six months of my job, I had been motivated by the ambition to prove worthy of Aditi. She liked her man to be successful. After she dumped me, I joined the bandwagon of workaholics, becoming a part of the matrix where each day began with a phone call over coffee; and each night ended in a pub, entertaining some client. Life had become some kind of profound competition, where my emotional loss was substituted by my professional success. I became a part of what they call the rat race.

It would have continued so, making me the stereotypical young, obese vice president who has a heart attack at thirty-five, and then finds solace in a hefty bank balance, a model wife, and two luxury apartments.

Fortunately, the great recession of 2008 happened, and I was asked to sack a couple of team members. Now, there are a few dominant personality traits that guide my actions. One of them is an exaggerated sense of accountability for people or things I am entrusted with. Aditi used to call it my Samurai Code of Honour. I refuted the company's decision, threatening to quit if any of my team members were terminated. I was confident that they would not risk losing me. I was wrong.

I gave my team members positive recommendations, and we parted. One of the sacked employees was Pranay, the technical advisor in my erstwhile team. We used to get along well, so it was only natural for him to move into my apartment to save on the rent. The reason why Pranay had become one of my better friends could be attributed to him possessing the rare talent of sitting with me over drinks, without feeling the need to fill the silence with mindless chatter.

With my new unemployed status, I suddenly had time. Lots of it. Pranay and I decided that we needed a break for introspection purposes, and zeroed in on Goa. We were sure that a few weeks of sea breeze and sunshine was what we needed to clear our minds.

Pranay managed to procure a shack on a beach. This turned out to be the wrong course of action, as a substantial part of our holiday was spent lying intoxicated on the beach, with a bunch of French people who subscribed to the philosophy of Epicureanism. It was difficult to ponder over future prospects of your professional life, while marijuana lingered in the air, a bottle of Jack Daniel was always at arm's length, and a couple of topless French girls applied buckets of sun lotion to their deliciously-toned bodies.

After a month of vegetating, I realised that I was too materialistic to spend the rest of my life waiting for spiritual enlightenment on a beach, and decided to come back. It was on the bus, during our journey back, that I had one of those epiphanies that led to my becoming a private detective. It must have been two in the morning, and all the other passengers were paying their tribute to Morpheus. I could hardly keep my eyes closed and I decided I was disillusioned and disgusted with the confinements of corporate life that demanded sycophancy as talent, and offered egotism as the reward. Translated, that meant the only other job offer I had in hand was at a salary reduced by thirty per cent.

The bus had stopped at one of those ghats. I looked out from the window, and was overcome by a sense of wonder. The pitch-black sky was lit across the horizon by millions of coruscating stars. There was deep silence, and I suddenly felt a sense of empowerment. I felt content with being rather than becoming. There was a time when I used to enjoy nature. During the past years in the success marathon, I had become oblivious to its joys.

It was mesmerisingly peaceful. I felt intrepid, and was possessed by a sense of destiny that mocked my worries, which seemed insignificant as compared to the vast cosmos of opportunities that existed before me.

What was I worrying about? I was born to die anyway. As I sat in the lap of nature with my new-found power, I suddenly remembered my maternal uncle's will. The old man had been my idol and used to run a detective agency in Bhopal. As a teenager, I used to visit him during the summer vacations. I had distinct memories of sitting in his one-room office, and being regaled by tales of his cases.

The pattern was the same. He used to recall a case, and lay it in front of me. I was supposed to guess who the culprit was. When I got it right, he used to make a big fuss over me. Enthused by his encouragement, I used to promise myself that I would be a part of the fraternity that restored order in people's lives. It was the closest-guarded secret till I was fifteen or sixteen. Then one day I had given it up. I wondered why. The passions that I had indulged in as a boy, an eternity ago, did not feel silly now.

On the contrary, I was surprised how conveniently I had subdued my dreams and chosen a vocation, which had much to do with circumstances rather than free will. A month before I lost my job, a relative had called informing me that my uncle had died of kidney failure brought about by diabetes. He was sixty-six, and had died alone, and broke.

The only worthwhile possession he had had was the one-room office on the first floor of a rundown building. I was informed that he had left the property in my name, and its approximate valuation was eight lakh rupees. It's not every day that you can gamble on someone else's money to pursue your whims. In Goa, a French woman had said to me, "Everything happens for a reason. You may not know it yet, but wait and see. Do not doubt the wisdom of the universe."

Could it be that the universe was sending me a signal now? I was suddenly excited. Pranay was asleep next to me when I jabbed his abundant midriff at two-thirty in the morning.

"Dude, I think we need to start a detective agency. You know...solve mysteries, create order from chaos and all that. What do you think?"

He replied with a thunderous snore. I took that as an omen. To cut a long story short, we joined as apprentices in one of the globe's biggest detective agencies, or so they claimed. During the first two months of my training, I was oscillated between domestic, and corporate and banking fraud investigations – getting more training in mechanical gadgetry and corporate communications rather than the real stuff. As soon as the training period was over, I opted for domestic investigation. It seemed that I had made the correct decision as, very soon, I developed a reputation of being an effective resource; and finally, the director of the agency was allocating all the tough cases to me.

Eight months later, I had travelled to Bhopal and sold my uncle's property, returned to Bangalore, taken a small office on lease and started my own private detective agency with Pranay and Aarti. Things were running pretty much to my satisfaction. It was all fine, until Aditi called that Sunday afternoon.

Lost in thought, I almost missed the yellow hoarding, where Aditi had told me to take a turn. I pushed the brakes hard. Pranay's upper body merged with the dashboard.

"Sorry, dude. You okay?"

"No, I am not!" He put his hand over his heart, and breathed in dramatically, "I feel a faint pain. Right here!"

Pranay suffered from a subdued form of hypochondria – courtesy his mother, who was some sort of quack, and owned a homeopathy clinic.

"Just your heart fluttering. I don't see anything."

"Uh ... no, but it could be something internal. Feel this." He put my hand on his chest, and looked at me in anticipation. "Do you feel this?"

"Feels like a lump. Could be breast cancer."

The road was too narrow for a U-turn, so I reversed the vehicle into an arterial road next to the hoarding. Soon we arrived at a gate surrounded by a wall that was at least twenty feet high. The driveway took us past lawns and flower beds. I was soon in front of an enormous house that looked like it could house a family of two hundred.

I parked my car behind a red Porsche. I pressed the horn to give the bereaved family notice of my arrival. The front door opened. It was Aditi.

I got out of the car, and started walking towards the house. Each step was heavy, and my heartbeat had trebled. She looked different. She had let her hair grow, and had put on just the right amount of weight that accentuated her womanly curves. Her breasts were fuller, and hips rounder. The eyes were the same, black holes pulling me towards them.

She nodded to me in her idiosyncratic style. No enthusiastic wave; no superficial hug. She was called the ice queen in college. To everyone else she seemed callous and emotionally undemonstrative, but I had experienced the passion that existed beneath that serene exterior. She was wearing a yellow diaphanous negligee that stuck to her tall and statuesque frame like second skin, and gave me a glimpse of her round breasts. Behind me, Pranay gasped audibly.

I nodded back at her because I didn't trust my voice. I saw she had been crying. The first and last time I had seen her cry was when her father had had a heart attack, just before we became lovers. Or rather, before she *decided* to take me as her lover.

I felt angry at myself for falling victim to this recurrent nostalgia. *She dumped you, you fool.* Her shapely pink lips curved into a faint smile as she approached me. I took a deep breath and said in a matter of fact tone, "Hi. Tell me what happened."

She ushered me into the house. The grandeur of the hall made me feel under-dressed. The decor was obviously the work of a connoisseur, who knew how to achieve a pretentiously elegant effect.

I observed the scene before me. The setting was one of obvious melancholy, with various people sobbing in varying degrees of sorrow. I was pleasantly surprised to see everyone weeping quite soberly. No one exceeded the decibel beyond which sorrow becomes hysteria. If I hadn't known that a murder had been committed in that house, I would have thought they had just had a domestic squabble.

The controlled sorrow had an air of inevitability about it, as if the death was brought about by old age, or a prolonged terminal disease. Not the kind of grief I would have expected in a household that was still coming to terms with the murder of a family member. Seated on the divan sobbing silently, was the father of the deceased, Paras Kapoor. Even in his grief he looked regal. Sunil sat next to his father, trying to comfort him. On seeing me, his surprise was evident.

"Vishal?" he asked, stunned.

Aditi rushed to him and whispered why I was there. If he was rattled, he didn't show it. It struck me that Aditi had called me out of genuine panic, and hadn't even bothered to consult her husband. It gave me a perverse kind of satisfaction to know that I was foremost on her mind for comfort when she was distressed. What sentimental creatures men are!

I glanced cursorily at each person in the gathering. There were eight people in the room, including Aditi. Seven of them were family, or friends, and the eighth person standing in a corner was evidently a servant or caretaker, judging by his posture and attire. And, of course, a corpse somewhere in the house. So that made them nine in all.

I felt awkward standing in the middle of the room. I caught Aditi's eye, and gestured that I needed her to join me and Pranay in a corner. I asked her to tell me exactly what had taken place. She filled me in on the details.

The Kapoor family had gone to the farmhouse the previous night to celebrate Paras Kapoor's sixtieth birthday. The old man had wanted a quiet family affair over the weekend. They had started partying at nine the previous night, and had continued their merrymaking with drinks and games till about two in the morning. At two, all of them had retired to bed. Anil, the victim, had the habit of sleeping outside, in a hammock on the lawn, behind the building. He had adhered to his alfresco sleeping habit, and that was the last anyone had seen him alive.

Expecting hangovers all around, and a late start to the day, the Kapoor family had instructed Ram, the caretaker of the farmhouse, a man in mid-forties, to come late the next morning. It was the unfortunate Ram who had discovered the body at ten thirty in the morning, while watering the garden.

I glanced at Pranay, and was pleased to see him making notes in his illegible, microscopic handwriting. Those notes would be as helpful to me as a French poetry book, but at least it made us look professional. I asked Aditi to acquaint me with each person in the room. She obliged. I had already identified Paras and Sunil, the father and younger brother of the deceased respectively.

A young man with features so similar to Paras, that they could only be justified by a common gene pool, was comforting an exquisite beauty. He was the youngest son, Vimal; and the grief-stricken lady he was comforting was his wife, Reena.

Another attractive, swarthy lady was sobbing inconsolably into an elderly man's arms. She was Shalini, the wife of the deceased, and was being comforted by her father, Mayank Tripathi. I caught the uncomfortable, blank look in Mayank's eyes, and was puzzled by it. He was obviously feeling ill at ease. Shalini held on to the old man, oblivious to his discomfort.

Aditi must have read my mind, for she came closer and whispered, "Mayank Uncle suffers from amnesia after his second heart attack. Doctors think it may be an advent of Alzheimer's. You may find his actions strange."

I engraved the family tree in my mind.

An engine spluttered and coughed outside, heralding the arrival of the police. I went out with Pranay, and filled the senior cop in with all that I had learnt from Aditi, the intent being to give him a head start. It was a wasted effort. The police inspector appeared amused on hearing who I was. He shook his head like a teacher addressing a toddler. He looked at his two subordinates, and deliberately repeated, 'Private detective' as if it as endearing a term as 'Santa Claus'. The two subordinates laughed vigorously, as was expected.

The inspector looked over his shoulder. "Is that your car, the white Honda City?"

"Yeah," I answered.

"I should take you in for driving rashly on the road. You almost got us killed."

That was not correct. They had been at no risk, as I had overtaken their vehicle from the side overlooking the valley.

I apologised sarcastically. "Emergency, sir. I was getting late for the matinee."

One thing I had learnt from my experiences was that the police would despise a private detective anyway, so it was better if you started throwing around some attitude right from the start. This would confuse them. The police inspector was a practitioner of the oldest intimidating tactic, intended to awe people – staring deep into your eyes, while caressing his moustache. He stared at me for an eternity and, when I didn't flinch, turned to Aditi asking for Sunil. His eyes latched on to her swaying hips as she led us to Sunil.

The police inspector dutifully offered his condolences to Paras Kapoor. He was quite obsequious, acting more like a waiter wheedling to earn his tip, rather than a cop. I didn't blame him. Paras Kapoor was a renowned real-estate developer, and would probably get a sympathy call from the police commissioner, and the chief minister. They would enquire if the inspector in charge was doing his job properly; not to forget the media coverage that the case would attract.

It had been ten minutes since the police had arrived, and the inspector was still offering his condolences. I looked at his name inscribed in the plate on this shirt said impatiently, "Inspector Babu, I think we should examine the corpse."

"Oh, should we? You will tell us what to do now!" he replied with condescension. I was punished again with the accusatory stare. I was tempted to confess some past crime – maybe the time when I was four, and had deliberately peed in the pool when no one was watching.

Inspector Babu turned his attention to the corpse, and followed Sunil with the confident gait of a man who knew what he was doing. Only Shalini and Reena, who were obviously still in shock, stayed back in the house.

"Did he examine the corpse before we came?" Babu asked Sunil, pointing at me.

"No, he didn't.

"Good. We don't want amateurs spoiling the show." He smiled sneeringly at me.

Sunil ushered us through the hall, into the kitchen. The kitchen had sliding glass doors that opened into a lush lawn covered with grass similar to that on a golf course. The gardens extended to the south, with an artificial beach in the centre; and beyond that, a cerulean pool touched the twenty-foot high compound wall that ran along the perimeter of the property, and was, for all practical purposes, insurmountable.

There were lights hanging between two trees on the right side of the beach, obviously for illuminating the beach and the whole garden. The dimensions of the rectangular beach, situated between the garden and the pool, must have been approximately thirty by forty feet. There were four pine trees exactly in the middle of the beach, and supported a hammock.

Anil's body was stretched out on the hammock. He was lying on his stomach. The outline of a wallet protruded from the trousers' rear pocket. I bent and saw the black handle of a knife that had been plunged into his heart. The sand had absorbed most of the blood, judging by the dark patch beneath the hammock. I observed the various approaches to the hammock. With the pool blocking off access to the hammock from one side, there were two ways by which someone could have got on to the beach, to reach the hammock. Either someone could come en route from the kitchen of the bungalow, or walk from the direction perpendicular to the pool that led to the rear portion of the property. Was there an opening or a gate on the other side? I made a mental note to check that.

I was lost in thought for a few minutes, studying the various approaches to the hammock. When I turned around, I saw to my dismay that Babu was lifting the corpse with the help of the two junior inspectors. The Kapoors were a handsome, well-built clan, and each brother was at least six feet tall if not more. Even with three of them at the task, they were struggling.

I lost my temper.

"Inspector, don't you think it would be better to take some photographs for records before you begin your investigation?"

He was stupefied for a change, and replied meekly, "I was trying to see the weapon."

I walked towards the corpse and lay under the hammock, still staring at the inspector in disbelief. The murderer had aimed the knife for Anil's heart, and had hit the bull's eye. Anil had been stabbed once. I examined the corpse for a few more minutes. Rigor mortis had set in, making the face stiff. He had a Rolex on his wrist. I noticed that it had stopped at 3.30. The deceased had a gold chain around the neck.

Inspector Babu joined me beneath the hammock, and started scrutinising the wound with adroitness that would have given a complex to the most accomplished surgeon.

Sunil spoke. "Inspector, there is one more thing. Ram found that the lock of the back gate had been broken. I think someone from the village committed the murder ... Ram, get the lock."

Sunil pointed towards a place perpendicular to the pool. That confirmed my doubts about an entry from the rear side of the property.

I stood up, and saw Babu struggling to do the same, thanks to a tub of wobbling jelly for a stomach. I extended my hand for support. He ignored it, and signalled the junior cops to help him get up. Ram rushed back with the fresh piece of evidence and handed it to Babu. I stood patiently while Babu held the lock and looked at it from all angles.

I requested Ram to lead me to the back gate. With the front gate locked, and a twenty-foot wall running along the perimeter of the bungalow, this was the only other route that could have given access to an outsider. I requested everyone to get off the beach at once.

Paras looked surprised and asked me why.

"I will tell you in a moment," I said.

The back gate was open, implying that the intruder had broken the lock from outside, entered, murdered Anil, and then made his or her escape. I went to the gate, and tried to fit the broken lock into the latch. This was getting more and more interesting.

When I returned to the garden, Inspector Babu was speaking on the phone. "Yes, send the van right away. We need to get the body to Mr Kapoor's house in the city. Also send a convoy of ten men or more. Yes, we know who did it. Someone from the village."

Everyone had been summoned to the garden, and Babu was reassuring a distraught Paras.

"Don't worry, sir. As soon as the backup arrives, I will head to the village with Ram, and round up the ruffians. Third-degree treatment, and all of them will be owning up to their crimes in this life as well as their past lives."

I stood at a distance. I wanted to be away from the family while I observed them, lest the murderer saw the shock on my face, that hadn't melted away since I uncovered some new facts.

I walked towards the inspector and spoke loud enough for everyone to hear. "Inspector, I just heard you speaking on the phone. Do you think there are no other investigations required?"

Babu stared at me like a spider would stare at a fly before devouring it.

"Of course not! The case is solved. You can go home. We will take it forward from here ... kid."

"Please let me hear your thoughts about the murder."

Everyone was audience to my conversation with the inspector. That served my purpose well, as I wanted to observe everyone's expression.

The inspector felt his moustache confidently, and began. "It's an open and shut case. Some drunken fool from the village was attracted by the music playing through the night. When the lights were switched off, he broke the lock with the intention of stealing whatever he could lay his hands on. Paras Sir was just telling me that his son liked to have a few drinks lying in the hammock, before falling asleep.

"The thief would have been startled by Anil, who was evidently awake, and there might have been a scuffle.

Unfortunately, the thief stabbed Anil. I will catch the rascal, don't worry."

"So the intent of the murderer was to steal?"

"Yes."

"What did he steal?"

"What?"

"Anil's wallet, gold chain, and diamond-studded watch are intact. What did he steal?"

Babu thought for a moment, turned to Paras, and asked, "What was stolen, Sir?"

There was a flurry of activity as Paras, Sunil, and Vimal looked at the body.

Vimal said, "He is right. Nothing is missing!"

Babu said, "Well, maybe the thief got scared, and ran away."

"Scared of *what*?" I enquired.

He must have known how silly he sounded, for his voice faltered when he said, "Scared of the murder that he had committed."

"So he entered the premises with the intent to steal, murdered Anil in cold blood, and then got frightened?"

Babu looked ill at ease, and said, "What's your point?"

"I don't think the intent was to steal."

"Then why would someone break in?" asked Paras, visibly appalled.

I decided it was time to tell them about the clues I had found. I looked at the crowd around me, and requested all of them to pay attention.

"I need some more information before I tell you my version."

I instinctively turned to Aditi. I wanted every chance to stare at that beautiful face.

"So the facts, I understand, are these. All of you reached here yesterday evening to celebrate Mr Kapoor's birthday. The party began at nine in the night, and ended at around two in the morning. All of you retired to your bedrooms, and Anil slept outside. I have some questions."

I was met with silent acquiescence. Pranay was standing right in the middle of the group. I touched my earlobe. That was our signal for him to hit the record button of the recorder he was carrying. I pulled my earlobe again. That was our signal for him to check that he had indeed pushed the record button, and not the rewind button, as he had done a few times before.

I directed the first question at everyone in general.

"Between nine and two, was the party restricted indoors? Did anyone venture out to the beach, or maybe to the pool?"

Paras replied after a moment's silence. "We wanted to come out to the pool side around midnight. But it was quite chilly outside, and Reena had been running a fever. So we dropped the idea, and stayed indoors."

"So no one ventured outside till Ram discovered Anil's body?"

"That is correct."

I nodded in appreciation at the old man. I directed the next question at Vimal. "What time did Ram leave?"

Vimal thought about it, and then replied in a thick American accent, "Ram left at nine last night. He helped us serve the drinks and snacks, and then we sent him off."

I hurled at the next one at Sunil. "We know it started raining sometime past midnight. Did anyone of you notice when it stopped?

He said, "It stopped at around one-thirty in the morning. I remember because I had come out to the veranda for a smoke."

I turned to the petite Reena and asked, "The access to the farmhouse is quite exclusive. Given the close proximity to the village, I assume that the front gate was locked by someone from inside after Ram left?"

Reena looked innocently lost, and Sunil replied on behalf of his sister-in-law. "That's correct. I locked the gate myself. It was my duty to lock the front gate before it got dark. Yesterday, I locked it at nine, as soon as Ram left."

"You walked the entire stretch from the front gate to the house? It must be at least fifty metres."

"So?" he asked, impatiently.

"It is quite a long and dark stretch. Did u carry a torch?"

"No, the lights in the garden are sufficient. Ram switches them on at six every evening, to discourage any trespassers."

I pointed to the lights hanging between two trees in the garden. "Those ones?"

"Yes. They throw enough light to illuminate the garden and the road."

"Okay, and where are the switches for the lights?"

"The switches are in the kitchen."

"Any other switches outside the house?"

He shook his head.

I asked Ram, "So it is your duty to switch them on at six every evening?"

"Yes, sir, but not every evening. We switch the lights on in the garden only when the family is visiting."

"And when do you switch them off?"

"In the morning."

"You went to the garden and saw the body first?"

"Yes, sir. I came at ten and rang the bell. Sunil Sir came out, opened the gate, and went back to sleep. I had just put the hose to the tap to water the garden, when I...."

He put his head in his hands dramatically, and shuddered.

I looked carefully at all of them. "I see the lights are switched off now. Who switched them off?"

This innocent question surprised everyone. A couple of people looked at Ram expectantly, who shook his head.

I thought aloud, "Ram was outside the house. When he saw the body, he would have panicked, and his normal faculties would have been affected. He would have screamed to get your attention. All of you would have obviously rushed to the body. So which one of you was composed enough to notice that two lights in the garden were still on, and switched them off?"

I didn't wait for an answer. "Did one of you turn the lights off before retiring to bed?"

Paras replied, "No, the lights were on when I looked out from my bedroom window last night at around two-thirty. Anyway, we deliberately keep the lights on at night."

I snapped my fingers. "Please pay attention. I need to get a confirmation for this one. Could it be that one of you turned off the lights this morning accidently?"

"Difficult. The switch for the floodlights is in the storeroom, in the kitchen," offered Vimal.

That confirmed my doubts. I requested Ram to switch on the lights. In two minutes the lights were on. An involuntary chill ran down my spine as I realised what this meant. The murderer was staring at me right now.

I continued, "So the bulbs are not fused. Someone must have deliberately turned them off from inside the house.

For the sake of convenience, let's assume that it was the murderer."

There was an expected cacophony of angry voices. I had made my statement slowly, trying to study each individual's reaction. There was indignation and shock, but no fear on anyone's face.

Babu's loud voice suppressed the rest. "You mean to say someone from the family committed the murder?"

He looked like he was going to murder me.

Paras said indignantly, "Young man, you'd better be careful about what you say!"

I took a few breaths.

"I am not saying that someone from the family *is* the murderer. All I am implying is that turning off the lights would have undeniably been a very big advantage for the murderer. With the lights on, most of the beach would have been exposed. Switching the lights off was the only thing he or she had to do, so that the murder could be committed without being witnessed. All the other facts evidently prove that this murder was planned. Come with me."

The angry mob followed me. "What do you see here?" I asked Babu, pointing to the beach.

"Sand," he replied.

"Yes, sand. And if you tax your delicate vision a little bit more, you will see footsteps on the sand, evidently made by all of us. The sand is damp from the rain last night, and we see a deluge of footprints. These include Anil's footprints, and all those who have subsequently come from the bungalow to the hammock, after the dead body was discovered."

I pointed to a particular set of deep footprints left by heavy boots. "These, Inspector, I believe, are yours."

Everyone looked at the marks on the sand. I walked over to the other side of the hammock, and looked at the untouched part of the beach facing the pool.

"There are no footprints leading to the dead body from any other part of the beach."

I looked around to see if all of them were with me. They were an avid audience. I walked to the side of the beach leading from the back portion of the property. Even as I walked, my footprints left their marks on the damp sand.

"There are three ways someone could have reached the hammock. There are no footprints from the pool side, or from the back gate. All the footprints visible are from the bungalow leading to the hammock. Not a single footprint from any other side of the beach leading to the hammock. Unless the murderer flew, he or she must have walked from the side facing the bungalow."

The inspector, and Paras, went to the other part of the beach to confirm what I had stated.

Babu said defiantly, "What if the murderer entered from the back gate, got on to the porch, and then came to the beach from the kitchen, knowing that his footsteps would be visible in the morning?"

A murmur of voices rose collectively, supporting this idea.

"He was pretty smart for a petty thief then. And yet he ran away without stealing anything, because he was scared of a corpse?"

"You also saw the lock," shouted someone behind me, with a ferocity that surprised me. It was Ram. He had suddenly become very interesting to me. I turned towards him, and said, "I am coming to the lock."

I turned to Babu. "So the murderer broke the lock after it had stopped raining, entered the premises, came to the courtyard outside the kitchen without being seen by Anil, managed to switch off the lights through a closed door – that shows no sign of a forced entry – murdered Anil, and then, instead of dashing to the back gate, retraced his footsteps to the courtyard again?"

Babu hesitated and conceded, "It does sound unnatural."

Paras looked pale. "I am sure one of us switched off the lights. Think for God's sake."

Everyone looked at one another.

I noticed Babu was perspiring when he asked Paras, "Sir, what do you think about his version?"

Paras looked aghast. "He is wrong, of course."

Sunil lent support to this father. "Insane! This is ridiculous."

I turned to Sunil. "The party dispersed at approximately two in the morning. I am sure people wouldn't have gone off to sleep right away. Your father said he was awake at two-thirty and saw the lights on. What time did you sleep?"

"Aditi and I went to the bedroom around two. But we would have fallen asleep at around two forty-five, or three – latest. Right, Aditi?"

She nodded at him. The casual words Sunil had uttered shook me, and I pondered the extent of the intimacy between them. Did they have sex last night?

Was he better than me? Did he understand her as well as I did? Did she moan and whisper 'I love you' when she came? I became aware of Aditi's gaze, and I was sure she knew what I was thinking about. I felt disgusted at the power of my sentiments.

"Well, what are you thinking?" asked Babu, giving undue importance to my blank stare.

I looked at the inspector.

"The entire exercise of the murderer creeping stealthily to the courtyard from the back gate, murdering Anil, and retracing his way via the courtyard to the back gate, would be a minimum of twenty minutes' process, right?"

Babu replied, "Yes. Twenty minutes or more."

I continued, "You will notice that Anil's watch has stopped at three-thirty in the morning. Most probably from a heavy impact, while struggling with the murderer. That means, in case the murderer was from the village, which I highly doubt, he or she would have entered the premise latest by three-ten in the morning. That implies he would have started the process of breaking the lock by three o' clock. It's a strong lock. There would have been some noise. If people were awake at three, someone would have heard something."

Babu rushed towards Anil's body, lifted the limp wrist, and nodded. "The glass of the watch is cracked, and it has stopped at three-thirty."

I addressed the crowd.

"Did anyone of you hear any noises between three and three-ten in the morning?"

Paras walked to his son's body and glanced at the wrist watch. He paled and nodded. He repeated my question to his family.

Sunil reasoned, "No, dad. But we were all intoxicated last night, totally sloshed. I don't think we would have noticed anyway."

I shook my head. "The lock couldn't have been broken. Follow me."

I led them to the back gate. I told Ram to stay inside the compound. I closed the metal gate behind me, so that we were outside the compound, facing Ram. I asked Ram to place the broken lock in the latch.

"Well?" I looked encouragingly at everyone.

They looked lost.

"Look at the size of the grill. Even a kid would find it difficult to get his hands inside to reach the latch."

I asked Aditi to try squeezing her petite hands through it. She could only get two fingers through.

"It would be impossible for a full-grown adult to put his hands inside. Look at the lock. Not a single scratch on it, no sign of it being broken by something heavy. It is neatly cut in half. Probably sawed."

Paras was the first one to observe the obvious. "My God! It would have had to be sawed inside the compound!"

I shook my head. "My guess is that someone who had access to the key, conveniently removed the lock, took it to some secluded place, and sawed it, before throwing it here. The murderer would not dare stand inside the compound and break the lock. The noise would have been too much of a risk.

"He or she probably anticipated the party would extend beyond the wee hours. The lock was broken, and put here *before* the party began. Everything was planned meticulously."

Paras showed a perceptible draining of colour. Sunil stared at me disbelief, Vimal's eyes widened in shock, and Shalini started shivering.

No one had asked me the most pertinent question, so I told them my ideas. "Some of you might be wondering why the murderer didn't switch the lights on after committing the murder. Probably because he or she had some blood on the clothes; or it could have been cuts or bruises that required urgent attention.

"He or she would have required time to dispose off the bloodstained clothes, wash, change back into night clothes, and get back into bed. With the lights on, there was always the risk of being seen, and getting suspicious at Anil's odd posture in the hammock.

"Plus, the murderer knew that switching off the lights would not attract as much attention as switching them on. Some of the rooms overlook the garden, and the risk was too great. I am assuming that the murderer planned to switch the lights on in the morning."

I studied their countenances carefully, hoping for a hint.

"Someone wanted to make it look as though a villager had committed the murder; but I am very sure the murderer was from inside the hou ... eh ... inside the compound."

This time I caught the look. It was not a look of fear or guilt. Two eyes stared at me with hatred and anger. I was surprised at the hatred exuding from her eyes, clearly hinting at homicidal intentions towards me. For a moment, I locked my eyes with Shalini's. The beautiful widow was radiating negative vibes towards me. It immediately made her a suspect. I stared at her for a couple of seconds, and she showed no sign of lowering her gaze.

Everyone was silent now.

I said to Babu, "During the autopsy, you will realise that there was a struggle between Anil and the murderer. Either *after* Anil had been stabbed, or *before*, there was a struggle, the evidence of which can be found in the bloodstains on Anil's right-hand finger nails."

Three men rushed towards the corpse, and observed Anil's bloodstained fingernails. I reconstructed the crime scene for everyone's benefit.

"Since there was a struggle, let us assume that Anil was awake or semi-awake. It is certain that Anil was lying on his back when he was stabbed. But the body was found lying on the stomach.

"It would be terribly inconvenient for the murderer to creep in stealthily, get beneath the hammock and aim for Anil's heart. But if he had been lying down when he was stabbed, how did he turn? So let us assume that Anil had judged the murderer's intentions, stood up, struggled, and managed to scratch the intruder before being stabbed. He was then pushed so that he fell on his stomach, and the additional pressure drove the knife further into his heart."

All eyes were fixed on me, and I stared at Shalini. Intuition told me that the murderer was standing there.

A little later I casually asked Ram, "How did you scratch your neck?"

Everyone understood the implication of this question, and all eyes shifted to the scratches on his neck.

"What ... oh ... this is from the branches, sir – from the branches in the forest in the village, sir!" he said, pleading.

"Okay. Just concerned. Use some antiseptic."

Babu was sitting in my car while waiting for the backup to arrive. We had exited the house to respect the family's privacy. The grief associated with the death had been overshadowed by the shock of the macabre possibility that the murderer could be an insider. The Kapoors had become hysterical after I told them my thoughts on the murder. Paras had requested Babu and me to excuse the family for some time. They were seated in the living room, engaged in a sort of confused, tearful conference as we left.

Babu said excitedly, "If what you said is true, this will be one hell of a case! The media will go berserk!"

There was a twinkle in his eyes. "You are quite a sharp guy. For how long have you been doing this stuff ... hey ... what's that?"

I caught the familiar sweet smell of weed, and cursed Pranay silently.

"You are smoking drugs?" the Inspector yelled, and held Pranay by the collar.

It took a few seconds for Pranay's placid pupils to register that he was doing something wrong by smoking a joint in front of a police officer. His looked at me in alarm.

"Put that away."

I pulled the cigarette from between his lips and extinguished it against the steering wheel. I apologised on Pranay's behalf.

"I am sorry, Inspector. This is the first time he has seen a dead body at such close quarters. He is not thinking straight."

"That stuff is banned. I should have him arrested."

"Let him be, Inspector. We have bigger things to worry about. How will you handle the media when they come to know that Anil Kapoor has been murdered, and *you* have found clues that incriminate a family member?"

He let go of Pranay's collar, and stroked his moustache in ecstasy.

"It will be big! They would want to know how we found that, of course?" He looked at me slyly. "You will give a statement to the media?"

"Not a chance. I will leave it to your judgment to issue the statement."

He beamed at us, and both Pranay and I breathed easy. He continued, "I will tell them how both of us uncovered the clues together. That should keep us in the headlines for a few days."

"Maybe you should check with Mr Paras Kapoor before issuing any statements. And please don't mention my name."

He ignored the first part of my statement.

"You don't want me to mention your name to the press? They would want to know who found all the clues."

"Oh no. I got lucky. You were the first one to examine the corpse, remember?"

He looked at me and an unspoken agreement was sealed between us. He would forget the dope Pranay was carrying, and I would forget what a dope he was. An excruciatingly painful hour passed in the car.

Babu was attacking me with a paroxysm of idle chatter that was slightly more interesting than watching snails race. I thought of the repercussions of pushing him out of my car, and realised it would only make things worse. I wanted to shut out his mindless babble, close my eyes, and concentrate on how to deal with the tempest of past memories. I wanted to see Aditi again. I wanted a drink.

Thankfully, Ram came running and said, "Please come in, sir. They are waiting for you."

I followed Babu and Pranay into the living room, and found the Kapoor family sitting stiff and impassive. Count Dracula and his family assembled for their annual Halloween portrait. Six pairs of eyes gazed at me with a sense of anticipation reserved for a surgeon, who walks out of the operation theatre after trying to save a man's life. I noticed that Shalini and Mayank were missing, and asked where they were. Paras said that Shalini had had a nervous breakdown after hearing my assumptions about the murderer, and was resting in her room. Her father was with her.

Paras spoke in his commanding voice. "Please sit down. What will you have? Tea or coffee?"

His voice didn't quiver; his manner didn't falter. Here was a man who was a true fatalist, an indefatigable master of emotions. I could see the truth in the myriad versions of his rags-to-riches story I had read about – the migrant who came to the city forty years ago, with only a suitcase and a legacy of bad debt.

Babu opted for tea. I considered the propriety of asking for beer. Empty bottles were strewn all over the carpet from last night's party mocking my sobriety. I regretfully remembered the glass of Scotch I had left untouched at my office.

Paras asked me in a cautious voice, “What’s on your mind?” *Beer. Aditi.*

“I beg your pardon?”

“I mean ... what do you think?”

“What about?”

He gave me a stare of distrust. I looked at the waves of anticipation on the faces surrounding me. I realised what this was all about.

“I don’t know who did it! Do you actually think I do?”

Paras looked crestfallen. “Oh! You sure you don’t have any idea at all about the identity of the murderer?”

The old guy looked disappointed that I didn’t indict one of his family members. Something was wrong about his behaviour. They were still staring at me in anticipation. I retaliated with what I hoped was the most incredulous stare. They really thought I could discern the identity of the murderer, sitting in a car with Babu! The only person I knew who could do this was Sherlock Holmes!

Paras said politely, “Your presence here was highly appreciated today. We would like to know what your next step would be.”

“Well, if you appoint me as a private detective, I can formally look into the case.”

Paras looked at his sons, rebelliously.

“Vishal, I don’t know why you came here, or what are you trying to imply. But my son has been murdered. I want you to try and find the bastard who did this.”

Tears surged into his eyes, but he fought them back heroically. Sunil and Vimal did not look very happy, and Aditi had an imperceptible smile of triumph on her face, that only I could decipher. Apparently, some of them did not want me to work on the case. Anyway, the king had spoken, and the commoners could go to hell.

"I need someone to sign a standard agreement. I can send that tomorrow."

"Catch the murderer. We will sign the agreement tomorrow. Don't worry about money."

I immediately decided to double my retainer.

He continued, "I hope I can count on you for complete confidentiality."

"Yes, sir."

I gave my card to Paras. Aditi stretched her neck to catch a glimpse of it. I offered her one too. She took it shyly.

One of the junior inspectors entered the room, and informed Babu that the backup team had arrived. He looked at me.

"Umm ... in that case, do we go need to go to the village now?"

"I can't comment on that," I told him. "I have put forward my views on the crime. Going to the village is your call, Inspector.

I looked at Paras and realised I hadn't offered my condolences till now.

"I am very sorry for the loss of your son, sir. I hope we are able to bring the guilty to justice."

With these parting words I nodded farewell to Babu, and turned around to rush to the nearest liquor shop.

Babu spoke in a slightly high-pitched tone. "You are not leaving? At least wait till they take the body away."

I scowled furiously at him. "I think we should leave the bereaved family alone."

Paras spoke again. "Please stay. Maybe you will find some more clues."

When Paras spoke, everyone listened and agreed.

"Okay, but we shall wait in my car until they take the body away. I am sure you would like some time with your family to discuss things."

"It is hot outside. You can wait in one of the other rooms," Paras offered.

"Oh." I looked at Pranay.

"Oh." He looked back at me.

I said to Paras, "It is hot, but I insist that we sit outside. It would be nice to have a couple of beers just to keep us going."

"Ram will bring them outside."

Paras scowled at me for the first time. He was probably beginning to doubt my temperance. Not that I blamed him. It was hardly sensitive on my part to demand alcohol. But I needed strength to insulate my mind against Aditi, and against Babu's verbal attack, while waiting for the ambulance.

"Thanks."

Babu remonstrated with me for my insensitivity as soon as we were outside. "How could you ask for beer in a situation like this?"

I ignored him and spoke to Pranay.

"Call Aarti and tell her to lock the office and leave. Tell her to come tomorrow, and take her weekly off some other day."

It was two hours and three bottles of beer later that I was able to leave the farmhouse. The ride back home was much slower. I tried to concentrate on what I had learnt at the scene of the crime, evaluating various possibilities. The mind, however, takes masochistic delight in suffering. I found myself thinking more and more about what I had lost three years ago.

I opened the door and tripped over Bruno again.

"Fat bugger," I growled, and he responded by rolling on his back and inviting me with his paws to tickle his exposed belly. Bruno was an obese and lazy Labrador.

Pranay, sensing that I was in no mood to dissect the case, and probably pleased by it retired to his room. He came out five minutes later and asked formally, "Do we go over the case now?"

"Nah, let's do it tomorrow."

"Okay. You want me to do anything for you?"

"Yeah. Shoot the dog!" I said, rubbing my painful knee.

I tried to watch a movie, listen to music, and read a book – all futile attempts to isolate the past, but the mind insisted on wallowing in self-pity. Out of despair, I went to Pranay's room to see what he was doing. He had stripped to his shorts, and was just about done with making a joint. Then Pranay poured some beer into Bruno's bowl, and the beast lapped it up eagerly. Both of them knew that I got irritated when Pranay gave alcohol to the dog.

I told him off without conviction or malice. "Listen, you brewery – dogs are not supposed to drink."

Pranay replied without looking up from his joint. "He's not a dog; he's a superdog."

To show his support, Bruno licked the bowl clean. Pranay was laidback, pleasure-seeking, and rebellious. I was meticulous, responsible and deliberate. He looked at me and said, "You want a whiff? You look like you could use one today."

For a moment I was tempted, but then decided against it. I left Pranay and Bruno to their Bacchanalian excesses, and retired to my room. I took out a bottle of Scotch. This would be one long night.

It was dark. We were on top of the hill again. The light from the moon lit her face, and her silky hair cascaded in the strong wind. Her eyes glistened with sad emptiness when she asked, “Do you think I am a bad person? Am I responsible for Chetan’s death?”

“No, you are not,” I lied.

She looked into my eyes, searching my soul. “I believe you.”

Seconds later we were kissing. It was the first time I had touched a woman, and my technique was awkward. She took the lead, drawing me to her. My fingers trembled as I lifted her T-shirt and brushed my lips against her nipples. She moaned and bit her lower lip.

The scene changed, and I was alone on the hill. I turned and saw Chetan, his arms outstretched. Blood was trickling from his slashed wrists. He had the wide grin of a madman. I followed his gaze, and saw Sunil and Aditi standing in front of me, holding hands, smiling down at me derisively.

I woke up drenched in sweat. I got up, went to the refrigerator, and drank a litre of water. It was nine in the morning, and Pranay was still asleep. I didn’t have the zeal to go to office. With consciousness creeping in, I felt a sense of destitution. It was one of those hopeless moments when your life hangs precariously from the edge, and it can only be saved if you are able to conjure up a reason for your existence.

I sought mental inactivity in the comfort of my bed, and tried to go back to sleep. I lay on the bed staring at the empty walls. The thing about lying in bed and staring at the wall is that you gravitate towards past memories. Again and again I felt the emotion which I loathed – self pity. Like a vulnerable puppy shivering in the rain. Like the one she had helped that damp night.

We were on a bike, getting drenched in the rain, ecstatic with our new-found understanding of each other. Aditi had her arms wrapped around my waist, leaning forward so that her face rested on my shoulder. I was totally soaked, as I zipped the bike on the long and empty road, but her soft breath on my neck kept my spirits warm. Her nipples were taut, pressing hard against my back through the thin fabric of her blouse. I felt content and carefree. The sky was being challenged by stray streaks of lightning that reflected my own spirit that night.

We stopped at a dhaba on the highway to have tea. A newborn puppy was shivering uncontrollably in the downpour, snuggling against a newspaper. She wanted it. When Aditi wanted something, it was a challenge that invoked your machismo. The owner of the dhaba gave me a silly smile as I traded my leather jacket for the stray puppy. We got back to college, and she was ecstatic with the dog. Then she got bored with the responsibility of feeding it thrice a day. She had dumped it in a month. I should have learnt my lesson from that.

I groaned, and pinched myself to come back to the present. I had spent three years immuring myself against her. One glimpse of her couldn't pull me back into the labyrinth of past memories. I got up from bed and thought of calling Kalpana. She was a thirty-year-old divorcee, who would do anything to please me. Kalpana and I had a great relationship. Our relationship had the passion of lovers, and the comfort of two people who know that it is only about sex.

That was before she started pestering me for commitment and insisted on moving in my apartment with me. That too with her cat. It turned ugly when I broke up with her two months ago. I had decided never to call her again. Yet, I felt tempted to call her. Anything to get out of this sudden abyss.

I imagined Kalpana naked, with her ivory smooth skin, enticing breasts, and shapely legs. Junior stirred into action, demanding her presence. Sex, the greatest panacea for loneliness, albeit temporary.

I was dialling Kalpana"s number when the phone rang. It was Aditi.

"Morning."

"Hi. How are you?" she asked politely.

"Good. How are you?"

"Well, still recovering. You created quite an impact yesterday. We are still coming to terms with what you discovered. "

"Yeah, I can imagine it was unpleasant."

"Kind of. Dad wants you on the case as soon as possible."

"Dad?"

"My father-in-law. I call him Dad. He is quite impressed with your deductive abilities."

"He's a gracious man."

"Actually, no. He is a hard man to please. So ... you have some paperwork for us?"

"Yes. A basic agreement."

"Can I sign the agreement?"

"Sure. You are the client."

"Great. How do we go about it?"

"My colleague Pranay will bring the hard copy of the document for you to review, and if everything seems fine, sign it and hand it back to him."

I forced myself to say, "Along with the retainer cheque."

"Oh ..."

She sounded disappointed.

"The retainer is negotiable," I added quickly.

"Silly, I am not worried about your fee. I was wondering if you could come instead of your colleague; maybe meet me outside somewhere. There are a lot of guests here today, and we would not be able to ... discuss things freely."

I could think of a thousand reasons why I should say no. Instead I said, "Sure."

"Great! What time will you come?" she asked enthusiastically.

"Let me call you back and confirm."

"Okay. Choose a place near my house. I can leave the house for an hour at the most."

"Okay. Let me call you back in ten minutes and confirm the place."

"Okay. Will wait for your call," she said in a voice that seemed filled with eagerness.

I hung up. Junior had gone flaccid, receding into its shell with shame and remorse at the sound of Aditi's voice. I sighed. "Developing a conscience, are we?"

The monologue wasn't getting me anywhere. There was not going to be any relief today.

I reached the place at eleven. I had chosen a quaint and modest coffee shop that was run by an Iranian named Ali. He served the best chocolate desserts in town. I knew the regard Aditi had for chocolate. She had sent me a text message, informing me that she was running half an hour late. Punctuality had never been her strong point. I walked across rows of tables, to the counter.

Ali saw me and opened his arms in a mock hug. "Vishal! Long time. You forget your friend."

I sat at a table close to a window and was soon lost in memories of the past.

My reverie broke as I saw a chauffeured Mercedes stop in front of the bakery. Aditi got out of the Mercedes. She was dressed in white. Hers was a graceful walk, and I tried not to stare. The young teenager sitting in the corner elbowed his companion, who whistled softly when Aditi entered the shop.

"Hi," she said, and leaned forward as if expecting an embrace. I stood stiffly and extended my hand.

She shook my hand and grinned. "So it's going to be like that, huh?"

"Uh-huh."

We walked to a table in a secluded corner. "Please sit," I said courteously.

"How have you been?" she asked, putting her Armani sunglasses on the table.

A waiter approached us. I looked at her and enquired, "Chocolate mousse with coffee?"

She nodded, and smiled. "You remember!"

There was a pregnant silence for a few seconds.

"You created quite a stir yesterday. We all are shocked with the possibility that someone ... you know ... from the house ...."

"What's the reaction?"

"It's still not sunk in ... the fact that the murderer could be someone Anil knew."

"Yeah, I can imagine the shock although I must confess that the family is taking the murder quite well. Very resilient in conquering grief."

She raised her left eyebrow. "And is that a bad thing?"

"No. Just an observation."

"Oh? What have you observed?"

"That his wife and his brothers were not very attached to him. And vice versa probably."

She smiled. "You are good. Yes. Let us say he was the black sheep of the family."

"Black enough for someone to butcher him?"

She brought her hand to her lips in a subconscious gesture, and averted her eyes before replying.

"I won't bullshit you. Anil rubbed many people the wrong way. He was a spineless spoilt brat. But I can think of no one who would kill him."

"And yet someone did."

"You suspect someone?" she asked, anticipation evident in her voice.

I had found Shalini's behaviour suspicious, but Aditi didn't have to know that.

"Of course not! It is too early. That would be speculation."

She sighed. "I am here only for half an hour. Let's not talk about the murder now."

"Then what should we talk about?"

"You know ... things in general. How have you been? What's new in your life?"

I smiled and pushed the copy of the agreement towards her. It was a three-page document, printed on my agency's letterhead that used an obnoxious font, and sported a silly logo, chosen by Pranay.

She made no effort to pick up the agreement, so I said, "You only have half an hour. The agreement will take some time to read. Please pay special attention to clauses 4 and 5. You have to sign each page."

She took the agreement and signed each page with a flourish. She did not bother to read even a single word. She pushed it back to me.

"There, we are done with that. Dad will have the cheque sent to your office tomorrow. I assume the amount is mentioned in the draft?"

"Yes, it is."

"Good. Now that we have that out of the way, tell me about yourself. Three years. Any girl in your life?"

"Many."

She arched an eyebrow. "Is it? So when are you getting married?"

"I will send you a card."

She smiled coldly. "Hmm ... I am happy for you. Good, good. You should settle down."

"Yeah, I should," I replied curtly.

"Are you serious about anyone at present?" she persisted.

"Nope," I said truthfully. It would have been futile to lie, as she would have read the truth on my face instantly. I wished she would stop probing. While I courted her, she used to keep a tab on every movement of mine.

Her eyes glistened with grief. "I hope it is not due to me."

I looked in those sympathetic yet conniving eyes. I knew there was nothing genuine about her guilt. She wanted to reassure herself by establishing that I hadn't got over her. I wondered why I had agreed to meet her. The answer came back promptly. I wanted to relive the past. Meet her alone, just like the old times. Coffee and conversation.

She read my thoughts.

"Coffee, you, and me. Just like the old times. I can't believe that three years have passed us by. It seems like yesterday."

"No."

"No?"

"No. You couldn't have grown your hair by four inches, put on weight, and bought a Mercedes in twenty-four hours."

She smiled thoughtfully. "Yes, that is correct. I couldn't have done all that in a day."

I realised that even after three years, her smile could interfere with my breathing. She sensed my mood, and her smile was replaced by a serious, penetrating look. I was transfixed, and made no attempt to break the eye contact. There was the same intense attraction that had possessed me then. It was happening again – the flame and the moth story. And like the moth, I would always be drawn to the flame, even if it threatened to destroy me.

I forced myself to think about the day when she had told me that she was confused, that she loved both Sunil and me. It worked, and I looked away in disgust. The waiter placed the mousse and coffee on the table.

She took a bite. "Delicious!" She dropped a few crumbs on her shirt, and grinned sheepishly at me.

"So, when are you and Sunil starting a family?"

Her liquid black eyes became sad. “Oh, we are not ready now. Sunil and I are still in the process of ... accepting each other. It is not as uncomplicated, as it was between us”.

Us. I was getting tired of her subtle manipulations to keep reminding me of the past.

She mistook my silence for acquiescence to her line of conversation and continued, “I still get goose bumps when I think about us sometimes.”

She looked at me in anticipation.

“Aditi, why did you call me?”

She thought for a moment. “Instinct. When Anil was found murdered, everyone was scared. Usually, we look up to Dad for direction, but he was shattered. I felt helpless and scared.”

“Fair enough. Let me assure you, Aditi, I have no hidden agenda or ulterior motive to get on this case other than what my profession endows.”

I waited till she had registered the import of my words and felt sufficiently hurt.

“Please don’t embarrass me by talking about the past, or by divulging details of your relationship with your husband. A man has been murdered, and I am trying to do my job. You are my client.”

She gave me a mournful look, and her lips quivered. So did my heart. I softened and said, “Look, Aditi, we are beyond the point where we had to confide everything to each other. Let’s not complicate things.”

She nodded, and bit her lips. “It’s just that I used to feel so close to you that I ....” She terminated the sentence abruptly, and I didn’t persist, although I would have given my left hand to have her complete that sentence.

I waited for her to finish her mousse, and signalled to the waiter for the bill, hoping to bring the meeting to an end.

"Can I have another coffee, please?" she said suddenly. "You have a little more time?"

"Sure."

"Let's talk about you. The last I heard you were doing amazingly well in your corporate job. What made you become a private detective?"

"I realised that I was fascinated by corpses."

She said adamantly, "Come on! Please! Start from the beginning."

"From the beginning?"

I leaned back, clasped my hands behind my head, and closed my eyes thinking hard.

"Well, in the beginning, there was the Big Bang about one and a half million years ago. Then the earth was .... "

She gave me a disarming smile, and I had to smile back.

"Are you happy?" she enquired at an impulse.

"Immensely."

I was tempted to ask her whether she was happy. But I resisted the urge. Then I gave up the effort and asked, "Are you? Happy?"

She was prepared with the answer. "I am fine. Sometimes I feel lost, but then, you always used to say that I was prone to depressive spells and dark moods."

Depressive spells. I had encountered some of those myself when she had dumped me. I said those words to myself. *Dumped me*.

I replied gruffly, "Yeah, shit happens."

She must have noticed the change in my temperament, for she was about to say something, but then decided against it and drank her coffee.

"Well, Mrs Kapoor," I smiled, laying emphasis on the *Mrs*. "I have to ask you some questions. Please cooperate."

She looked at me expressionlessly and nodded.

"I would like to speak to some of the family members tomorrow. Can I?"

"Sure. Anyone specifically?"

"Shalini, to start with."

She arched an eyebrow in mock shock. "So you suspect her?"

She was not surprised by my first choice. Did she know something about Shalini that I didn't?

"Maybe. I see you are not shocked that I suspect her."

"Yes, I am not. We all noticed Shalini's strange behaviour yesterday. One moment she was crying, and the next moment she had a nervous breakdown. She has been a wreck ever since."

"Hmm ... Tell me about her father."

"That is a tragic story. Mayank Uncle has been Dad's

accountant for the last twenty-five years. His loyalty is legendary."

"Interesting. I didn't know that. Tell me about his amnesia."

We were interrupted by her phone.

"It's Sunil," she told me, and started speaking.

"What!" she said excitedly in a second.

Who?" she said, even more excitedly after a while.

"I am with Vishal. Signing the agreement. We are coming over right now."

"What happened?" I asked.

"They know who murdered Anil!"

I could sense the atmosphere was charged when I entered the house.

Paras was indignant. "We won't need the police, Babu! I will hunt and kill the bastard myself."

It was the genuine anger of an incensed father, who had just discovered the identity of his son's murderer. His face was flushed. I could see a heart attack lurking somewhere. He tripped over a vase and broke it.

Inspector Babu seemed to be at a loss for words. Vimal came to the rescue.

"Don't do anything rash, Dad. The last thing we need is a scandal."

I registered the word *scandal* for future reference.

Paras disregarded his son's words and said angrily, "That bastard! He thinks he will get away with murdering my son."

Before we could pre-empt his actions, Paras was out of the door. I didn't know what to make of it until I heard the roar of an engine revving up, followed by a screech of tires.

Reena cried out in distress, "Vimal, Dad is going to murder him! Do something!"

Vimal looked at the inspector, who looked at Sunil, who looked at me. I had heard enough to understand what had happened.

I said, "We need to follow Mr Kapoor. Do you know where he is going?"

"Yes, he is going to Leo's apartment," replied Sunil.

"You know the address?"

"Yes."

"Come on then. I will drive."

Two minutes later I was in the driver's seat, following a Land cruiser. I had seen a Porsche, a Mercedes, and a Land cruiser so far. How could I have competed against all this opulence? Aditi blended into this. Paras was driving like a madman. I lost sight of him occasionally. Sunil was sitting in the co-driver seat, helping me navigate. Vimal and the inspector were seated at the back.

I asked Sunil, "Who is Leo?"

The inspector had been waiting for this question. His tone was mocking. "Your theories were wrong, Mr Dee-tec-tive! We found the real murderer."

I waited for him to proceed. He held out an elegant gold chain in front of my face. A diamond pendant in the shape of a heart had the letter *L* was ensconced inside – one of those ridiculously shiny and expensive things that would be gifted to a lover.

"This belongs to Leo?"

"Yes, we found it outside the back gate of the farmhouse this morning. So you see, I was correct all along. The murderer had actually entered from that gate."

I was curious at this unexpected display of aggressiveness on Babu's part.

"You went to the farmhouse this morning to investigate again! Why?"

"Shalini remembered that she had indeed heard a distant sound the night of the murder. She heard metal scraping against metal somewhere near the back gate. I put two and two together, and concluded that it had to be the sound of a lock being broken. And I was correct! I would have spotted it yesterday itself, but you misled us with your fairytales about footsteps on sand and narrow grills."

A million questions ran through my mind. I picked up the most pertinent one. "Hmm ... Why didn't Shalini mention these noises yesterday?"

Vimal sounded protective as he answered, "She must have been in shock, poor woman."

Sunil lent his support. "And thank God she remembered it this morning! We were lucky that the inspector found the locket before any villager got his hands on it. You almost had us believe that one of us had committed the murder. You should be stopped from pursuing detective work."

I ignored his threat, and wondered at the possibilities. I was sure that there was no locket outside the gate yesterday. I had scanned every inch of the property near the gate. It was highly likely that Shalini had placed the locket there herself to mislead us.

"So, it would appear that this Leo entered from the back gate, and murdered Anil. But the lock could not have been broken from the outside."

Babu said, "Leo was Anil's friend. They used to come together to the farmhouse frequently. It would be easy for Leo to get a key."

"Okay. That's possible. Motive?"

"Uh ... motive ... yes ... that we will find out when we arrest him."

"This Leo ... do you know him?" I asked the brothers.

I looked in the rearview mirror, and saw Vimal glancing quizzically at Sunil. Sunil widened his eyes at Vimal, a signal to be covert and cautious.

"Leo was a close friend of Anil's," said Sunil.

They were hiding something.

"And what about you? Is he your friend too?" I questioned.

Sunil looked at his lap uncomfortably and replied, "No. He was close only to Anil."

I persisted. "You have seen Leo wearing this locket?"

"Anil had given the pendant to Leo."

It was too intimate a locket to be gifted by a man to another. Then reality hit me suddenly, and I slowed the car to concentrate. The pattern seemed clear – Anil sleeping alone, Shalini's behaviour, Vimal warning his dad of a scandal, Anil and Leo coming to the farmhouse together, and the heart-shaped locket. I chose my next words carefully.

Sunil's temper had been legendary in our college. An incident that occurred back then was still entrenched in my mind. We had been sitting in the mess during the lunch hour. A mess worker had accidentally slipped and dropped a bowl of curry on Sunil's expensive designer clothes. His normally calm and pleasant demeanour had changed into something ugly. His face contorted into an all-consuming anger, and he punched the poor kid in the stomach so hard that the chap lost consciousness.

I remembered that punch now, and deliberated on paraphrasing my doubts without provoking him, in case I was wrong. He was already angry at me, and my left eye was directly under threat if he did decide to sock me in one.

"So, Anil and Leo were lovers," I said nonchalantly. I had slowed the vehicle down already, to duck in case Sunil retaliated with violence. However, I was relieved to see him turn pale.

Vimal was surprised. "Who told you that?"

I pointed at the locket. Sunil gave me a look of awe, or fear, or probably both. He asked slowly, "Did Aditi discuss Leo's relationship with you?"

"No. I guessed."

Inspector Babu asked, "What do you mean lovers ... oh ... OH ... OOH!"

I asked Vimal, "What can you tell me about Leo?"

Sunil interrupted, "Nothing. We don't keep contact with him at all."

"Where is Mr Kapoor heading?"

"Dad is going to Tox town. Leo has an apartment there."

"You don't keep any contact with Leo, but your dad knows where he stays?" Curiosity was evident in my voice.

"Yes. Leo stays in The French Boulevard."

"That's not what I meant. How do you guys know where he stays?"

I looked at Vimal in the rearview mirror, expecting an answer. He averted his eyes.

"You used to visit Leo for cocktails then?"

Vimal replied drily, "The apartment was gifted to Leo by Anil."

"Aha," I nodded, understanding.

There was a blind corner at the edge of the road, and I turned only to be greeted by commotion. The Land cruiser had banged into an Alto. Three irate teenagers, evidently the occupants of the Alto, had surrounded Paras and were shouting at him.

I braked hard, heard some curses from the driver behind me, and tried to steer to a corner of the road. Babu responded with a speed surprising for a man of his build, and was between the three youths and Paras even before I had managed to bring the car to a halt.

Babu took charge immediately, and said something to the youths that made them scoot faster than chilled beer through a digestive tract. The only major damage was a nasty dent on the Land cruiser, and a cut on Paras's forehead that kept bleeding. It was decided that Sunil would drive Paras to a hospital in the Land cruiser. Babu and Vimal joined me in my car, and we continued our journey to Leo's house.

The French Boulevard was one of those classy apartments. The lawn was covered by grass that you see on tennis courts on Star Sports, and the women wearing stilettos blew flying kisses at each other while walking their poodles. Two towers touched the sky overlooking a gigantic pool. The architecture was gaudy and rich. I wondered why it was called The French Boulevard.

"What's so French about it?" I asked no one in general.

"The architecture!" said Vimal. "Look at the tiled courtyards, red and green roofed terraces, expansive windows, and open spaces."

I laughed sarcastically. "Obviously, the developer mistook Amritsar for France."

"The developer happens to be my father," said Vimal drily, "and I assure you, he's been to France quite often."

I found myself in one of those embarrassing moments that no amount of improvisation can salvage – like the time when you start peeing against the imposing wall of a secluded bungalow, and just as you are concentrating on the exodus, the owner of the house, with the personality of an army colonel, and a German Shepherd at his heels, confronts you. You are at your most vulnerable, anatomically, and any attempt to salvage your pride is futile. You just ignore them and get out.

I pretended to fiddle with the car radio. Vimal was still sulking when I asked, "By the way, how does Leo look?"

"I have never seen him."

We parked the car in the visitor's parking area and walked towards the entrance of the building.

"Do you know the exact address?"

"House number 203. Second floor," said Vimal, pointing to a terrace. There were some clothes drying on the railing of the terrace.

Babu marched to the guard sitting at the reception and spoke authoritatively, "We want to see Leo."

He turned to Vimal and asked for Leo's full name. Vimal didn't know.

The guard opened an orifice decayed with years of tobacco abuse and said, "Leo sir is out since last evening. He hasn't come home."

"Are you sure?"

"Yes. He informed me that he would be back only tomorrow night."

We came out disappointed, and Babu charted out the future course of action.

"I need a search warrant. I will phone the station and get it issued. I will also call for a backup, so that we can wait here and ambush him. You may have to drive me back to the Kapoor residence. My jeep is there."

"Well, I guess there is no point waiting here. I will drive both of you to the house and—"

"What's wrong?" Babu noticed my puzzled expression.

"There was a brown towel in the balcony when we came. It is not there now," I said, pointing towards the terrace.

"Are you sure?"

"Positive. Also, the door leading to the room from the terrace is open. Why would someone leave the door to the terrace open if he is out for a couple of days? Leo is inside! He must have instructed the guard to lie."

I looked at the pipe leading to the terrace, and quickly told Babu of my plan. "I will climb up the pipe and enter from the terrace. Once I am inside, I will dash to the main door and open it. We can capture him then. When I am halfway up, you, Vimal, and the watchman, walk up to Leo's main door and wait there. If I don't open the front door in five minutes, break it open and charge in."

I assumed that everyone was in acquiescence, and made a sprint for the pipe. To my amazement, I hadn't moved an inch. I looked behind and saw the reason for the impediment. Inspector Babu was holding my T-shirt. He said disapprovingly, "I am afraid I can't let you do this."

I gave him a disbelieving stare. "Why not?"

"It is too dangerous. If anyone has to climb up the pipe, it has to be me," he said nobly.

I looked at the chaotic mass of his stomach, and pleaded with my eyes.

"Inspector, please understand that in this case, procrastination will make us culpable of helping the criminal escape. Leo has instructed the guard to lie. That means he is trying to buy time, maybe fix evidence. I think I may be faster than you."

He growled. "Ha! You are a bloody civilian. I have been trained in countering obstacles you can't even imagine."

I looked at Vimal for help, but he did not register any emotion. I was sure the guard would have informed Leo that an inspector had come snooping around. We were losing precious time.

I said with full conviction, "I know that, inspector. I wouldn't dream of trying any other obstacle in your presence. The only reason I volunteer to climb up the pipe is because I have the relevant experience in all kinds of activities related to acrobats."

"What do you mean?"

I looked at Vimal. "Tell him about my pedigree."

"What?" Vimal asked me stupidly.

"I am a natural in trapeze acts. It's in my blood. My ancestors were amazing acrobats. They did that for a living."

"Really?" Babu asked and relaxed his grip.

"Cross my heart and hope to die. See, I am still alive. Let me go."

The inspector looked guiltily at Vimal. "You are witness that he is going up, even though I offered to go."

So this was what this was all about. And I thought Babu was concerned about my welfare.

I replied on behalf of Vimal. "Inspector, *in case* I fall and break any limb, or Leo hurts me, it is my responsibility. For the record, even though you wanted to go up, and confront Leo yourself, I insisted and ran to the pipe before you could stop me. Vimal is witness to that."

"And you told me that you were experienced in climbing. *Acrobat* is the term you used."

"That is absolutely correct. Now let go of me."

He released his gorilla-like grip and asked, "What did your family do exactly?"

I sprinted a few steps away from him before replying. "My ancestors were apes. You should have seen them swinging from tree to tree."

I tied my handkerchief on my right hand to handle the friction between the metal and my skin. The developer had planted creepers along the walls of the building, no doubt to achieve the 'French effect'. They sprang in all directions along the pipe, making my climb difficult. It took me five minutes to cross the first floor. I looked up and saw that Leo's terrace was still about twelve feet above me. I looked down, and signalled to Babu and Vimal to make their move. I was almost there. My legs were trembling, and I was out of breath. I hadn't played Spiderman since I was a toddler, and I could feel my arms and legs revolting at the unnecessary effort. I halted for a few seconds and then began the vertical ascent again.

It took me another five minutes to finally reach Leo's apartment. I lifted my left hand off the pipe and grasped the terrace railing. I looked down, and my hands went cold anticipating my next move. My right hand let go of the pipe and grasped the railing as well. I dangled from the railing for a few seconds. Then I raised my body against the railing, slowly pulling myself up till I could swing one leg over the railing. I fell onto the terrace and huddled in a corner.

There was no sign of Leo. I crawled to the door that was ajar, and peeped into the room. It was a sparingly furnished bedroom with a double bed, a wooden cupboard, and a television. There was an open suitcase on the bed, carelessly filled with clothes. Someone had been packing in a hurry. The other door of the bedroom was partly open, and I could see a passage. It would probably take me to the main door. I decided to make a dash to the front door, and confront Leo, after taking refuge behind Babu's gun.

I had just got on to my knees in the on-your-marks position, when Murphy's Law prevailed. An athletic, tall man appeared from a hitherto hidden bathroom adjoining the bedroom. He was bare-chested, and carrying a shaving kit in one hand. He had a brown towel wrapped around his neck. He saw me, and shouted something nasty. Before I could react, I saw his hand thrust forward in a bowler's action and a metallic object hit me below my left eye. Intense pain, and a fountain of lights, seemed to explode in my eyes. It left me dazed. I stumbled, tripped, and fell backwards on the floor.

I lay there dazed, and touched the wound below my eye. I felt some loose skin drenched in thick liquid that I hoped was blood and not some liquid leaking through the cranium. I glanced sideways. The son of a bitch had thrown a deodorant bottle at me! I tried to assess the damage to my eye, straining to open the partially stuck eyelid. I lost precious seconds, and Leo was standing over me. He delivered a powerful punch to my solar plexus, cutting off my breath, and I groaned at the sharp pain that burnt my intestines. He pinned me down to the ground with his body weight, and started to strangle me.

"Who the fuck are you?" he asked.

Maybe it was the subconscious awareness that a half-naked gay man was sitting on top of me, with my hips under his legs; maybe it was the cheap pub that Pranay and I had started frequenting, that always showed wrestling on television ... Whatever the reason, I felt a sudden rush of testosterone, and locked my legs around his neck in a classic wrestling style, and pushed him back.

Our position had reversed, and I was on top now. I had always preferred the missionary anyway. His fingers found my windpipe, and I started choking again. My knees were burning from the climb, my left eye was numb, and my stomach was experiencing slight cramps. Leo was struggling violently under me. I felt my grip relax. I jammed my right knee with great force into Leo's abdomen. His pupils dilated, and his grip slackened.

I got up as quickly as my legs would permit, and tried to run for the door. Leo tripped me with his leg, and I fell face down on the bed, hitting something hard. My tongue tasted something salty. I was not on the beach, so it had to be blood. I felt too dazed to get up. From the corner of my eye, I saw Leo get up and walk towards me. I looked at the object I had fallen on. It was his shaving kit. I zipped the pouch open, and scrambled around to find anything that could be used as a weapon.

I found a metallic can of shaving spray and held it tight. Leo's superhuman strength became evident when he lifted me effortlessly, with his hands under my armpit, so that we were face-to-face. I had the can in my left hand. I thrust my right hand forward, pushed his chest away with all my might. His grip slackened, and my toes touched the floor. He pulled his fist back, held on for a few seconds, and then catapulted it towards my face. Within milliseconds his fist would hit my nose. I jerked my arm up, pushing the can towards his jaw. It hit him before his fist touched me. I heard some bones crack. He released me and collapsed on the ground, groaning in agony. There was no time for congratulating myself. I heard the doorbell ring, and limped to the main door swearing at Babu. He should have broken down the door by now.

The door bell rang again. I opened the door and said to Babu accusingly, "I thought I told you to break the door open."

Vimal and Babu both said in unison, "My God! What happened to your eye?"

I counted till five, and breathed normally again. "Why didn't you barge in?"

"I thought ringing the doorbell would be better. What happened to your eye?"

"Got into a scuffle with Leo. He's lying injured in the other room. Why the hell would you ring the bell if I wasn't at the main door, you fool?"

"How does it make a difference?" Babu asked defiantly.

"What if he had put a bullet in my head and escaped from the pipe?"

I didn't wait for an answer, and guided the inspector to the room where I had left Leo a few minutes ago.

"You overpowered him?" Babu sounded surprised.

I felt some kind of movement as soon as I entered the room, and immediately ducked, missing the cricket bat by a couple of inches. Leo swung the cricket bat blindly once more, and Babu ducked too.

"Don't come towards me!" he yelled and rushed towards the door. Only the gentle Vimal stood between it and Leo. I expected him to be wise and step aside. However, Vimal brought his fists up in a boxer's stance and stared boldly at Leo. Leo hissed in anger, and waved the bat menacingly at Vimal, who bent backwards as though his spine were made of elastic. The bat missed his face, and Leo was thrown off balance. Vimal landed a left-handed punch on Leo's jaw, and almost carried him off the floor. Leo lay stone cold on the floor. Babu and I looked at Vimal in admiration.

"Wow. You took good care of him," I commended him.

"Three times gold medallist in boxing. University level," he said shyly.

Babu handcuffed Leo to a chair, while I picked up parts of my personality strewn on the floor. My shirt was torn, and one of my shoes was missing. Vimal helped me pick up my wallet, car keys, a pen, and some fabric from my shirt.

I took stock of the damage to my eye in the bathroom mirror. A small plum had formed where my eye used to be. The pain was increasing with time, and I needed immediate medical attention. I went to the hall and took out a bottle of vodka. There was nothing else in the refrigerator. I was not much of a vodka drinker, but these were dire straits. I joined Babu and Vimal in the room. Leo was semiconscious now, and trying to understand what was happening.

Babu looked at the bottle of vodka in my hand, and stared at me disapprovingly. "You can't drink that."

"Why not?"

"It is personal property."

"So was my eye."

"You need proper medicine for that, not vodka."

"I know. But the bugger has no whisky or beer in the refrigerator. You know what they say. Patients can't be choosers."

I dispensed with etiquette and took a direct swig from the bottle. That was for the eye. I immediately took another one for my bruised knees. I concentrated on the faint pain in my abdomen and took another gulp. The vodka burnt my throat, reduced the pain, and I immediately felt better. I even smiled good naturedly at the morose Leo, who was regaining consciousness.

"What's your name?" barked the inspector in an intimidating way.

Leo stared at us insolently and said, "I want to make a phone call first."

Slap.

"Answer the question."

Leo looked at Babu without an iota of fear.

"You don't know my contacts. All of you will be sorry. Watch it. Do you even have a warrant for me?"

I pitched in. "Listen, you are a suspect for the cold-blooded murder of the city's biggest real-estate developer. If anyone needs to be sorry, it is you."

Reality dawned on him, and he became aware of the reason why we were there. His eyes widened.

"What? I am a suspect for Anil's murder? Are you crazy?"

I spoke to Babu, "He is Leo all right."

The inspector jubilantly took out the heart-shaped pendant inscribed with the letter *L* and suspended it before Leo's face.

"We found this at the scene of the crime."

For a moment Leo paled, and his tone sobered.

"This is not mine! I mean ... Anil had given it to me, but I returned it to Anil a few weeks ago. I didn't murder Anil."

"Every madman says he is a genius, and every criminal says he is innocent," said Babu philosophically.

I took out my trustworthy tape recorder and hit the record button. Babu's pearls of wisdom were priceless.

"Do you have some proof that you returned the pendant to him?" I asked.

He thought for a moment and spoke excitedly. "Of course! I threw the locket at him in front of at least twenty people at The Clocker's Pub."

"The Clocker's Pub?"

"It's a pub on Wilson Street. Some of the occupants that night were regular visitors. And wait ... the bartender –

Reddy – he would remember the incident. I threw the locket at Anil, and it fell into his glass. He asked Reddy to get him another drink. I am innocent and I can prove it. Just let me make the phone call."

"You can make your phone call. But we want to ask you a few questions first. If you are innocent, you need not be scared. This will be part of a routine investigation, okay?"

He nodded. I realised what this meant. If Leo could prove that he had returned the pendant to Anil, not only would my original theory of the murderer being an insider hold true, it would also incriminate Shalini. It was the usual mistake a first-time criminal made. It was supposed to be a flawless murder. In his or her panic, the murderer had planted the locket outside the back gate; and going by the circumstances, I was inclined to believe that Shalini was the culprit behind this.

I asked Vimal, "If Leo returned the locket to Anil, who would have access to it?"

"Umm ... Anil would probably have kept it in his room. All of us would have had access to it."

I could see the realization dawn in his eyes, as he answered my question. I knew he was evaluating the same person I was – Shalini. Babu made a phone call and asked someone to talk to Reddy, the bartender, at The Clocker's Pub. Leo was white as a sheet now and, unless he was a very good actor, he was telling the truth.

Babu tried to extract more information from him. "Your real name is Leo?"

"Yeah."

"Leo as in Leonard?"

"Leo as in Leo."

The Inspector was not convinced. "What type of name is that?"

"I was born on 23rd July. My parents named me after the zodiac sign."

"Lucky you," I chipped in.

"Why?"

"One day earlier, and you would've been called Cancer."

Leo didn't find the joke funny. I looked at the carelessly half-packed suitcase, and grinned.

"If you are innocent, why were you packing? Why would you assault a police inspector with a bat and make a run for it? What are you hiding, Leo?"

"I ... I ... thought ... you were thieves."

Babu turned a nasty shade of crimson. "Do I look like a thief to you?"

I was not convinced. "So that is why you attacked us. Why would you instruct the guard downstairs to lie?"

I went to the suitcase and emptied its contents – casual wear, undergarments, and toiletries. I could feel Leo's eyes on me. I walked to a table in the corner and opened a drawer. There was an envelope there. I could see his reflection in the mirror next to the table. He licked his upper lips nervously, and moved his gaze from my back to the cupboard. He was nervous about something in the cupboard. I opened the cupboard. There were clothes, some documents, and a large black leather bag that was locked.

"Key?"

"What are you doing? Don't touch my bag. I will sue you."

"Silly boy," I said, and picked up a pair of scissors lying on the table. The scissors had been lying there all along. A murderer, who could stab someone in the heart, would not have used a deodorant bottle or a cricket bat to attack an intruder. He would have used the scissors. I dragged the blades of the scissors along the width of the bag and emptied the bundles of currency notes on the bed. There were one-thousand-rupee note bundles. Babu whistled. There were five hundred bundles, and each bundle had a hundred notes.

"That's a cool five crores in cash. Care to explain this?"

Leo had aged two years in two seconds.

"They are my savings, from my modelling assignments."

"Who were you modelling for? Reserve Bank of India?"

Babu stared at the notes in hypnotic wonder. Vimal walked to the bed, picked up a bundle, and remarked casually, "The currency is authentic."

Five crores in cash. The inspector was stumped, the detective was tempted, and the rich dad's son was nonchalant. Life was fair.

Babu looked at Leo menacingly and said, "You better have an explanation for this."

"I ... I earned it".

I placed the scissors below his chin, and lifted his face. "Either Anil gave it to you, or you stole it from him. Which one?"

All that crap about the eyes not lying is actually true. He knew that I knew, and he knew that he was cornered. His eyes conceded defeat and he said, "I didn't steal it from Anil. He gave it to me. Can you light a cigarette for me, please?"

Vimal spoke up. "That is a load of bullshit. Anil would never give that kind of money to you."

"I think he did," I said.

I picked up Babu's keys from the bed, and unlocked Leo's handcuffs. He took a cigarette from his pack, lit it, inhaled deeply, and immediately relaxed.

"Thanks a lot."

"No sudden movements," Babu threatened him. Then, turning to me he asked, "How do you know Anil gave him the money?"

"If he had murdered Anil, he would have left the country yesterday with the cash. I am assuming he became aware of Anil's death just now, and was trying to escape with or without the money. He knew that if he was found with the cash, he would become the prime suspect. He was desperate to escape. That's why he attacked us."

Leo nodded. "Yes! If I had murdered Anil, why would I stay? I saw it on TV an hour ago, and panicked. That's exactly how it happened. The money belonged to Anil."

"I believe you. But you need to give me more dope."

Vimal intervened. "You people don't believe this scum, do you?"

I looked at Leo and said, "Depends on our friend here. As of now, he does seem to have a motive. Five crores is big enough a motive for someone to kill Anil."

"Bullshit! Anil didn't have that kind of money. He got peanuts from his family. Ask him," Leo pointed at Vimal.

Vimal looked at him with hatred.

I turned to Leo. "You have attacked an inspector. Your locket was found at the scene of the murder. You have a motive. Unless you tell us what's been happening, you are going to the noose."

Leo sighed. "We were supposed to go to Paris on Thursday, three days from today. On Saturday night Anil called me, all excited, and instructed me to postpone the tickets to next week. They are in the envelope that you took out from the drawer."

I found two international tickets and handed the envelope to Babu.

"Why did he ask you to postpone the flight?"

"He didn't tell me. He was excited, and mentioned that he had hit a jackpot. He said we would have to wait another week to collect the payment."

"Okay. How much?"

"I don't know. He didn't speak much. He seemed in a hurry."

"What about this? Five crores?"

"He got this money last week. He didn't tell me from where. We were planning to leave India for good. Everything was settled. He called me on his father's birthday, and told me to postpone the trip by a week.

"He didn't show up this morning. Which was normal. He usually spent weekends at home, or his old man burst a vein and didn't pay him his pocket money. I heard about Anil's murder on TV. I panicked, and decided to leave the city. I was packing when you showed up on the balcony. That is the truth."

"At what time did he call you on Saturday?"

"Around seven in the evening."

"So let me get this right. The cash in the apartment is Anil's, and you are unaware of the source. Both of you were planning to leave the country this Thursday. Something happened on Saturday evening, that got him excited about another big payment, and he asked you to postpone the trip, correct?"

"Yes."

I looked at Vimal.

"Anil was Paras Kapoor's heir. Why would he leave the country with just five crores, jeopardizing his inheritance?"

Leo interrupted with a sarcastic laugh. "Inheritance? The old man had already declared that Anil would not get a penny when he found out about me. Anil was on a weekly allowance." He looked at Vimal and continued, "And with the financial mess these guys are in, they will be lucky if they can avoid bankruptcy. Their debts for their dream mall project run into hundreds of crores. Anil always said that the project would ruin them. He hated his family. And they hated him. He had to leave."

I had read about the mall that Kapoor Developers were building in the central business district. Land acquisition had been a tedious process, and the media had had a field day writing about the malpractices the Kapoors had resorted to, to get their hands on the property. The property itself was at a prime location, at the junction of two main shopping streets. I had passed the site many times, and it was hard to miss the barricade with *Kapoor Developers* emblazoned on it.

I turned to Vimal. "I am confused. Is five crores a big amount for someone like Anil?"

"What kind of question is that?"

"An important one. Is there any truth in what Leo is saying?"

Vimal replied reluctantly, "Yes. We are coming out with a flagship mall project in the city. When the market tanked, our bank loan was cancelled, just like with every other developer in the city. The land is on lease from the government, and we have to complete the project within a certain period, for acquisition. We had borrowed money from the market at a high interest. So yes, liquidity was tight. From that perspective, at this time, five crores would be a big amount for Anil ... and us too."

"What's all this about Anil getting a weekly allowance? What does that mean?"

"That is not concerned with the case, and I request you not to go there."

Leo sprang to my defence. "It is true! He was never involved in their work. He was even disallowed the measly financial support when the old man found out about the locket he gifted me – paid for with the company's finances."

Vimal moved threateningly towards Leo, but Babu intervened.

Vimal restrained himself, but said disgustedly, "You must have stolen it all. Anil would not have that kind of money. He was always short of cash."

I faced Leo. "Anil called you last Saturday. That was the night he was murdered. What did he tell you?"

"What I just told you – to book tickets for a week later, and wait till we got the subsequent payment."

"You look like a curious guy to me. I am sure you would have insisted on knowing what was happening."

He took another drag, and averted his eyes. "I don't know. I swear."

I decided he was lying. Whenever a person ends a sentence with 'I swear', rest assured he or she is lying.

"Liar Liar, pants on fire," I pulled the cigarette from his lips, and extinguished it on his thigh, burning a small hole through his trousers. He yelped more with shock than with pain.

He raised his hands in a placatory gesture and said, "I really don't know! Maybe he sold another one of his father's leased buildings. He had attempted forgery once."

"Forgery?" I asked

"Ask him." Leo looked at Vimal again.

I looked at Vimal too and he answered, "Anil had some bad habits. He had forged Dad's signature twice to sell some space in one of our buildings to an investor. He was caught both times."

"Aha," I nodded, understanding.

Babu frowned. "You are onto something. Tell me what it is."

"Nothing. I swear."

I asked Leo, "So Saturday was the last time you spoke to Anil?"

He grinned slyly, now that a few things were dawning on him. "You yourself said that I am not the murderer. The flat is in Anil's name. I am sure that the Kapoors would want to keep the cash. I will get nothing. You guys don't have anything on me! I shan't say another word till I speak to a lawyer."

Babu walked up to me and whispered, "My men checked on Reddy. He is a bartender in the pub, just like Leo said. He has confirmed that Leo returned the locket to Anil during an argument last week. So Leo's alibi is confirmed. It is all very confusing."

I realised that the poor man hadn't deduced the implications of this discovery, so I enlightened him. "If Leo is telling the truth, then the locket was in Anil's custody, and the only people who would have access to his closet or room would be immediate family members. This, coupled with the fact that an eyesight as fine as yours failed to notice the pendant outside the gate yesterday, points only at one thing."

He thought for a moment, and awareness dawned on him.

"To tell you the truth, I already had my doubts! I found it

hard to believe that I had missed an essential piece of evidence like the pendant at the scene of the crime yesterday."

I looked at Vimal. "See. I told you, Vimal. The inspector always supported my theory. He was just playing along."

"Yes, yes, I was just playing along."

I searched the flat for a couple of minutes, but found nothing consequential save some pieces of an airplane ticket. Air France. I looked at Leo.

"These are the ones I was telling you about. For this week."

Ten minutes later, a couple of sub-inspectors came in to apprehend Leo.

"What do you intend to do with him?" I asked Babu.

"Well, I can definitely take him in for attempting violence on a police inspector. But I have intruded into his house, with some civilians. If he really knows someone influential, it could mean unnecessary trouble for me.

"The flat is registered in Anil's name; the money can easily be attributed to the Kapoors' affluence. If Anil forged a signature again, the family will stick together, and the money will be accounted for. Nothing out of the ordinary.

"I think I will take Leo in for questioning, just to shake the rascal up, and teach him some humility. But I will have to release him in two or three hours."

It was almost six when I left Leo's house. Leo was not even taken to the police station. Reddy, the bartender, had affirmed Leo's version, and arranged five more people who had witnessed the fight between Anil and Leo that night. All of them remembered Leo throwing an ornament at Anil's face and marching out in anger. While we were on our way back, Vimal phoned Sunil, and told him about what had happened at

Leo's apartment, exaggerating my heroism and undermining his contribution in capturing Leo.

"How is your father?" I asked Vimal after he disconnected.

"He is fine. He needed two minor stitches, but they want him to be admitted tonight for an entire check-up. You need some help for your eye too."

Vimal drove the car through the imposing gates of his bungalow, guarded by two gunmen, who looked only too trigger happy to me. Vimal had offered to drive my car so that I could rest my eye. At least that was what he said. I had a nagging doubt that he was nervous about me driving with all the vodka in my bloodstream.

"I see you keep gunmen for security."

"Yeah. The business of real estate is such."

Vimal got off near the house and thanked me. A driver was waiting for him to take him straight to the hospital.

"Your eye looks nasty. Would you like to accompany me to the hospital? Get it checked. I am going to meet Dad there anyway."

"Nah. I will be fine. But thanks for asking."

He brought his phone close to my eye, the light from the display screen illuminating the damage. His concerned expression told me it was bad.

"Well, get some treatment. It looks terrible."

"I will," I paused. "Incidentally, I need a favour. I would like to intrude upon your house tomorrow and talk to some of you. Is that okay?"

"Umm...sure. I will inform Dad."

I drove out of the gate. The cheeky guard made me roll the window down, and checked the vehicle again.

The sun was setting, leaving behind a residue of a dull pink and orange. It looked tired and serious, reflecting my own state of mind. I thought about Aditi in the café, and felt my own heart sinking with the sun. A man had almost taken my eye out of the socket, my knees had whitewashed an entire apartment block, my intestines were flattened; and yet, the only pain I felt was within ... when I remembered Aditi. I was hopeless.

I opened the door of the apartment, and was greeted with the sweet smell of weed in the air. Pranay was lying on the bed, looking at the ceiling. Bruno was lying with his head on Pranay's lap, and also staring at the ceiling. The lights were switched off, and trance music played softly. I switched on the lights, and Pranay cringed in pain.

"Nasty man. I was just getting transported."

Bruno looked at my eye and started barking in terror – part charging, part retreating. "Shut up, stupid dog. It's your master."

"You need a doctor, man," Pranay commented noticing my eye.

"I need a drink." I was exasperated.

I went to the mirror and looked at the wound. It was ghastly. The plum had bloated to double the size. The only good thing was that the major impact of Leo's blow had missed the eye, and landed upon the upper cheek, so the wound was more cosmetic.

"What are you drinking?" I asked Pranay.

"Standard. Rum."

I took the bottle lying on the table and poured myself a generous amount of rum and coke. I refilled his glass and raised a toast.

"Cheers. To swollen eyes."

"So how did you get that eye?"

"Long story."

"I can spare some time from my busy schedule."

I filled him in on the details, starting from the car chase with Paras, and ending at the commando-confrontation with Leo.

"So, you think Shalini is the murderer?"

"Don't know. But I do know that she is trying to throw me off the case for some reason."

We drank in silence and soon Pranay closed his eyes and smiled. Transported, perhaps.

I sat there drinking alone, until I had wiped off more than six inches from the bottle. The music was soothing, and I poured myself another drink. A lazy warmth pervaded me. I remembered Aditi's smile at the café. It must be a masochistic need in people to think about their biggest losses after getting drunk. The glass fell down and broke into a million pieces. I took a swig from the bottle. The darkness was whirling in concentric circles, and I felt the familiar pull into the vortex of promised love. My sentinels were defeated, and I gave in to the past.

"I want to become a monk," she said.

Just minutes ago we had been kissing passionately. If anyone else had displayed this transition in mood, I would have laughed my guts out. But not with Aditi. Such impulsive introspection was natural to her. I was used to her transformation from a seductress to a pensive woman, to a chaste monk, in a single moment. It fascinated me.

"When did you decide that?" I asked.

"I have always been exploring the idea. I tried chanting mantras, and visited shrines. It brought me peace."

Her eyes had a distant, dreamy look. Yet they were attentive, examining the surroundings with purpose.

"I don't think you are cut out to be a monk."

She looked up and locked her eyes with mine. I had that familiar, eerie feeling that she could read my mind and tell exactly what I was thinking.

"Why do you say that?" she asked.

I grinned. "Monks are supposed to be celibate. Your passion could be a hindrance."

She smiled back. "Well, I could be celibate if you were nowhere near. It's only with you that my animal instincts are aroused."

"Then maybe I should stay away from you. I hate to be an obstacle in your spiritual quest."

She smiled, and ran a finger down my cheek. "No, that will make me sad."

In the west the orange and red glow of the sunset was beginning to fade away. We were sitting on the edge of a hill, and I could see eternity in the depths of the valley below. I sensed her sadness, and knew she was feeling guilty about Chetan.

She asked me almost on cue, "Do you believe in God?"

I pointed to the red and velvet ribbons emerging from the sinking sphere. "I believe in nature. It never betrayed a heart that loved her."

She looked in the direction my finger was pointing at. "That's a beautiful thought. But nature is neutral. Do you fear that there is a God who keeps a tab on our good and bad deeds? And that we will have to atone for our sins?"

"I don't know. But if there is some sort of celestial justice, I wouldn't mind. It's fair."

"Yes. I hope so too. It is only fair. But do you fear that?"

I put my arm across her shoulder and reassured her. "Listen, what happened was not your fault. He was weak ... and let me assure you, you don't have anything to fear. It was his infatuation that drove him to suicide, not your encouragement."

Even as I said that, I diverted my gaze lest she see the doubt in my eyes. "There are other tangible fears that should be occupying your mind – like what nerve racking dinner the mess will serve tonight."

She smiled. "Hmm ... I think I have one of those ... tangible fears."

"What's that?"

"Public singing."

"Public singing?"

"Yes. When I was nine years old, I was asked to sing at a birthday party. I started singing, and all the other children started laughing. I've never sung in public after that."

"Sing for me."

"Why should I?"

"Because I want to hear you. And I could never laugh at you."

"That is because you are biased. But I will sing anyway. I always wanted to sing to someone."

"Great."

"There is this song by Bette Midler. It reflects my thoughts. Have you heard of it?"

"Nope."

"Okay, here goes ..."

She looked down shyly and started singing. I couldn't understand much of the song, and her voice was out of tune and untrained. But sitting on that hill, being an audience with the trees, it was the sweetest voice I had heard.

It's the hope of hopes, it's the love of loves,
This is the song of every man.
And God is watching us, God is watching us,
God is watching us from a distance.

She ended the song and looked at me intently, trying to gauge my reaction. I was entranced and replied after a few seconds, "That was quite good. You have an innocent voice."

"You have to say that."

"I don't have to."

"Yes, you have to. That's what lovers do. Hide each other's flaws."

I woke up with elephants stampeding in my head. It was ten in the morning, and I vowed for the umpteenth time not to have rum. It was strictly for the dogs. I went to the refrigerator and made my customary hangover destruction drink – the ephemeral battle of refreshing the senses only to intoxicate them.

I looked at my eye in the mirror, and was pleased to see that the depressing purple had transitioned into a rebellious red. I was debating whether to sleep my headache off or keep my appointment with the Kapoors, when the phone rang. It was Vimal.

"Hi."

"Good morning. Did I wake you up?" he asked in surprise.

"No, I was up hours ago." I lied for the heck of it.

"Oh ... I have been trying to reach you. You were not taking the call."

I saw the missed calls on my mobile screen.

"Yeah, I was meditating."

"Oh ... okay. I told Dad you wanted to talk to some family members. He has requested that you meet him before you speak to anyone else. There is a prayer meeting for Anil starting at one today. Some relatives and guests are expected. We are a little busy, so we wanted you to come a little early."

I looked at the time. It was already ten-fifteen. There was throbbing pain at my temples, and my back demanded a soft mattress. I tried to keep the relief off my voice.

"Not a problem, I can come tomorrow."

"Okay ... hold on. Let me ask Dad."

There was an exchange in the background.

"Dad says it would be nice if you could come today, before the ceremony starts, and talk to Shalini. He would also like to speak to you himself."

"Uh ... thanks, Vimal, but I didn't say I wanted to speak to Shalini."

I must have been on speakerphone, for Paras responded, "I assumed that you would want to talk to Shalini. Was I wrong?"

His tone was confident and mocking. Obviously, he suspected her too. Maybe he had some evidence and wanted me to confront her.

"No, I did want to speak to her. I will be at your place in an hour."

I took a shower and dressed quickly. Bruno followed me around, growling at my eye. I put on sunglasses to relieve him. I woke Pranay up, and told him to meet me at office for lunch. An hour later, I was at the Kapoor residence. The gate was opened by one of the trigger-happy guards. He opened the boot and searched the car. I took off my sunglasses, hoping that he would recognise me from last evening.

"Sign this," he said gruffly, thrusting a register at my face.

"I was here last evening with Vimal."

"Many people were here last evening. Sign it."

I filled in the details and handed the register back to him.

"You can pass."

Maybe it was my car that pissed him off. He probably wasn't used to searching cars that were anything less than flashy SUVs. I blew him a kiss, and drove in.

A spacious tent covered half of the lawn that was witness to a flurry of activity, with cleaners and waiters running around. I parked the car and walked to the main door. I rang the bell, and was surprised to find Ram at the door.

"I thought you were the caretaker of the farmhouse. What are you doing here?"

"I come to the city whenever there is a big function, to supervise things."

"Good for you. I am here to see Mr Paras Kapoor."

"Yes, he is expecting you. Please follow me."

He led me through a claustrophobic hall, meshed with grandeur and pomposity. He stopped in front of a door and knocked. Paras was sitting on a rocking chair, turbaned in a white bandage. It was a plush set-up with neat and tidy woodwork. Long rows of books in oak shelves ran along the perimeter of the room. A home library. Nice. Ram was exiting when I called him back.

"Ram, I would like to talk to you after this. Where can I find you?"

He turned around and asked cautiously, "Talk? Regarding, sir?"

Paras intervened. "That's okay, Ram. Stay in the kitchen till he calls you."

That settled it. The general had ordered the valiant soldier to stand in front of the firing squad. Ram took a half-bow, and left.

"How is your head?" I asked Paras.

"It's a minor scratch." He pointed to my sunglasses. "How is your eye?"

"Playing rainbow. It has already changed three colours. Should be back to the normal colour soon."

"Vimal told me what happened yesterday. It was very brave of you to apprehend Leo. Babu called this morning. Leo was speaking the truth. He has more than six witnesses who saw Anil return the locket to Leo that night. What can this mean?"

The old man smelt of deception. He knew precisely what it meant. I played along.

"Well, it would seem that someone planted the locket to frame Leo. Probably the murderer. He must have got nervous."

Paras got up slowly from the rocking chair, and walked towards one of the book racks. He picked up a book and glanced through it. He put the book down, came back, and sat down on the rocking chair. He rocked the chair for a few seconds, building up suspense.

"Yes. You are probably right. When Shalini remembered she had heard some noises outside the gate, and Babu found the locket, it gave me hope. But if Leo is innocent, then it can only mean one thing."

He said the last sentence with resigned acceptance, and looked at me, anticipating some comment. I raised my eyebrows questioningly. He rocked his chair for a few seconds, and then said firmly, "This is going to be complicated. I assumed you would want to speak to Shalini today."

"Yes, I was planning to start with her."

"Do you suspect her?"

"No. Do you?"

He looked at me in disbelief. "You don't suspect her! Then why do you want to interrogate her?"

"Not interrogate; talk to her. To start with. I would like to talk to each family member subsequently."

He stared at me. "Why don't you start with me?"

"I have nothing to ask you now, unless you want to tell me something on your own accord."

"Hmm ... how old are you ... if you don't mind me asking?"

"Nope; age I am okay with. Just don't ask what my salary is. I am twenty-eight."

"You are smart for your age. I was surprised when you showed up at the farmhouse. I asked Sunil, and he mentioned that you had been classmates." He paused. "She is a beautiful girl. You must be regretful."

I was glad I was wearing sunglasses, and the old man couldn't see the wild movements of my eyeballs. I said in a mind-your-own-business-tone, "Forgetful, not regretful. How did you know?"

"A guess. I noticed Sunil was not particularly fond of you when you showed up at the farmhouse that day. That drove me to grill him about you. You can always tell with your kids".

"Well, I don't have the luxury of having grievances against my clients. Bad for the business."

I didn't want him to digress from the topic. "Okay, sir. I want to start with you, ask some basic questions. Tell me, what is bothering you? Do you have a gut feeling about who the murderer is?"

He stared at me for a long time. It was an intimidating stare, used to make people nervous. I stared back. Finally, he said in a weary voice of a sixty-year-old man, "Yes, I have suspicions. And so do you, young man. Maybe we suspect the same person. Anil had his shortcomings, but no one would want to murder him. And yet everything suggests that he was murdered by one of my own. If that is the case, then that person is Shalini."

He said it as a matter of fact, devoid of any anger or resentment.

He continued, "I want to tell you something that will help you put things in better perspective. Anil was our first-born, and we pampered him. He was very close to his mother. When she died, I immersed myself in work and could not give him the time and attention he needed. Let us say he had a misunderstood adolescence. The others were still young when my wife died, so they were easy to distract. Anil was a rebel. He was always creating problems. Some were big problems."

He was silent again, and I waited for him to continue.

"I tried to make a last effort to change him. You know about Leo?"

I nodded, and he said, "It was very hard for me to come to terms with the fact that Anil was a ... you understand?"

He continued, "Mayank has been my accountant for more than twenty-five years. His wife died when Shalini was just two years old. I treated Shalini like my own daughter. She went to the same school that my sons went to, her birthdays were celebrated with equal pomp as my sons, and I sponsored her college education.

"The point I am trying to bring forth is that I loved her like a father. And I felt prouder than Mayank when she turned out to be such an intelligent and mature lady. When I found out about Anil's preferences, I panicked, and asked Shalini to marry him."

He waited for my reaction. I nodded in encouragement.

"She refused. She was in love with someone else. I was being unfair. Of all my sons, Anil was the least deserving. But I was desperate. It was a cruel joke on me. I was sure physical contact with a woman would reform Anil. He was my blood after all.

"I tried to make Mayank coerce Shalini into marrying Anil. He was a loyal employee. Perhaps too loyal. She refused. I showed my displeasure towards Mayank. He was a weak man, and easy to manipulate. I am ashamed, but I admit that I was instrumental in the deterioration of his health.

"After his first heart attack, I went out of my way to ensure that Mayank got the best treatment possible. I saw it as my chance to convince Shalini to marry Anil. When Mayank recovered, I asked for my reward and got it. Shalini married Anil. I won."

He smiled bitterly at me. I debated over switching on the tape recorder. This was too much information to process. I looked at Paras's grief-stricken eyes and decided against it.

"It has been one year since Shalini married Anil. It has also been a year since I saw her smile. She hasn't smiled since she entered this house. Can you believe it? She has become a ghost. She just reads, and takes her father for walks. Reads and walks! Both father and daughter have reduced to vegetables in front of me. There is nothing I can do.

"So you see Vishal, I am guilty. They are my kids, and I have failed. I have failed as a father and as a protector. That is a very big guilt to live with. You will understand when you are a father."

I was tempted to tell him that the only way I would be associated with the term *father* would be if I renounced the world, embraced Christianity, and became a priest. He was silent now.

"Thank you for telling me this, sir. I understand now. You believe Shalini murdered your son, but you are morally haunted by your own guilt, since you believe she was driven to such dire straits by her forced marriage. Right?"

He nodded. "Her mental balance is affected. She is the only one who had a motive."

"I am still not clear about her motive. What would make her hate Anil so much as to murder him?"

"Anil was responsible for Mayank's second attack. That attack brought him to this unfortunate state. Anil, in a fit of anger, had pushed Shalini down the stairs once. Mayank tried to intervene. Anil ... shook him up. Mayank had a heart attack right there."

"When was that? The second heart attack?"

"Around three months ago. Is that enough of a motive?"

"Maybe. Is there anything else that might have added to her hatred?"

"Anything else?"

"Did he harass her, or abuse her physically?"

Paras looked at me with infinite sadness. "I wouldn't know, son. I wouldn't know. I hope not. But if he did, I never witnessed it. He didn't consummate his marriage though. He told me that just to spite me. He married Shalini only because I had threatened to cut him out of my inheritance."

Paras's lips quivered, and I thought he was going to break down, but he maintained his composure and said, "When you talk to Shalini, please remember not to be harsh with her. I want one promise from you."

"What is that?"

"When you do discover the identity of the murderer, the information should not go out of this house. You will tell me, and disappear from this household forever. I will deal with it. I hope that is okay with you."

"Okay. Sure."

"No one. Not the police, not your friends, not anyone. Are we clear?"

"Crystal."

"Thank you. I am indebted to you forever."

"Don't be. I take cash."

"It's not about the money. We need you much more than you need us."

"How come?"

"It would be difficult for me to confront Shalini unless I have proof. You have to break her. God knows she is a tortured soul, but Anil was my son. I can't have her in the house. But I won't let her go to jail either. I have spoken to some of my psychiatrist friends, and there are lots of places where she can live peacefully.

"All I want you to do is get her to admit to my son's murder, so that we can put this behind us and get on with our lives."

The headache was distracting me. The old man was leading me to believe that Shalini was the murderer.

I said, "Mr Kapoor, do you believe that someone from the family could be involved in the murder?"

He was taken aback and seemed confused. "Yes, of course. You have already established that. I had begun to hope again that you may have been wrong when we got a lead on Leo yesterday. I hoped he was the murderer. I hoped desperately that he was the murderer, because that would've helped me hide my failings as a father. But we know that the entire thing was fabricated, to throw us off the track."

"And you are telling me that Shalini is the murderer?"

He nodded sadly. "Of course! That is evident."

"Mr Kapoor, let me get this straight. Whatever you have told me just now is with the intent of attributing a motive for Shalini to murder your son?"

"It is for your benefit, Vishal. You have to know this to get a confession out of her."

"Do you have any proof that Shalini murdered your son?"

He looked surprised. "Proof! What proof is needed? There is no one else who could be involved!"

"There is unaccounted-for cash in Leo's apartment. Are you aware of that?"

"Yes, I wanted to thank you for helping us recover that."

"You are welcome. My point is – have you accounted for that money?"

"Yes, we know how Anil got the money. You don't have to know the details. It is not related to his murder."

"Anil called Leo the evening he was murdered, saying that he had hit a jackpot. I think I need to investigate this further."

"You don't have to do that." Paras said firmly.

"Okay, then please tell me what jackpot Anil was referring to."

"There was no jackpot. The friend of his is lying. Anil realised that he didn't want to leave his family, and had a change of heart at the last moment."

The old man stared at me stubbornly.

"The five crores in cash? How did he get that?"

"That is immaterial to your investigation."

"I was told he had forged your signature to sell some of your assets in the past. Did he forge your signature this time too?"

He maintained an obstinate silence for a few seconds, sighed, and then said in an exasperated tone, "Yes, he did. He forged Sunil's signature. That fool! He undersold one of our best-tenanted properties ... at half the price."

"That was how he got the money?"

"Yes."

"What was the total amount of the transaction, if I may ask?"

"He sold it for sixty crores. I had offers for ninety crores for the same property."

"Sixty crores? But we found five."

"A certain component of the amount is always paid in black to save on tax. I checked with Mr Asrani, the buyer. In this case, Anil had asked for fifty percent black and fifty percent white."

"That means he got thirty crores in cash?"

"Yes. We haven't been able to find the rest. I am trying to look in all the places. Twenty-five crores have vanished."

"And the remaining thirty crores, the white component?"

"That would have been credited to the company's account. Anil had asked Mr Asrani to deposit the amount on Thursday."

"That was the day he was leaving with Leo?"

"Yes."

"I think I need to investigate the forgery and see what I can find."

Paras said threateningly, "Don't dig into his past! Let his soul rest. You know as much as I do who the murderer is. That is why you wanted to speak to her today. So speak to her and break her!"

"Yes, I suspect her," I said politely. "But I have a hunch that the money could give us a better understanding of why Anil was murdered. Not to forget, we have no proof that can incriminate Shalini."

Paras's nostrils flared. "Don't talk like a damn fool! There is no proof needed. This is my family, and we know what happened."

He was fuming. If looks could kill, he would have killed me. I rubbed my temples to subdue the headache.

"Mr Kapoor, unfortunately, the justice system in our country does not count intuition. Nor do I. You are implying that Shalini is the murderer, and you have provided a motive too. But unless you have seen her committing the crime, or have some tangible proof, please don't use terms like 'breaking Shalini'. All I want to do is have a chat with her."

"Don't get carried away, Vishal," he said, trying hard to control his anger. "You know perfectly well that Shalini is the murderer. She had a nervous breakdown when you reconstructed the murder at the farmhouse. We all saw her.

"What about the locket? Only Shalini could have had access to it. Now, for God's sake, go in and get a confession from her. I can't stand her being in the house."

"Shalini is a suspect," I admitted controlling my own anger. "But unless I prove her guilty, I look at all the people present in the farmhouse on the day of the murder, with equal suspicion."

He closed his fists and leaned towards me threateningly. "If the murderer was at the farmhouse that day, it *has* to be Shalini. It would be crazy to even suggest that someone else committed the murder."

His eyes sparkled ferociously. "Crazy! You understand? I know my family better than you do. So prove Shalini guilty and make my task easier, like I have made yours. Then take your fee and leave. No need to get carried away."

Headaches always made me impatient. I snapped.

"Well then, old man, you don't need me. You need to hire a truth fairy. It would be easy for her. She will just wave her magic wand over Shalini's head and ... Poof! ... you have your confession. After that, you can hire the angel of death to execute her. You can hang her from the stout mango tree I saw in your garden. That can become the Kapoor Tree of Justice."

I got up and walked purposefully towards the door. I had just opened the door to make my exit when there was a cry for help.

"Please stop! Please!"

I turned around and raised my eyebrows. He smiled.

"I am sorry. I guess it was wrong of me to impose my version on you. Please continue your investigation in a manner you find suitable. Just let me reiterate what I believe, and then I will not repeat it. Okay?"

I nodded and he continued, "I am one hundred per cent sure that we will see eye to eye on the identity of the murderer before the end of the day. You are a smart man. I am sure you will be able to think of the right way to make her confess. I have full faith in you.

"Let me assure you, you will spend very little time with Shalini. I know my sons and their wives, Vishal. They are my flesh and blood. They cannot be murderers. The only person who had a motive was Shalini. That is all I wanted to say."

He smiled, and made a gesture of zipping his lips. I was still standing at the door. I had almost stepped out, when I turned back and told him, "You are right, sir. Everyone has a motive. Sometimes it so subtle that the person cannot see it himself."

"Everyone has a motive? Nonsense! What about my motive?"

"You may have a motive for wishing to believe that Shalini may be the murderer. If she is innocent, and the murderer is someone else, you would have failed as a father again. And as you said, the guilt can be unbearable. I will see you around."

I left the distraught father staring into infinity, and went in for my long overdue chat with Shalini.

I walked across the living room, and towards the kitchen. My heartbeat doubled as I caught a whiff of her fragrance. I realised I had been hoping to see her since the moment I had entered the house.

"Hi, Vishal."

I turned around slowly. Aditi was wearing a short red terrycloth bathrobe. Her feet were bare on the cold marble floor, and her hair was wet. She looked as though she had just got out of the shower. Her long, sculpted legs were visible below the robe, which ended about three inches above her knees. The curves of her breasts were perceptible through the robe. She was wearing nothing underneath. Her breasts heaved softly as she started walking towards me.

"I just had to see you! I heard about your eye," she said in a concerned voice.

Her expression was serious, but her eyes were laughing, daring me to resist her.

I grinned. "A good thing you came too. That's a sight for a sore eye."

I knew she must have planned her entry. She lifted my sunglasses and observed my eye. I felt her breath on my face. She was as tall as I was, five nine, making her tall for a woman.

She was lithe, slender, and it made her look even taller. I was broad, by virtue of years of hitting the gym, and it made me look shorter.

"That must hurt, baby," she said removing my sunglasses, and gently blowing cool air at my eye, almost challenging me with her pink, shapely lips. Her face was devoid of any make-up, and her natural beauty bewitched me. It was happening again.

She was twirling my sunglasses in her hand, fully aware of her control over me. I caught hold of her petite hand and held it still. Then I wiped the sunglasses against the fabric of the robe, between her breasts. I made sure my fingers lingered on her nipples for a few seconds. They were hard.

"Oh ... Vishal!"

I waited until her lips had almost touched mine.

"Sunil!" I exclaimed.

She jerked back violently and turned around. There was no one there. She looked back at me with a petrified expression. I grinned.

"You shouldn't play with fire, baby, unless you want to get burnt."

She looked at me angrily and marched away. I knew she was hurt. I also knew she was vindictive. With her, a misdeed never went unpunished.

Her breath lingered over me, and my headache increased. I wanted a drink. Many drinks. I walked into the kitchen. There was a young woman cooking something. The aroma teased my hunger. I realised I hadn't eaten anything since morning. Ram was nowhere around, so I requested her to guide me to Shalini's room. We passed through the kitchen, down several corridors, and up some flights of stairs, before arriving at a room with the door ajar.

She pointed to the door and hurried back to the kitchen. I entered the room. The lights were switched off, and the blinds were drawn. The room had been plunged into melancholic darkness. Shalini was sitting at the corner of a bed, staring at a laptop. She was oblivious to my presence. I noticed two single beds separated by a dressing table, the size of a tank. I felt sorry for her as I remembered Paras's words that her marriage had never been consummated.

I coughed softly. Shalini's head jerked, and she stood up, almost dropping the laptop. She looked terrified, and transfixed, like a rabbit caught in the headlights of a speeding vehicle. Her eyes were hollow – eyes that had been open for too long and needed rest.

"I am sorry. I didn't mean to scare you."

"Don't you have the basic courtesy to knock?" Her recovery was fast, too fast for my comfort. She had been expecting me.

"Sorry," I went outside and knocked at the door. There was no reply. "Ready or not, here I come."

She had walked to the other corner of the room, and was sitting on a sofa. I was rewarded with an intensely hostile stare. I saw faint traces of fear beneath her hostility. Her shoulders were arched with tension. I sat down opposite her. She was playing with her fingers. She avoided eye contact now, preferring to stare at a distant wall. The white sari she was wearing contrasted against her complexion. Her hair flowed in waves down her shoulders. I realised that Shalini was an attractive woman, the kind of woman a man would like to comfort and take care of.

Her eyes interested me. They darted everywhere, unable to focus at a single place. I stood up and walked till I was right behind her. She immediately stiffened and turned around, watching each step, paranoid. I walked to the closet and opened it. It contained a woman's clothing and cosmetics. I opened the adjoining closet. This one contained a man's clothes. I opened the drawer and saw a few watches, a mobile phone, some credit cards, and a gold wristband. I turned towards her.

"You heard about Leo?"

She lowered her gaze. "Yes."

"It seems Anil carried the locket home. Probably kept it in the drawer in this closet."

She was still staring at the floor, and made no attempt to indulge me. I said in a matter-of-fact tone, "Shalini, Mr Kapoor has given me a carte blanche to question all the family members. Is there a problem with that?"

She locked her fingers, and then flexed them again. "No, no problem."

"Good. I know this must be an unpleasant time for you, but I need to ask some questions. I will make it quick. May I?"

She remained quiet, and hunched her shoulders in a defeatist gesture. I thought about her sharing this depressing room with a man who despised her. I imagined her watching her father fall into a life of oblivion. It must have been a lonely existence.

"The police have established that Leo had returned the locket to Anil. The locket could have reached the farmhouse in two ways. Either Anil carried it there with him, or the murderer took it from this closet. I would be worried if it was the latter case."

She looked at me with cautious interest as I continued, "If the murderer carried the locket to the farmhouse, then we are dealing with an extremely perceptive person, who was smart enough to pre-empt the need for framing Leo, in case his or her plan of incriminating a villager failed. What I am sure of, however, is that the person who put the locket outside the gate is the murderer. Do you agree?"

Always ask the suspect questions that have to be answered in the affirmative. His evaluation of the import of his answer will either slow down the answers or make him nervous. She answered quickly, almost as if she had prepared the answer. "I know nothing of the locket. I knew it existed only because Sunil created a ruckus when it was delivered."

"Ruckus? What kind of ruckus?"

"The bill was charged to the company's account. It was an expensive ornament. Each diamond in that thing must be worth lakhs. When Sunil discovered that Anil had gifted it to Leo, there was a big fight between those two."

"Diamonds?"

"Yes."

"The ones on the letter *L*?"

"Yes."

"I didn't know they were that expensive. You reckon they were worth lakhs?"

"Yes. There were at least ten of them on the pendant," Shalini replied.

"I thought you hadn't seen the diamond pendant in your life. You only knew it existed because of the ruckus that night?"

Her face turned white, and her eyes widened. She said in a barely audible voice, "I haven't seen it."

"Then how did you know that the chain had the letter *L* engraved on it, studded with diamonds?"

"I ... I heard about it."

"From whom?"

"From Sunil."

"When?"

"Yesterday. He described the locket to me." She was perspiring in the air-conditioned room, and I noticed her hands trembling.

"What time did Sunil speak to you?"

"After dinner, I think."

"So after dinner he discussed the pendant in intricate detail with you?"

She whispered something inaudible. I could see she was on the verge of tears.

I said loudly, "Speak up. I can't hear you."

She said in a quivering voice, "Yes. I think so."

"Okay. I think I will speak to Sunil, just to be sure. You have a tendency to forget important details. You also forgot to mention that you heard metallic sounds at the back gate that led us to the locket."

"Frankly, I don't remember who it was," she said defiantly. "It could have been Vimal who told me about the locket this morning, or I might have heard the servants talking."

She was not going to be cornered so easily.

"Okay. Were you aware of Leo's ... eh ... involvement in Anil's life?"

"Yes," she said, visibly relieved that I had stopped asking her about the locket.

She was still not looking me in the eye. There were a million questions looming in my mind, like meteors attacking, and I picked the least incriminating among them.

"Did you love your husband, Shalini?"

She looked up guardedly, surprised at the question.

"What kind of question is that?"

"An insignificant one. You don't have to answer that."

I had succeeded in making her look directly at me, so I asked her a significant one. "Inspector Babu told me that you heard distinct sounds, metal against metal, just before Anil was murdered."

"Yes. It was a faint sound, and I gave it no thought."

"Funny. I remember where your room is at the farmhouse. If I remember correctly, your bedroom is the last one along the passage. And yet you heard noises that no one else heard – not even your father, whose room is closest to the window overlooking the back gate. Of course, one can always argue that you and your father were the only sober people that night. So, if you were able to hear noises, maybe your father heard some too."

I could see the panic in her eyes. She replied slowly. "My father has a weak heart, and suffers from high blood pressure. That is why I don't allow him to drink. He takes sleep-inducing tablets."

"I didn't know that BP tablets were sleep-inducing. I will take the prescription from him and check ... just to be sure."

"Check? What do you mean?" she was alarmed.

"Well, considering that the murderer was cutting the lock on the gate barely half an hour after all of you retired for bed, and your father's room was closest to the gate, I am surprised he could not hear the noise."

"I am telling you he was asleep."

"I know. But just to make sure, I have sanctioned a lie-detector test for him tomorrow," I lied without batting an eyelid.

Tears ran down her cheeks. She said amidst sobs, "Don't harass him. He's been through a lot already."

The sensitivity of the female tear gland always confounds me. I stared at her with cold detachment. I looked around the room, attempting to ignore her sobs, and was elated to discover a small liquor cabinet housing all sorts of colourful elixirs. I had half a mind to go to the bar and take a drink. I diverted my eyes to the wall above it to curb the temptation. There was a family portrait on the wall that caught my attention. I walked towards it, my eyes fixed on one face in the multitude of faces.

Anil and Shalini were seated on the divan, while the rest of the family stood surrounding the bride and the groom. Aditi stood next to Sunil, looking radiant in a traditional red lehenga choli that parted slightly at her midriff. I realised I had stopped breathing. Suddenly, all my senses were active and conscious of Aditi's presence in the wretched house. There was an immense emptiness I felt in the house. I had to get out fast.

I tore my eyes off the portrait and walked towards Shalini, who was still sobbing. I placed my hands on her shoulder and said softly, "Shalini, there was no sound. There was no outsider. It was only after it was proved that the murderer was an insider that you panicked and conjured up the story about hearing a sound. Then, to throw the cops off the track, you placed the locket outside the gate. We can do a fingerprint analysis to see if you touched the locket. There are not many options now except for telling the truth."

The fingerprint stuff was pure bullshit. It had fallen into so many hands, that an exact analysis was not possible.

I had shot an arrow in the dark. The cold accusation hung in the air. My heart beat like a tom-tom. All she had to do was throw hysteria at me, feign a nervous breakdown, excite sympathy, and I would have to back off.

She had her head bent over a table. Her body shook with tearful convulsions. She stopped crying after a minute, wiped her face, and asked me with a look that Eve would have given Adam before he relented and tasted the forbidden fruit.

"Why are you intent upon proving that the murderer is someone from the family?" Her eyes were pleading with me.

"Why are you so intent upon proving that the murderer is *not* an insider?"

"You don't understand. There was no other option."

My heart started pounding at her last statement. Was this a precursor to her confession? The recorder was inside my shirt. I had switched it on the moment I had entered her room. I knew my moment of triumph was a few cajoling statements away.

I spoke very softly. "Shalini, the murderer is an insider. The lock was broken from outside. The steps on the beach..."

She interrupted me with a renewed light in her eyes, speaking with the excitement of a person who, after being sentenced to death, is given a chance at pardon.

"Maybe the murderer didn't get on the beach, and threw the knife from a distance. That would explain the missing footprints on the sand."

I panicked slightly at this new turn of events, and tried to make her relinquish control.

"Shalini, it was pitch dark! The lights were off. Anil was lying on his stomach. You mean to say that the murderer aimed for Anil's heart from that distance, in that position?"

"Yes. And I can prove it!"

"How?" I asked, stupefied.

She ran to the laptop. That made it clear that she had been preparing for our little interview.

She spoke energetically. "I have been doing some research on village gypsies. They are expert knife throwers, and can aim from as far away as thirty feet. Have a look."

There was a buoyant spring in her step, propelled by a desperate need to convince me. She kept the laptop on my lap, and stood behind me. She maximized a web page that showed pictures of silly people dressed in sillier clothes.

"Look at the pictures of this gypsy tribe. They are renowned for their knife-throwing accuracy. Read this text."

She placed the cursor at a certain portion and read aloud. "... successfully aiming at targets as small as an apple placed on a person's head, while blindfolded, from a distance of thirty feet or more."

She opened another webpage and said excitedly, "Read this. These ones are so skilled that some mafia groups employ them as professional assassins."

In her eagerness to prove her point, and harpoon my theory, she had leaned close ... too close. Her soft breasts were pushing hard against me, and exuding warmth that left me cold. It was a deliberate move. I wondered whether, in her naiveté, she actually thought she was distracting me.

My headache took control of me, and commanded that I march to the liquor cabinet. I placed the laptop on the table, got up, and walked towards the bar. There was no whisky or rum in the cabinet. Only gin and vodka. I cursed silently. What was wrong with the world?

I had picked up a glass to pour myself a drink. I remembered my manners and asked Shalini, "Can I pour you one?"

She grabbed the glass from my hand. "Let me. I am quite good at making drinks."

She gave a smile that seemed too eager to please. She carefully measured an exact amount of vodka in my glass, mixing a viscous blue liquid from an unlabelled, transparent bottle. She handed me the glass.

"Try it and tell me how it is."

I felt sorry for her. I knew she was playing around, her enthusiasm a facade to cover the tremendous pressure she was under.

I took the glass from her, and was struck by the unpleasant thought that if she could research gypsies, she could research viscous blue poisons that went along well with vodka. I stared at the drink in my hands. What the heck! You were born to die anyway. I took a sip and relished the taste. It was actually good, and I smiled at her. I could swear she blushed.

She smiled and said, "So you see, there were no footprints on the sand because the knife was thrown from a distance by a gypsy. You can convince people about that. Would you do it for me?"

I finished the contents of the glass before replying, just in case she decided to snatch it back.

"A gypsy from the village? Hmm, the idea is strange."

"Why? Every village has gypsies!"

"No, that is fiction propagated as truth by Bollywood movies. I assure you most Indian villages do not have knife-throwing gypsies picked up by the mafia to become assassins."

Her face contorted angrily and she said, "You just saw the pictures. The murderer is most certainly a gypsy. I am going to show the results of my research to Babu."

She made the last statement with triumph. It was a false effort though. Her eyes belied the terror she felt, and her voice was high pitched, reflecting her insecurity.

"I would advise you not to share this with Babu."

"Why? Because then he would know that your theories are silly?"

I remembered Paras's reference to her madness, and wondered whether she would really be better off in an institution.

"Nope. You shouldn't share your theories with anyone for a good reason. The initial pictures you showed me were of a gypsy tribe from Hungary. The other picture was from a remote village in Africa. You may find it difficult to find their descendants in your local village."

She sighed wearily and looked at me sincerely and said, "Vishal, Anil was a bad man. I swear he got what he deserved. I had endured enough, and this was God's way of giving me justice."

I gauged the implication of this sentence. I had it on tape. I waited with bated breath for the impending confession to follow.

"Please, let it rest. It will not harm you to tell Inspector Babu that some villager committed the crime. Please." Her eyes glistened with tears, imploringly.

I tried to sound shocked. "Rest! Shalini, your husband has been murdered! Why would you want me to stop the investigation when I have a hunch that I may catch the murderer very soon?"

I walked a few paces towards her, so that her next words would be recorded properly. She surprised me by walking faster towards me, and putting her hands around my neck.

She spoke firmly.

"Just back off, Vishal. How does it matter to you? I will do whatever you want. You want to sleep with me?" She pulled me towards her, grabbed my hand, and placed it on her breast. Her eyes made her look like a mad woman. I felt the heat radiating from her body.

I reacted instantly, roughly pushing her away. She fell down on the floor and started crying. However, there was some fatalism about her crying now. I felt sorry for her. I realised that my anger would only worsen her battered state of mind. I poured a glass of water and offered it to her.

"I am sorry, Shalini."

Tears were cascading down her pale face. "I am sorry. This is so embarrassing. I am not like that," she said amidst breathless sobs.

It was heart wrenching to see her cry. I knew there must have been a compelling reason why she had debased herself in front of me. I just hoped the reason was not murder.

"Will you take money?" she asked suddenly, all attentive.

Again, I was surprised by her quick recovery. I shook my head.

"Shalini, I am sure you have a reason for your actions. I want you to know that I see you as a woman of substance, and that will not change, no matter what. I promise you one thing, however. If I find the murderer, I will tell only Mr Paras Kapoor.

"I will not disclose anything to the police, or to any other family member. If it is any solace, Mr Kapoor is not going to hand the murderer to the police. He may only transfer the person to a psychiatrist."

She started to shiver. Her body was trembling. I saw her pupils enlarge. There was a cold knot in my stomach, as I remembered the poison theory. But she hadn't tasted the vodka. I went towards her just before she passed out. She wasn't faking it; she was out cold. I lifted her up and placed her on the bed. I held my finger beneath her nose and checked her pulse. The breathing was normal, and the pulse was steady. She needed rest. I covered her with a blanket. I hadn't got a confession, but a bond had been created. Between a detective and a criminal. Ironical. The bond of common suffering.

I picked up the mobile on the table next to her bed. I went to call-register and checked her received-calls. The last ten calls were from the same person – Raj. I checked her dialled-numbers folder. The last six calls Shalini had made were to Raj. The last one was made at eleven-fifteen, minutes before I came into her room. I checked her messages. The inbox was empty. She had deleted all the received and sent messages. I flipped through the deleted-messages folder. One of the messages was still there. It had come at eleven-twenty. It read,

Just thinking. The gypsy theory is weird. Just offer him money. Relax. You will get thru this. I am always there for you.

I dialled the number. He picked it up at the first ring. "Hi baby. How did it go?"

"It went just fine."

He was silent for a few seconds. "Who is this? Where is Shalini?"

The tone tottered between panic and anger.

"I am Vishal, a private detective hired by Mr Paras Kapoor. You are Raj?"

"Where is Shalini?"

"She is asleep."

"Wake her up. I want to speak to her."

"Not a good idea. She needs some rest."

"If you have harmed her, you will be sorry! I know about you."

"Listen Raj, why don't we meet?"

"I am on my way. Stay there until I come."

"Splendid. How much time will you take?"

"I will be there in twenty minutes."

"Great. I am waiting."

I exited Shalini's room with mixed feelings. I should have felt euphoric, but I felt dismayed. I had nearly solved the case. But the solution would also bring an end to Aditi's presence in my life. Paras's words resounded in my head, *Do your work and leave*.

It had been a mistake to get onto this case. Like cancer, her magic was engulfing me, and each cell in my body had turned traitor, prompting me towards her. I hoped I would see her again.

I tried to subdue my thoughts about Aditi, and concentrated on what had transpired with Shalini. I had almost got her to confess. The corridor led to a balcony. I walked into the balcony, and felt the warm sunshine and crisp air. A colossal tent covered the lawns filled with hundreds of neatly stacked chairs. A portrait, the size of a billboard, was placed at the centre. I focused on the handsome, young face of Anil that smiled at me from the portrait. It was a pity to die so young, no matter how fiendish he was. I saw Vimal barking orders, and supervising the caterers who were laying food on the tables. The waiters lingered around carelessly. There was no sign of Aditi.

"I am here, sir," I heard a familiar voice behind me. I turned around and saw Ram.

"Ah ... here you are. I was looking all over for you," I lied.

"I have been waiting for you to come out of Shalini madam's room, sir. Malti told me you had come to the kitchen. I am sorry; I was out on an errand. Do you want to talk to me now, sir?"

The excitement was evident in his eyes. I could almost imagine him telling his grandchildren the story of the great detective, who interrogated him regarding the gruesome murder of Anil Kapoor.

"Who's Malti?"

"She is my niece. She took you to Shalini madam's room."

All my suspicions were fixed on Shalini. The poor lady had almost acknowledged her crime. I decided to interrogate Ram purely out of habit, rather than agenda. Maybe I could get an insight about Shalini's relationship with Anil.

He led me to the dining room, so that he could keep an eye on the cooks. The aroma of the various delicacies being prepared tantalised my nostrils, and I remembered I hadn't eaten a thing since morning. Ram turned out to be a mind reader.

"Sir, have you had breakfast?"

"Yeah," I lied. I didn't want any digression.

"Would you like some tea or coffee?" he asked obsequiously.

"Sure. Coffee. Black. Thanks."

Ram yelled at a servant in the kitchen, and asked him to make some black coffee for me.

"I heard how you caught Leo, sir. It was a very brave thing to do. Could I look at your eye?"

"Sure," I said, removing my sunglasses, and let him make a fuss over it.

I gave him the same bullshit about Paras having given me the rights to question him, and began his interrogation.

"How long have you been working with the Kapoor family?"

"Seven years, sir. Since the time they built the farmhouse near my village. I helped Paras sir procure the land, and then supervised the construction of the farmhouse. My main responsibility is to take care of the farmhouse whenever the family comes visiting."

"Not much work, eh?" I winked at him.

He appeared shocked. "Oh no, sir! I travel to the city at least twice a week – whenever there is a function, or whenever the family travels abroad, like today I am here to supervise the cooks and the other domestic servants. In fact, my presence here is so important that I have a permanent room in the servant quarters."

"Point noted. So you are indispensable to the family."

His chest swelled up by at least a few inches. A servant came in with my coffee. I was just about to pick up the cup when Ram stopped me.

"Idiot!" he shouted at the servant. "Get the other crockery. Do you know who he is? He is from the police. How many times have I told you to get cream biscuits for important guests? The ones Vimal sir got from America."

The servant vanished, depriving me of the hot coffee, but I said appreciatively to Ram, "I see what you mean. You are the man in charge."

He gave me a grovelling smile. I was not actually from the police, but I hated the idea of telling him the truth and disappointing him. The coffee gave me a rush of energy, and I decided to shake Ram up a bit.

"How is your neck? I see the scratches have almost disappeared."

He paled visibly. "Sir, I got them from the trees in my village. I will cut a tree and bring it to the city, so that you can see how densely they are covered with thorns."

"No, no, not required," I said hastily.

I pretended to stare at a non-existent mark on my nails, and said casually, "Anyway, Babu will get the fingerprints report by tomorrow. There were some fingerprints found on the body. You needn't be afraid, since you didn't touch the body."

He looked terrified. "Sir, I did touch the body when I found it. My fingerprints would definitely be there."

"Did you touch the knife?"

"No, sir."

"Then there is no need to worry. The police would most probably take the fingerprints on the weapon. I will inform them that you touched the body accidently though. Rest assured."

His face regained the entire lost colour, and he offered me the imported cookies.

"But then of course, if the murderer was smart, and wearing gloves ... as I suspect he or she was, then the police would have to rely on the fingerprints on the body to zero in on the suspect. In that case, there would not be much I could do."

"Oh no!" he gasped. "I need to talk to Inspector Babu."

I almost choked on the cookie. "No need for that. I will take care of you."

He folded his hands in appreciation.

"I know an innocent man when I see one, although..."

"Although what?" he shrieked.

I whispered, "Well, we have firmly established that the murderer is an insider. And remember, Ram, blood is always thicker than water."

"What does that mean?" he said, confused.

I looked at him, picked up another cookie, broke it dramatically into half, and gobbled one piece. I paused dramatically.

"Do you know what our first lesson is, while investigating a murder case like this?"

He shook his head.

"That in ninety per cent of the cases, the person who discovers the body is the murderer."

His legs wobbled, and his hands started trembling. I quickly leaned towards him and said reassuringly, "I am your best friend here, okay? Who do you think is the murderer?"

He gulped, looked in all directions to ensure that no one was eavesdropping, and whispered, "Sir, I haven't told this to anyone because no one would believe me. They think I am an old fool."

"They are snobs," I urged in my most bourgeois tone. "Tell me,"

I was barely able to bear the suspense. Would he name Shalini? Detectives have many a time relied on the careless and frank testimony of the domestic help, to solve a crime.

He whispered, "Sir, Anil sir was an evil man. He was punished for his bad deeds."

"Well, for God's sake, who did it?"

"You just said it, sir."

"What did I say?" I controlled the urge to shake him.

"God."

"God?"

"Yes, sir. When Paras sir bought the land, and was clearing the site, we found a small Shiva idol in the middle right where the beach is. I begged sir to construct a boundary and give it the respect it deserved. The place of worship was demolished for people to lie half-naked in the sun. You know what Paras sir did? You know what he did?"

I could guess, but I dutifully shook my head.

"He removed the idol, and gave it to the construction labourers working at the site. God has taken revenge."

He was livid at the memory of the blasphemy.

"How come?" I was too dazed to react.

"Don't you see, sir? The hammock was right at the position where the idol had been. You know what happened one day? I was requesting Paras sir to consider shifting the beach somewhere else, and build a small temple there instead. Anil sir heard me. He laughed at me and urinated on the beach – right where we had found the idol."

Ram trembled with anger, remembering the act of desecration.

"One day my friend Kishore, while returning from the city at midnight, saw a white spirit sitting on the beach and crying ... *at the same spot.*"

Was he pulling a fast one on me? I noticed his wide eyes, the pulsating veins on his forehead, the terror-struck posture, and gave him the benefit of the doubt.

"So you are saying that a white spirit killed Anil?"

"It was an act of God, sir."

"How is that possible?" asked the non-believer.

"With God, anything is possible," said the believer.

'With God, anything is possible,' I repeated slowly. I squinted to look in another direction to suppress a rude laugh. I took a few deep breaths before speaking again. Knife-throwing gypsies, and God, would be a formidable opposition for anyone.

"Well, let's hope God doesn't take care of all retributions himself. I would go out of business!"

Ram looked shocked.

"Okay, Ram, I have a few more questions."

I didn't want him to gauge my suspicions about Shalini, so I kept her for the last. "Tell me about the brothers – about their nature, and the relationship between them."

He spooked me by looking for imaginary white spirits in either direction before replying in a whisper, "Sunil sir and Anil sir used to fight incessantly. Every day, sir. If it wasn't for the timely intervention of Paras sir or Vimal sir, one of them would have killed the other a long time back."

"They used to fight over—?"

"Over everything, sir. They were two opposite planets sir, Rahu and Ketu."

"Focus, Ram! What was the most common reason for their fights?"

"Anil sir was lazy and cruel. He was wasting his father's money. Sunil sir is a good man, but he can't control his temper. Everyone is scared of Sunil sir's temper, including Paras sir. They always fought over money and business."

"Were the fights serious?" I asked.

"Oh yes, sir. Very serious. The servants tell me that the night Anil sir was murdered, there had been a big fight between the two in the evening. Very bad, sir!"

I leaned forward. No one had mentioned a fight to me.

"Okay. Tell me about this very bad fight."

He leaned towards me, till he was practically on my lap, and spoke with an ultrasound frequency that even Bruno would have found difficult registering.

"Speak up. I can't hear a thing."

"Paras sir has forbidden the servants to speak about it in front of the police."

"What exactly has he told the servants?"

"Well, I was not a witness to the fight, sir. I was at the farmhouse. But Malti saw the fight. She's my niece. Paras sir has instructed her not to talk about it to anyone."

I tried to maintain a deadpan expression.

"Hiding important information from a police officer, who is investigating a murder, is a crime with a minimum sentence of two years. Tell me everything you know about the fight."

"I can't, sir. Malti will lose her job, and I my respect in front of Paras sir."

"Listen, Ram, your telling the truth will help me capture the murderer. I have already hinted to you that you are our prime suspect. I am your only friend, remember?"

He muttered weakly, "I can't be disloyal. I have had their salt, sir."

"Don't be stupid. It must have been Tata's. And it will taste the same whether you have it here or in jail."

I could see he was considering the options.

"You promise not to tell Paras sir that I told you?"

"I swear!"

He said, "The fight took place on Saturday evening, before they left for the farmhouse."

"Would you know what the fight was about?"

"Well, I have spoken to the other servants, and have an idea. They are building something big in the city, sir ... something very big, and very costly, at MG Road junction. Sunil sir is handling it."

"Yes, I am aware of the mall they are building."

"It was a cursed project, sir, the root of all problems," he paused dramatically.

I was sarcastic. "Why? Did they find an idol there too?"

"No, sir! Please don't make fun of such things. A lot of money was borrowed for the project ... from illegal sources. Rowdy people started coming to the house and shouting at Paras sir. Vile things, sir ... very vile things. Since Sunil sir was handling the project, Anil sir used to blame him for the financial distress of the family. Of course, I am not the one to gossip. I just heard some servants talking."

"This is not gossip; this is a healthy discussion. Please go on."

"Have you heard of Muktiar Ali? The Don?"

"No. Who is he?"

His eyes became the size of saucers.

"Muktiar Ali? He is going around with Rakhi, the film actress! You must have heard of him?"

I had no idea what he was talking about, so I nodded vigorously. "Yes, Mukhi. I remember now. What about him?"

"On Saturday, his men came to the house. They started throwing the furniture around. Malti hid behind this cabinet when they came in. Sunil sir rushed down to confront them. Malti told me that Sunil sir tried to pacify them, but they wouldn't listen. They carried a piece of paper that they threw at Sunil sir's face, and accused him of cheating the lenders."

"What was that paper?"

"One of those stamp papers that we use to buy and sell properties."

"Okay. What else did Malti tell you?"

"They left threatening dire consequences if the money was not arranged. After they had left, Sunil sir read that paper and lost his cool. Soon he was shouting at Anil sir, and Anil sir was abusing him. Malti told me, they were yelling at the top of their lungs.

"The servants told me that the fight escalated when Sunil sir said something about Anil sir's boyfriend. Anil sir slapped Sunil sir. Sunil sir picked up a knife, and chased Anil sir around the house. Malti swears that Sunil sir would have stabbed Anil sir. He was a madman that evening!"

"What happened next?" I asked

"Anil sir locked himself in the bathroom. Sunil sir kept banging on the door, striking the door with the knife shouting in anger. He calmed only when Paras sir arrived. He had ..."

"Wait! Sunil chased Anil with a knife on Saturday evening?"

"Yes, sir! Malti saw it with her own eyes."

"Get Malti here now."

He was reluctant about that. I gave him my don't-argue-with-me stare.

Ram ushered Malti into the room in a few seconds. He introduced me. "Malti, this is Inspector Vishal from the CID. Tell him the truth."

From the police to CID over a cup of coffee. That must have been the fastest promotion in the annals of the Indian police.

I decided to benefit from the prestige bestowed upon me. "Yes, Malti, I am from the CID. Tell the truth, all right?"

"Yes, sir." she trembled.

"Was there a fight between Anil and Sunil the day Anil was found murdered?"

She looked at Ram, who encouraged her to go on.

"Yes, sir."

"Tell me, what happened exactly?"

"They were shouting at each other. We expected the fight to stop quickly, since they often fought. But that day they came to blows. Sunil sir said something and Anil sir slapped him."

"Then?"

"Sunil sir picked up the knife from the fruit basket, and chased Anil sir around the house."

"You saw this with your own eyes?"

"Yes, sir. All the servants were scared."

"How did it end?"

"Anil sir ran and locked himself in the bathroom. Paras sir came in and put a stop to the fight."

I wondered if Aditi had witnessed the fight.

"Where were the women of the house at that time?"

She thought for a while and replied, "Aditi madam and Reena madam had gone to the club to play tennis. Only Shalini madam was at home."

"Right. How did the knife look?"

"Very sharp, sir! I have cut my finger countless times while washing it."

"That is not what I meant. What was the colour of the handle?"

"It was black, sir."

I remembered the black handle of the knife that was used to stab Anil.

"Malti, I want you to think carefully about this. What happened to the knife Sunil used to threaten Anil with?"

"I looked for the knife all around the house, sir ... that day and the next. I could not find it. So I replaced it with an identical knife from the set."

"When did you last see the knife?"

"Sunil sir had marched out of the room with the knife. I searched his room thoroughly the next day, but I did not find it."

I controlled my rising excitement. "No one found the original knife?"

"No, sir."

My heart was beating faster than ever now. "Is the replaced knife from the set similar to the one that was lost?"

"Yes, sir. Only, this one has a red handle."

"Bring it to me."

Malti brought the fruit basket. I picked up the knife and stared at it. It was a replica of the knife that had been used to stab Anil. I tried to subdue my thrill at this discovery. The Kapoor family had deliberately hidden this incident from me. Could this be one reason why Paras was eager for me to get a confession from Shalini?

I realised that Malti and Ram were waiting for my orders. I needed another testimony, lest the uncle-niece team were misleading me. I saw a man come out of the kitchen.

"What's his name?" I asked Ram.

"That is Raju, sir. He is a cook."

"Raju!" I yelled, and he immediately paled on seeing me. Apparently my reputation preceded me everywhere.

He came towards me with folded hands. I wasted no time. If it was rank they wanted, they would get it.

"Raju, I am the chief of the CID, and demand the truth. Was there a fight between Anil and Sunil on Saturday evening? The night Anil was murdered?"

He looked accusingly at Ram, and said in a visibly upset tone, "Yes, sir. There was a fight."

"Who attacked whom?"

He looked at Ram again. I held Raju by his shoulders and repeated, "Who attacked whom, and with what instrument?"

"Sunil sir attacked Anil sir. With a knife."

I dismissed all of them, and pondered over this new twist. Even if Sunil was innocent, Paras was smart enough to gauge the import of the events on Saturday night. If the police came to know of this, they would definitely take Sunil in for questioning. So he had instructed everyone to remain quiet. Even Aditi had not mentioned this to me.

My belief that Shalini was the murderer was based on three facts: her suspicious behaviour at the farmhouse, her attempts to mislead the police by planting the locket near the back gate, and the message sent to her by Raj.

The suspicious behaviour could easily stem from nervousness; I had no evidence at all that she had planted the locket; and the SMS was cryptic to say the least. Not to forget, Paras definitely had a clear motive to prove that Shalini was the murderer, in case Sunil was involved. I remembered my meeting with Aditi in the café. She was the first one who had mentioned that the family suspected Shalini. Had she met me because of our past, or had she come just to reinforce my suspicions about Shalini?

I let it all sink in. Sunil had chased Anil with a knife. The knife was missing and, most probably, was the murder weapon. Shalini had just become my number two suspect. I needed to get in touch with Babu.

"Hi buddy!" a cheerful voice called behind me.

I turned around to see Babu walking towards me. I had never thought I would ever be genuinely delighted to see Babu, until that moment.

"They told me I would find you in the kitchen. Found anything else?" he winked.

"Yeah. Your timing couldn't be better. I think you are my lucky mascot. What did you find out about Leo?"

"He returned the locket all right. It is an inside job. Shalini, isn"t it?"

"What makes you say that?"

"You were in her room when I came. I was chatting with Paras sir. He said you would break her and get a confession. So did you break her?"

"I have only broken wind so far. But ... do you recognise this?"

I handed the knife to him. He looked at it cautiously, trying to decide if this was a trick question. Then he said meekly, "This is similar to the one that Anil was killed with. But the colour of the handle is different."

"Correct. What if I tell you that the night Anil was found murdered, someone had chased him that very evening with a knife similar to the one you are holding in your hand?"

"What! Who?"

"Sunil."

"What! Who told you this?"

"The servants."

"I want to speak to them."

"Do it after I leave. Paras had specifically instructed everyone not to mention the incident to either you or me."

"That rotten scoundrel!"

"So tell me now, Inspector, with the new-found evidence, do you think there may be a possibility that Sunil is as strong a suspect as Shalini?"

"Umm ... maybe ... yes. No, Shalini planted the locket. She must be the murderer."

"It doesn't prove anything. We have been speculating so far."

I could hear the cacophonous honking of horns outside the house.

"Looks like the guests are arriving. I will catch you later. I need to think."

"Wait. I wanted to talk to you about something. In private."

He said it in the conciliatory tone you use when you need a favour from someone.

"Regarding?"

He leaned towards me, till I could smell his cheap after shave lotion. He looked over my shoulder, and then behind him.

"Shoot, Inspector!"

He said in a low voice, "Someone has spoken to the press. They know we suspect an insider. I got a call from a lady named Anjali Singh, who, incidentally, happens to work for my favourite daily. She enquired if it was true that we suspected a family member. I didn't comment, of course. But there's a lot of undesirable interest the case is generating."

I expressed my surprise. "How could they know that? But it is good you brought this to my notice. I understand your concern."

"Not concern; excitement!"

"Excitement?"

"A lot of publicity for me ... eh, I mean ... for both of us. We will be famous."

"Famous? For?"

I was genuinely bewildered.

"Look, Vishal, my grandfather used to say that opportunity knocks only once. Let's make full use of it. Imagine if Shalini or Sunil were the murderer. The press would go crazy. What after that? How do we get the maximum credit?

"I will tell you how. You inform me as soon as you have solved the case. Both of us will inform the press together. What do you say to that?"

My bewilderment gave way to indignation. I had a nagging feeling that he had leaked the information to the press himself. I said jovially, "Aha! Team work, eh?"

"Yes," he said winking at me. "I will assist you in finding the murderer. Once you identify the murderer, I will make the arrest. Then we can call some of my trusted journalists, and issue a common story about how we cracked the case together."

"Sure thing. But what if I am not able to solve the mystery?"

"You just told me that it is Sunil."

"Must have been my holy ghost. I did not say anything like that."

He looked confused and asked, "Then it is Shalini?"

I beckoned him to come closer, and whispered, "What about gypsies? From the village? Did you know that gypsies can throw a knife from a distance of thirty feet? Blindfolded! I need you to check on all potential knife throwers in the village first."

Babu's confusion turned into indignation. "What! Oh ... okay, I get it! You want to solve this yourself, huh? You don't want to involve me? Take all the credit."

If he was going to leak information to the press, I needed him off my back.

"Look, Inspector, my grandfather used to say that opportunity is like a woman covered by a veil. You have to grab her, and take your chances. Even if there is a minute possibility of the murderer hailing from the village, we have to explore it. The important thing is to solve this case together, and then reap mutual benefits. Right?"

"You mean it?"

"Cross my heart and hope I die."

He beamed and said, "Thanks. What do you want me to do?"

"You can go and talk to Shalini about the gypsies. She is taking a nap now, so maybe you can come back tomorrow. You need to explore her theory and see what you can find in the village."

"Splendid. So we have a deal?"

"Yes, sir. We do."

"And remember, Vishal, such a case will not be forgotten in a hurry. We will be in the limelight. You know what I mean?"

"My thoughts exactly."

He winked at me and I winked back. The inspector buzzed off like a drunken bee.

"Vishal," I heard a voice behind me.

It was Paras. He looked as excited as a four-year-old waiting for his gift from Santa on Christmas Eve.

"What did Shalini say? Did she confess?"

I took out the knife from my pocket, forgetting my non-disclosure agreement with the servants, and threw it on the floor.

"No. But Ram did."

He looked at the knife. I was prepared for any reaction. Denial. Amnesia. Shock. But he was steady as a rock.

He sighed. "No. This is not what it seems. I told the servants not to tell you about the incident, because it would have misled you. It was an unnecessary detail which would have confused you."

"Sunil chased Anil with a knife the same evening that he was murdered. You didn't think that was an important detail?"

"No, because it was an unfortunate coincidence that Sunil had a knife in his hand that day. Sunil would never hurt Anil. He is my blood. Trust me, son, it is Shalini. I know it. I thought you would have managed to get a confession from her by now."

I looked carefully at the stubborn man in front of me. Either he was a lunatic; or he did not know that the knife was missing, or that it was probably used to stab Anil. Either way, he was going to write me a cheque, so I couldn't dispense with decorum.

I said patiently, "The knife used to kill Anil was the same one Sunil chased him with. Would you consider that an important enough detail to make me doubt the sanctity of your blood as an alibi?"

The reaction came now. It was late, but genuine. The old man paled, and had to lean against the front door for support.

"What!" he exclaimed.

"What part did you not understand?"

"The knife was the same?"

"Yes. It has been missing since the day of the fight."

His legs gave way, and I rushed to him for support.

"You did not know that the knife was missing?"

He whispered as if he were short of breath, "No! How do you know that the knife is the same?"

"Because I saw it when I was examining the corpse. The handle had the same engraving."

He was at least four inches taller than me, and had placed his entire body weight on my shoulder. I led him to a sofa in the living room, and offered my standard reassuring words for trying times.

"Would you like a drink?"

He shook his head. His complexion had transformed from baby pink to jaundice yellow. He sat down thoughtfully, and then exclaimed, "Oh my God! She witnessed the fight, and planned it. She picked up the knife. My God!"

"We need to prove that."

"You don't understand!" he yelled. "I have been fair and just till now ... fair in forgiving her for the murder of her husband and my son. But if she thinks she can frame Sunil! Don't you see? First Leo, and now Sunil. I demand that you talk to her right now."

The old man was up on his feet, and rambling.

"I don't think she did it," I wanted to see the old man's response.

"See? She has convinced you too. She is a parasite. I have to take care of it myself."

He was rushing towards the staircase.

"I don't think she did it… alone," I repeated.

He stopped and turned around. "What do you mean?"

"Who did what alone?" Sunil stepped in. He was carrying fifteen-litre canisters of mineral water in either hand. He had stripped to his vest, and his muscles bulged. I imagined him chasing Anil around the house with a knife, in a fit of anger.

"Vishal tells me that Shalini had an accomplice?" Paras looked at me warily.

Sunil kept the canisters down and walked towards me. "Oh? What makes you say that?"

"Anil was stabbed while he was standing. It was a single, powerful stroke. There is evidence of a struggle. Shalini was at least eight inches shorter than Anil. If you remember the angle of the knife, the blade had pierced him so that the handle was slanting upwards towards the sky.

"If Shalini had stabbed him while he was on his feet, the handle would have slanted towards the ground. The murderer was at least as tall as, if not taller, than Anil. I think Shalini is involved. But there is no way she could have overpowered Anil and escaped unhurt, unless she had an accomplice."

Paras pounded his right fist on his left palm excitedly. "So you *do* think she is involved. You found something, didn't you?"

I switched on the tape recorder, and played selected parts of our conversation.

Paras looked at Sunil and said animatedly, "Did you hear that? The bitch is telling him to stop investigating my son's murder. That does it. We have proof!"

Sunil spoke up. "No. Not enough proof." He looked at me cautiously and asked, "What else? You haven't played the entire recording."

I didn't want them to hear the part where she was trying to seduce me so I replied, "There's nothing else of significance on the tape. There are other facts that point towards her being the murderer."

"What?" They asked in unison.

"Two things. First, she lied about not having seen the locket before. Second, I found an SMS on her mobile phone that may be incriminating."

I handed her mobile to Paras.

"She has been dialling and receiving calls from a certain Raj," I said, as both Paras and Sunil read the text message on the phone. "Any idea who Raj is?"

Paras read the SMS and raised his eyes. "Gypsies?"

For their benefit, I played that part of the recording where she was talking about the gypsies.

He was shocked. "That proves it! This was a premeditated murder. Whoever this Raj is, he was her accomplice. Vishal, you just solved the case!"

His enthusiasm was contagious. Sunil butted in, "Raj is Rajesh. Remember Rajesh Pillai, Dad?"

"Oh ... yes! Of course! He was the man she was going around with before she married Anil."

"Yes. He came for the wedding. Tall guy."

Paras's expression turned ugly, and he spoke angrily. "So she used her old lover to murder my son! I will get both of them hanged!"

"What about the institution for Shalini?"

"Don't talk like a fool, Vishal! After learning about this, I will not rest until both of them are rotting in jail."

There was a constant noise of horns honking outside the house.

I said to both of them, "I took the liberty of calling Rajesh. He insisted on coming here. I think both of you should attend to your guests. I will speak to him."

"Shouldn't we share the tape with Babu at once and have them arrested?" said Paras.

"Not yet, sir. I need to work on it at my own pace."

"Are you serious? What else is required now? You have the damn proof in your hands."

I kept the tape recorder inside my shirt pocket. "I will begin with questioning Rajesh. If he was involved in planning the murder with Shalini, let me assure you he would have a few tricks up his sleeve. Then I plan to investigate the reason behind Anil's call to Leo on Saturday evening. I think it may be tied up with the cash found in the apartment."

"The cash is accounted for," barked Sunil. "I agree with Dad. We should tell Babu to arrest both of them right now."

"Yes, but there are still close to twenty-five crores missing, if I understand correctly. I can look into it."

"That is not your job. Dad?" he looked at Paras.

Paras thought for a few seconds. "I think Vishal may have a point, son. This Rajesh may not be an easy nut to crack. Moreover, with so many relatives in the house for the next two days, I don't want to create a scene."

Sunil was adamant. "What if both of them run away, Dad?"

Paras spoke decisively. "You got to admit, son that he has been very effective till now. If there is a chance of finding the money, I want him on the job. We haven't been able to trace it till now. So I don't see any harm in it."

He looked at me. "Two days, Vishal. In two days, you will break Rajesh, and submit the recording, along with your testimony, to the police. She isn't going anywhere. And if you do find the cash, remember that one per cent is yours. That is twenty-five lakh in cash over and above your fees."

Sunil picked up the canisters and walked out looking disgusted.

I waited on the terrace for Rajesh. I leaned against the railing, and observed the activity in the garden below.

People dressed in white were placing garlands in front of Anil's photograph. Paras was shouting orders to the waiters. Vimal was guiding the guests to the garden. Sunil and Aditi were sitting in a secluded corner of the lawn. Aditi had changed into a white sari that looked very becoming on her tall and slender frame. Sunil looked tense. Aditi ran her fingers over his head, and tousled his hair reassuringly. Sunil smiled and caressed her cheek. She leaned forward and gave him a wifely kiss on the cheek. It was a harmless intimate moment between a husband and wife. And my stupid heart stopped beating for a few seconds.

Aditi looked up at the terrace precisely at that moment, and saw me standing there. The heart started beating again. Time started ticking by, and noises were audible again. I turned around and walked into the house. I stood outside Shalini's room deliberating my next move.

Ram walked up the staircase leading a tall, thin man. "Sir, this is Mr Rajesh Pillai. Paras sir said that you would like to talk to him."

Mr Rajesh Pillai overtook Ram and galloped towards me. "Where is she?" Pillai asked sounding tough.

"In her room."

"Where's her room?"Rajesh asked urgently.

I pointed to the door, and he rushed inside. I dismissed Ram and followed Rajesh. He was standing next to the bed. His eyes wandered all over Shalini's face, studying every detail carefully. He gently touched her forehead and said in despair, "She has a fever."

"Slight. She needs rest."

He looked at her, and a great pain flashed in his eyes. It seemed he loved her a lot. H sat on the bed warily. He was wearing a diamond ring on his index finger. It was not one of those colourful ones that are worn to ward off destiny's misfortunes. This looked like a wedding ring.

"You are married?"

He looked startled and remarked scornfully, "Yes! Oh ... so you have already started detecting on me! Well, mister, I am not weak like Shalini. Don't try to ... don't try to ..." he fumbled for the right word, gave up, and waved his twig-like finger at me threateningly.

Jeez, he was one of those sensitive ones. He was staring at Shalini again. I realized he wouldn't mind spending the rest of the afternoon sitting there staring at her.

"I was told that you are a good friend of Shalini's."

"Friend?"

He said it with such rage that I couldn't account for it.

"We were much more than friends, mister. You will not understand. Never. No one will. Ever."

He pouted. His face was a sponge reacting to everything I said. I would have loved to play a game of poker with this guy.

"Can you explain this?" I showed him the SMS on Shalini's mobile. He paled immediately.

"What?" he said stupidly.

With Rajesh as her support system, I was able to understand why Shalini was getting nervous attacks.

"This SMS came from a number registered in your name."

"So?"

"So ... you are a very smart man. My compliments."

"Listen, mister, don't try to ... trap me. I know all your tricks."

I had reached the point when I needed to have a few drinks and get smashed for sanity's sake.

"And for my last and much admired trick, I do the disappearing act. Watch closely."

He was listen-mister-ing me again when I walked out of the door.

In the kitchen, I gave Shalini's phone to Malti, and told her to hand it to Paras. I walked out of the main door. The case was solved as far as I was concerned. Shalini was cornered. If Rajesh was an accomplice, he would confess too. The idealists were the easiest to break. I had two days to find the missing cash and make twenty-five lakhs.

I tried to make an inconspicuous exit. The engine roared to life, shattering the peaceful ambience. The priest looked up from the *havan kund* and stared at me disapprovingly. Aditi stared at me disapprovingly. The guards at the gate stared at me disapprovingly. My reflection in the mirror stared back disapprovingly. This was too much hatred to counter in a sober state of mind. I drove out of the gates trying to remember the nearest pub in the vicinity.

Suddenly, a lady on a pink Scooty drove horizontally across the road, parking her vehicle in front of my car. She was off the Scooty in one swift movement, and walked towards me purposefully. She waved her hands in what seemed like a gesture of peace or apology. She took off a pink helmet, which gave way to a pink scarf. She was dressed in a vibrant pink top, and capris that were a lighter shade of pink.

She loosened her scarf, and I was relieved to see that her hair was not pink. She had a dazzling smile that ended with dimples on both cheeks. I decided to be civil. I always give the benefit of the doubt to cute ladies. Strappy pink heels accentuated her extremely toned and shapely calves, promising a great pair of legs. I waited as she approached me. I rolled down my window.

"Vishal Bajaj?" she asked sweetly.

"Who wants to know?"

"I am Anjali Singh from *Crime Busters*. Heard of it?"

Her name sounded familiar, and I remembered Babu mentioning her. I had heard of the publication all right. It pandered to readers who enjoyed glorified accounts of murders, rapes, and other crimes in the city.

I replied coldly, "Yes, I signed an online petition last night to ban the magazine."

She grinned and disarmed me. It was an infectious smile.

"We are covering the murder of Anil Kapoor at his farmhouse. A private detective has been hired, whose vehicle registration number matches yours. We would like to interview you."

Then she added quickly, "We will do a small write-up on you. Damn good publicity."

She spoke fast and directly. I tried to think of the correct words to dismiss her, without being provocative. No sense in making the press your enemy.

She sensed my indecision and added, "More importantly, I can give you information that will help you in your investigation. Useless information that may be useful to you."

"What sort of useless information?" I asked curiously.

"We have a plethora of Page 3 information that will shock you. Personal stuff about a member of the Kapoor family."

I was tempted. Then I realised that she was most probably alluding to Anil's homosexuality, in which case, any information she might have about his personal life would be redundant and useless.

She looked at me in anticipation and spoke with some impatience, "Listen, dude, let me buy you lunch. I am starving, and have been waiting for you in this goddamn heat for the past forty-five minutes."

"Well, if it is any consolation, the tan looks really good on you."

"Wise guy. So, are we exchanging notes?"

"Sure. Why don't you join me in the car? I suggest you remove your bike from the middle of the road though."

"How will I come back? The auto-rickshaws will charge a ridiculous amount, and I get sick if I travel in a bus."

"I will drop you back to your bike."

"Swell. Give me a minute," she said triumphantly.

"So, where are we going?" I asked her when she had slid into the seat beside me.

"Drive straight. I know this very good joint that serves the best Chinese food in town. And it's cheap too."

She took out a camera form her pink handbag, and took my picture. "What the hell are you doing?"

"Just clicking some pictures for the article, baba! Don't tell me you are the shy kind. I am only making you famous."

She held the camera protectively to her chest, and I knew I didn't have a chance of reclaiming my picture using coercion.

"No, no. I am a hardcore exhibitionist. But I am not Vishal. I work for him. My name is Pranay."

"O-h-ho, I knew it," she said with a gleam in her eyes.

"You did?"

"Yes. You don't look like a private detective."

"How are they supposed to look?"

"Well, for one they should be pot-bellied and shabby. And most of them are middle-aged. You look more like someone working in an MNC."

I thought about Pranay's appearance.

"Affirmative. Except for the middle-aged part, you are bang on target about Vishal."

"Boy, your boss pays you well!"

"My boss is a stingy bastard. Which part of my existence makes you think I am affluent?"

"Well if an assistant can drive a big car ..."

"Aha ... very perceptive. Actually, this car belongs to Vishal, and I get to use it as per the boss's discretion. Generally, I commute by bus."

"You should buy a Scooty. It is very convenient. My boss is also stingy. He pays me peanuts, but I need this job to make it big in the world of investigative journalism."

"Come to think of it, even you don't look like an investigative journalist."

"Why?"

"Too much pink. Maybe you need to start wearing blue or purple for effect."

She rewarded me with another one of her irresistible smiles.

"I hope I am on the right route."

"Shit! You had to take a right back there," she said a second after I had missed the turn. "Sorry."

I replied gallantly, "No problem. Just be alert now. This is a one-way."

I reversed the car on the one-way, and took the turn.

She suddenly asked, "Oh! Do you even like Chinese?"

"Yeah. Love it."

All solids tasted the same to me. It was only the liquids I was fussy about.

"Thank God! My father always tells me how dominating I can be ..."

"I think your Dad has a point though."

"Shit. You had to take the left!" she said, just as I missed another turn.

She smiled sheepishly.

"I am so sorry. Sometimes I can be so absent-minded!"

Not even gods could have resisted that smile. I smiled back graciously.

"No problem."

"Well, you are a sport, aren't you? And thank God for that. I have just about had it with all the rude, chauvinistic, lecherous bastards who can't get over the fact that I am an investigative journalist."

Her pretty face contorted in fury, and her cheeks blazed pink. She looked at me, calmed down, and smiled again.

"I am sorry. I get worked up when I think about all that. I guess I just need to hang in there, till I get my big break. Hopefully, this story can do just that."

The very good joint that served the best Chinese food in town was called Popeye.

"I didn't know Popeye was Chinese," I remarked.

"He is not. But don't let the name make you judge the food! I hope you are not one of those judgmental types."

"As non-judgmental as they come. And come to think about that, Popeye did have a slight squint, didn't he?"

"You will love the food. Wait and watch."

"Well, as long we order something with spinach in it, we should be okay."

She knew each waiter by name, and they all responded to her like drones to a queen bee, fussing all over her.

"You happen to be a frequent visitor?"

"Yes, I just love this place. My goal in life is to start a Chinese restaurant next to a beach, and make money from the restaurant to open a bookshop. I think that is my destiny. What is your destiny?"

I wondered how investigative journalism would blend with a bookshop that was funded by a Chinese restaurant. I smiled and shrugged my shoulders. Then I noticed a young couple sitting and canoodling in a corner over some Coke. There was a group of young ladies yelling at each other in a corner, again with Coke bottles on their table. I looked around in a state of panic. None of the customers were having liquor.

"They serve liquor, right?"

"No," she said disapprovingly.

"Not even beer?" I asked calmly, although I didn't feel calm at all.

She shook her head and looked at me suspiciously.

"Are you one of those guys who like to get drunk in the middle of the day?"

Served me right for falling victim to her wanton charms. All of a sudden she seemed less charming.

I looked at her expressive eyes and shook my head.

"Heavens no! I don't touch liquor before the sun sets. It is only when I am having Chinese food that I don't mind a sip or two of chilled beer."

"Good. I would hate for you to be a drunk."

The waiter came and I picked up the menu to order.

"Why don't you try their Tangy Mint? It is an out-of-the-world drink."

With her smile endorsing it, it could be stale milk, three days old, and I wouldn't have the heart to refuse.

"Sounds divine," I said.

She dictated the order to the waiter.

"Okay, get one Tangy Mint, and one Strawberry Blossom. We will order the main course shortly."

"How come you are not having the out-of-the-world drink?"

"Well, those are two of my favourite drinks. This way I can taste both," she said, with another one of her celestial smiles.

"I feel so exploited," I said.

She patted my hand and I immediately felt better. There is something infinitely reassuring about a woman's touch. Especially if the woman has a dimpled smile and a great pair of legs. I decided to forgive her for treating me to a teetotaller meal.

"So when will you introduce me to Vishal?"

It took me a few seconds to register that I was Pranay.

"Difficult. He's not very social."

"That is where you will help me. You need to tell him that this can be a symbiotic relationship."

"I know my boss. He would appreciate it if you do not mention his involvement in any of your articles."

"You are wrong. He would love this extra mileage that the publicity can bring. *Amateur detective employed by the Kapoor family to solve the murder of the eldest son*. And I will tell you what. If you give me his picture, I will take you out for lunch again someday."

"Tempting. With beer?"

"Okay, baba. With beer."

"And you will delete my picture that you clicked in the car?"

"Shy, aren't we? Okay. If you give me his picture, I will delete your picture. But seriously, Pranay, we will do the article on Anil Kapoor's murder anyway. Questions will be asked about the detective working on the case. If you are able to convince Vishal to meet me, I can write his side of the story. Otherwise, my editor will force me to cook up something fictitious, and I hate doing that."

I hated the idea of her snooping around to find out why I was involved in the case. It would be devastating for everyone concerned if they found out about me and Aditi. I decided to save her the trouble of prying.

"Vishal would hate that too. You got Bluetooth on your mobile?"

"Yes. You have his snaps on your phone?"

"Yes. Switch on your Bluetooth. I'll transfer the picture."

I selected the only sober picture of Pranay I had taken at office once.

She took out her camera from her purse, and I deleted the unsolicited picture that she had taken in the car.

She saw Pranay's snap and commented, "Yes. He looks much more like a detective. Shabby and fat. Now, tell me more about him."

"More?"

"Who is Vishal Bajaj? What's his agency called? And how is he involved in the investigation?"

"Vishal Bajaj is in his mid-thirties, is an irascible bastard who opted for voluntary retirement from the Indian Army a couple of years ago. His agency is called Hunt Detective Agency.

"The reason for his involvement in the case can be attributed to the excellent relationship he shares with an esteemed police officer, Inspector Babu. Babu recommended Vishal to Mr Paras Kapoor, and he was hired for the case."

"The police themselves recommended him? Wow, he's got good connections! Is he married, or single? Any other famous case he's worked on?"

"He's recently been married for the third time. Tell you what. I will arrange a meeting with him for you, and you can talk to him directly."

"Really? Promise?"

I shrugged.

"Sure." Anything to get you off my back.

"You are such a sweetheart."

"I know."

Our drinks came, and she waited until I had taken a sip of my Tangy Mint. She looked at me nervously, like a young bride waiting for her husband to comment on the first dish she had prepared.

Tangy Mint was a vile green, sickeningly sweet drink. It was the drink for man-eating, putrid aliens. She was staring at me, so I swallowed the liquid, smiled, and nodded.

"You were right. This does make me feel out of the world."

She cheered up instantly. "Well, I guess the picture should suffice for today. When can you get back to me with a date for the meeting?"

"Soon .... So what are you to going to write about in your article?"

She looked at me. "Can you keep a secret?"

"Sure."

"Well, we have an informer. There is a rumour ... you can't tell anyone about this, okay? The rumour is that that someone from the family is the murderer."

"What! Who?"

"You should know. Your boss was the one who found the first few clues."

"Really? He never tells me anything. What else?"

"Well, that is pure speculation from our side. But we will, of course, mention in the article that the suspect is an insider; write about the strained relationship between the brothers, generally mention the inheritance angle, and end the article there, leaving the rest to people's imagination."

"Dirty!"

"Yes, I know. I hate this shit. But I have no option. Jobs are scarce, and I need the money. I really do."

I believed her.

"So you would touch upon the inheritance angle, and indicate that one of the brothers could be responsible for the murder. But what about the Page 3 stuff you were telling me about in the car?"

She drew her chair closer to me.

"Well, there is a matter of sexual deviancy involved. That's the fodder for my next article. I can only tell you this right now."

"Sexual deviancy? How do you know that?"

"I got an anonymous call from an informer. He is the one passing me the information. I can't tell you more," she pleaded.

I didn't press the matter further. She was probably referring to Anil's homosexuality. I would have to warn Paras about this. Maybe he could pull some strings and tone the article down.

I said with a straight face, "I am only surprised that a publication as reputed as yours responds to anonymous phone calls."

She smiled triumphantly.

"I checked with Inspector Babu. He's in charge of this case. As soon as the informer called me, I spoke to Babu, telling him that we knew that the murderer was from the family."

"What did he say?"

"His first sentence was, 'How did you find out?' Then he tried to deny it. I pressed him till he gave me an affirmation. After that we became fast buddies. He is cute."

I silently cursed the imbecile. Even if he was not the informer, he had played his part in leaking the information to the media.

The waiter came to take our order for the main course. I had barely picked up the menu when she prompted, "Do you want me to order, since you are new here?"

"Sure. That would be out of the world." We had a chatty lunch that lasted more than an hour. She chatted and I listened. I dropped her back to the Scooty, and promised to expedite the meeting with my boss. I tried to reach Vimal on his phone, but my call went unanswered. The only other number I had was Aditi's.

Sunil picked up the phone. "Hi, Vishal. Aditi is busy. Can I take a message?"

"That's all right. Just wanted to inform you that *Crime Busters* is doing an article on your brother's murder. We can't do much about it, but I think they might publish something about Anil's sexual preferences. Just wanted to update your dad, so that he can pull some strings, if possible, and keep it from being published."

"The bastards! Any idea who is working on the story?"

"A journalist called Anjali Singh."

"Thanks again. I appreciate your kindness. Aditi has come. Do you want to talk to her?"

"Nope. That ... "My battery went kaput. I reminded myself to buy that car-charger.

It was almost four in the evening, and there was not one drop of alcohol in my body. Except for the vodka shots I had taken in Shalini's room. Vodka couldn't be counted as booze. It was milk for a grown-up man. I drove towards office.

Aarti was in a bad mood when I reached office. She pounced on me.

"Boss! Why don't you ever charge your phone?"

"My eye feels just fine; thank you for asking."

"Oh ... how's your eye?"

"Is Pranay here?"

"Yeah. He's been reading comic books since morning! I told him to talk to Mrs Singh for the remainder fee. He hasn't."

"Thank god for that! You should know better than to provoke Pranay into talking to clients!"

I marched into my cabin, and found Pranay asleep on my chair, with a comic book over his face. I took the comic book off his face and shook him awake.

"Good nap, Batman?"

"Yes, thanks." He stretched and got up.

I picked up an envelope that had arrived by courier, and tore it open. It was my retainer cheque for the Kapoor case. I handed the cheque to Aarti, and told her to deposit it first thing the next day. She saw the amount on cheque and cheered visibly.

"He's paid the entire fee in advance?"

"This is just the retainer, baby."

She looked at me in disbelief. "No kidding?"

"I never jest when it comes to money."

"That's almost double the usual retainer!"

"There's more where that came from, if I am able to locate some missing cash. So let me get to work."

I opened the drawer and took out a steel flask. I poured some whisky into it, and vowed never to make the mistake of leaving the office without it. Aarti exited my cabin, holding the cheque delicately in her hands. Pranay poured himself some rum, and emptied a packet of wafers into a big yellow bowl. He went to the fridge, and got out some ice cubes. I loved it when he displayed efficiency at work.

I walked over to the window and sat on the sill, looking at the busy scene below. I took a sip of the whisky and let it caress my tongue. Traffic seemed to be moving in slow motion, and the clamorous honking from vehicles drowned every other sound in the street. A dirty woman was carrying a malnourished child, and begging for change. Two street dogs were fighting. A formally-dressed man was talking on the phone, while eating what looked like a patty. Couples and children walked on the pavement. The whisky was still caressing my tongue when the phone rang. I gulped it down reluctantly and walked to the table.

"Hello, this is Vishal."

"Hello. I saw Shalini throw the locket. She threw it out of the back gate."

It was a woman. Husky and accented. There were three women who were present at the farmhouse. This was definitely not Aditi's voice, and Shalini would not call me to testify against herself.

"Who is this?"

"She threw it out, when you and the police had left."

"Reena?"

She disconnected the phone. I redialled the number. It rang a million times before someone answered.

"Hello?" a gruff male voice greeted me.

"Hi. I got a call from this number."

"This is a public phone booth."

"Where?"

"Lamington Road. Next to Thomas Bakery."

"Okay. I got a call from this number a minute ago.

Did you see a woman leave?"

"This is a local line. You can put in a rupee coin and dial the number. I don't have time to waste, observing who comes in."

"Fair enough. Can you ask someone else in the vicinity if they noticed a female leaving a few minutes ago?"

"Are you from the police?" he asked cautiously.

"No."

"Then fuck you."

He hung up.

I dialled the Kapoors' landline. Sunil picked up the phone. I disconnected, and dialled again after two minutes. This time Ram picked up.

"Ram, this is Vishal. Is Reena at home?"

"Ah, no, sir. The guests just left an hour ago. Paras sir insisted that everyone go out and get some fresh air. Reena madam has gone to the club."

"Which club?"

"Oasis Club. She plays tennis there."

"Thanks."

The Oasis Club was the most prominent club in the city on Chancery Street, which was parallel to Lamington Road. Evidently, Reena was not even trying to cover her tracks. That could mean one of two things: either she was genuinely dumb, or incredibly innocent. What bothered me was the manner in which she had spoken on the phone. It was almost as if she were speaking under pressure, waiting to get it over and done with.

Nevertheless, if Reena was willing to testify as an eye-witness, there was no need to wait. We would have to arrest Shalini and Rajesh right away. The only thing that bothered me was why Reena had decided to call me all of a sudden. Maybe she felt guilty, and was genuinely trying to help. She was definitely not trying to hide anything.

Half an hour later, I was negotiating an entry for Pranay and myself with the security guard at Oasis Club.

I said patiently, "Yes, Ms Reena Kapoor. Please check. We are her guests."

"She did not mention she was expecting any guests."

Oasis Club was strictly elitist. Entry only for the members, or guests accompanied by members.

"She must have forgotten. You must surely be aware of the tragedy that has befallen the Kapoor family. Besides, how would I know that she was here, if she had not personally invited me?"

"Sorry, sir. Maybe you should call her and tell her to send someone to the reception confirming this."

"She is playing tennis right now! This is very insulting. I will complain about your lack of civility to Mrs Kapoor. What is your name?" I began reversing the car.

He looked confused, and came running towards the vehicle.

"Sir," said the guard sounding worried, "She has not even paid the entry fee for guests."

"She told me to pay for it. How much is it?"

"Well ... it is five thousand rupees per head, sir."

I did not register any emotion as I handed him a credit card, and he swiped it. Besides me, Pranay clucked his tongue saying, "They better throw a complimentary Thai massage for this kind of fee."

As the guard made the receipt, he blabbered, "I am sorry, sir. It is on the orders of Mr Paras Kapoor that we are strict about the rules here."

"Yes, I understand."

"He is one of the club's committee members, and is very strict."

"Okay. I will recommend you to him. Good job."

I took my card back, and debated whether to tip him or not. In the end, I decided against it. He was probably earning more than me anyway.

I parked my car amidst a horde of Mercedes, Audis, and other shiny cars that I had seen in *The Fast and the Furious*. I walked towards the signboard in the middle of the parking lot. The tennis court was behind the card room, which was next to the library.

The card room was the last building on the plot. We had to enter it, walk to the end of the passage, and walk down a few steps to reach the tennis courts. The deserted courts were filled with water from the rain over the last two days. This was definitely not conducive for a game of tennis. I thought I heard a woman laugh. An L-shaped plot housed the courts.

Pranay and I walked through the puddles to reach the elbow of the plot and stopped.

In a secluded corner, Reena was sitting on a bench with a tall man. They had their backs towards me. They leaned against each other, as if conspiring together. With no shrubbery to hide behind, we couldn't risk standing where we could easily be seen.

The wall of the building that harboured the card room ran parallel to the L-shaped plot. There were two windows in the card room that could give us a good view of the bench, if they were open. We retraced our steps, and entered the card room. There were only a few old people there. I walked to the window at the end of the room. An old man, with a set of cards in his hands, looked at me suspiciously. I tiptoed to the window next to him. He brought his cards close to his chest and shot a warning glance. I smiled at him, shook my head to tell him that I was not interested in his cards, and pointed at the window.

The window hadn't been opened for decades, and I struggled for a few minutes trying to push it open. There was a thud as the window opened, and dust flew in all directions. The old man started coughing. I looked at him apologetically. He brought the cards close to his chest again, and scowled at me. I turned my back to him and stared at the bench. I could see Reena and her companion clearly now. Both of them were dressed in sports wear—T-shirts and shorts for him, a skirt for her; and sports shoes.

They looked fresh as daisies. They hadn't played any tennis today, which was understandable since the courts were flooded. They were both engrossed in their animated conversation, their heads close together. I could not hear them, but I noticed something strange about their posture.

They were sitting too close to each other. Reena was laughing uncontrollably, leaning her head against his shoulder. They reminded me of lovers meeting in a park. The fact that they were sitting on a rusty bench, hidden from public view, also roused my suspicions.

The man placed his arm around Reena's shoulder, and said something that sent her into convulsions of laughter yet again. He casually placed his right hand over Reena's thigh. Slowly, his hand began to slide up and down, suggesting that he was stroking her thigh. Reena leaned back, opening her legs wider. His hand crept up further. Reena closed her eyes, and threw her head back. Her thighs were now clamped tightly over the man's wrist. The skirt covered his hand, but from the gentle movement of his arm, I knew what he was up to.

Pranay whispered, "Dude, is he doing what I think he is doing?"

"Yeah."

"Is he Vimal?"

"No."

"Fuck! Why would they do this publicly?"

"Don't know. The forbidden fuels the passion, I guess."

There was a sigh – a lustful sigh. I turned around and saw the old man, who had been hiding his cards from me, standing behind me. He was hardly five feet tall, and I had not noticed him behind us at all. He grinned toothlessly at me and said, "Nice. Very nice."

His hands were no longer clutching the cards to his chest. In fact, the cards were now embarrassedly hiding a part of his anatomy in his trousers. He looked away from me quickly, and began staring out of the window again. I guess he must have been at least seventy.

"Careful, grandpa. You could get hernia." He was oblivious to everything except the sight in front of him. I decided it would not harm an old man to get some voyeuristic delights at his age, and made way so that he could get the front row. He grinned and walked forward. I had never given much attention to Reena. I reassessed what I knew about her. She seemed to be a typical rich father's daughter married to a rich father's son; a bit too vain, a bit too good-looking; and too fashionable to have any intellectual ambitions. I added *sexually promiscuous* and *exhibitionist* to the list now. The man's movements seemed to be getting more and more rapid and stimulating, and Reena threw her shoulders back, shaking with excitement, as the man conducted the symphony with his fingers. Reena jerked her neck to the right. We found ourselves staring at each other. She paused, and suddenly pulled the man's hand out of her skirt, signalling to the window. Both of them stared at me, shocked. Reena squinted to get a good look at me, and put her hand over her mouth. She had recognised me. I waved at them. My phone rang in two minutes.

"Hello?"

"What the hell are you doing here?"

"Who is this?" I asked sweetly.

"You know damn well who this is. Come out this instant!"

"Tell you what. Daddy knows you have been a dirty girl. Meet me at the cafeteria near the parking lot, with the gentleman."

I disconnected. Her voice had been shaking with anger, but I hadn't detected any trace of fear.

"Dude, I will interview Reena and her companion. Why don't you go and try to extract some information from the waiters?" I said to Pranay.

"About?"

"About Einstein's theory of relativity. What do you think?"

"Uh ... uh ... you mean about Reena?"

"Yes, Sherlock. About Reena and the gentleman with her. Question the waiters about their relationship."

"Why would they tell me?" he asked, doubtful.

I snapped impatiently, "Because you will pay them money! Offer them a thousand bucks each for any useful information they can give."

"Thousand bucks! That's too much."

"Just do as I say. Meet me at the parking lot when you are done."

Reena entered the cafeteria with her companion in ten minutes. Wickedness makes a woman more charming. I had always found Reena attractive, but today she looked downright sexy. Her face was flushed.

Her companion was a tall man with a goatee, and cold grey eyes. She stood next to me and glared, ignoring my offer of the seat in front of me.

I smiled. "Good game? You both look so flushed."

"What are you doing here? Who let you in?" she asked coolly.

"The guards did."

She thundered, "I will have you arrested for trespassing."

I had to admire her. I had caught her being fingered by a man, and she was the one threatening me.

"Okay, but then I would have to call your father-in-law, and request him for my release. I heard he is on the committee."

A black cloud formed over her head, and she had murder in her eyes.

"You bastard! You think you can blackmail me, huh?"

Her companion butted in, “Come on, man! Be mature about this. We were just having some harmless fun. Reena and I have known each other for a long time.”

I nodded at him.

“I like a reasonable man. Why don’t both of you sit? All I want to do is talk.”

The man whispered something in Reena’s ear, and she sat down reluctantly. She crossed her legs slowly, giving me a glimpse of her firm, shapely thighs, and black panties. Junior stirred, feeling claustrophobic, and demanding immediate release.

I diverted his attention by coming straight to business.

“Why did you make the call about Shalini?”

“Because—” she stopped abruptly, remembering just in time that she was not supposed to tell me.

“Why did you make that call?” I repeated.

She sighed. “Because Dad told me to.”

“Mr Paras Kapoor?”

“Yes.”

“And did you actually see Shalini plant the locket outside the back gate?”

“Yes. I walked into her father’s room on Sunday. I saw her hurling the locket out of the window.”

“What did you do?”

“Nothing. I didn’t make much of it that day. I had gone to her room to check on her, since she hadn’t been feeling well. She was not in her room. So I went to her father’s room. I opened the door and saw Shalini throwing the locket outside the window ... towards the back gate.”

“What time?”

“Umm ... just after you and the police had left.”

"Did you confront her?"

"No. As I said, I didn't think much of it that day. She was startled when I entered the room. I asked her what she had thrown out of the window. She said something about empty tablet sachets. I knew she was lying because I had seen something solid, made of metal. But the ambulance was waiting to collect Anil's body, and I was busy.

"I had completely forgotten about the incident, until the day Babu found the locket outside the gate. It was then that I realized what Shalini had thrown out from Mayank Uncle's window. It overlooks the back gate."

"Did you confront her then?"

"No. Dad had rushed to Leo's house. You were there. When I saw Dad in bandages yesterday at the hospital, I told him right away. I was afraid he would go after Leo again."

It made sense now. No wonder the old man had been so sure about Shalini being the murderer.

"Why didn't anyone mention this before?"

"Well, he was the only one to know besides me. I had forbidden him to tell you or the police."

"Why?"

"Well, Dad confronted Shalini this morning, as soon as he came back from the hospital. He forced me to say what I had seen, in front of her."

"What was Shalini's reaction?"

"She freaked out; panicked. She denied everything. She said she had not thrown anything out. I reminded her that she had thrown out some tablet sachets. She broke down and started crying. It was too much for me. I told Dad not to bother her again."

"Not bother her again? Even though you were sure she was the one who planted the locket?"

"Yes, even though I was sure she was the one who planted the locket."

"Why don't you want her arrested?"

"I would never hurt the poor girl! I told Dad that it was up to him, and the police, if they wanted to punish the girl. As far as I was concerned, the bastard deserved to die."

"Why?"

"The poor girl is a victim. Look, I can demand things. I come from a rich family. Aditi is shrewd and beautiful. She was able to compensate for her middle-class background with her personality. But poor Shalini has been a misfit from the start. She was forced to marry Anil. He was a fiend. I felt sorry for her, but never found the courage to stand up for her when Anil was alive. What right do I have to send her to jail, if she took justice in her own hands?"

"I am confused. If you didn't want her arrested, why did you call me today?"

There was a pause.

"Dad made me call you. I told him very clearly that I would not testify against Shalini if she denied throwing the locket out of the window."

"Then what happened to make you change your mind?"

"Two things. One, I read the SMS that her ex-boyfriend had sent her. Two, Dad mentioned that you have a recording in which she tried to bribe you to get off the case. If either you or the police are able to prove her guilty, I will testify. That was the deal between Dad and me. But her grave won't be dug based only on my testimony."

I said warily, "All this because you have a conscience?"

"Whatever. You will not understand."

She looked at me in disdain.

Her companion butted in. "I assume all your questions are answered?"

All this time he had been sitting quietly, listening to our conversation. It struck me that his expression hadn't registered any surprise or shock during our exchange. Reena had mentioned that she had only told Paras about Shalini, to protect her. Yet, she was perfectly at ease telling me everything in front of her companion, who had maintained a poker face throughout the interview. There was a possibility that he was already aware of Reena's version of events.

Reena placed a hand on her forehead, as if comforting a migraine. "Listen, what you saw inside...no one has to know...."

I smiled at her companion. "Hi, I am Vishal. You are—?"

He looked confused for a few seconds, and then said good-naturedly, "Hi. I am Abhijit Banerjee."

Reena glared at me. "Are you listening to me?" Then she softened and pleaded. "Look Vishal, I knew Abhijit before my marriage to Vimal. If Vimal finds out about us, he will be shattered. I love him. This is just plain fun. Do you understand?"

"Yes, I do. This is purely sexual."

"I beg you never to mention this to anyone."

"Don't worry. I won't. I have one more question, and then I will leave you lovebirds alone."

"What's that?"

"When you entered the room and saw Shailini throwing the locket out of the window, what was Mr Tripathi doing?"

"Uh...he was sitting on the bed, with the usual blank expression on his face, oblivious to everything around him."

"Thanks."

I got up and walked away.

We were hiding in the parking lot, in the shadows of a car bigger than my house. Pranay smacked his shoulder, missed a mosquito, and asked, "Can't we wait in the car?"

"We could have, if you had been able to find out something worthwhile from the staff."

"They are uptight, man! At least I found out Abhijit's address. What did you expect to find out anyway? She told you they were only having fun."

"I have a hunch. Let's see."

We had to wait for another twenty minutes before Abhijit came out. He started walking towards the parking, looking carefully in all directions. He took out his mobile phone and made a call. Reena came out and followed him to the parking lot. He walked past us and went to his car. Reena casually walked towards her own car. She sat in her car and reversed it till she had reached Abhijit. Abhijit had opened the boot of his car. It was dark by now, but the headlights illuminated quite a bit of the parking area.

I couldn't risk changing my position, so I strained my eyes to see what was happening. Abhijit took out a dark bag from his boot, opened the rear door of Reena's car, and threw the bag in. Reena drove away. Abhijit got into his car and drove away too.

I got into the car. "We will have a night out."

Pranay groaned. "What for?"

"To keep an eye on Abhijit Banerjee."

"Oh ... has Vimal employed you to tail his wife and her lover?"

"Nope. I don't think he is aware of this."

Pranay looked confused. "Why are we wasting time on Abhijit? He's just her fuck buddy."

"Night out it is. Didn't you find anything strange in the manner he threw that bag into her car?"

"No."

"What do you think there was in the bag?"

"I don't know. Tennis shoes?"

"You will see. We shall break into his flat when we get a chance. You got his apartment number?"

He sighed. "Can we go home and change into shorts?"

"Sure. And pick up burgers and booze."

Bells were ringing in my head. I was pulled out from a disturbed sleep. My phone was ringing. I looked at the time and groaned. It was five in the morning. I had been asleep for less than two hours. Pranay was snoring in the front seat. I whacked him on the head. He was supposed to be keeping watch.

I mumbled a dehydrated hello.

It was a woman's voice.

"Good morning. This is Anjali. We met yesterday. "

"Morning. Do you know what time it is?"

"It is five in the morning. Were you sleeping?" she asked amiably.

I tried to think of a sarcastic answer, but all my grey cells were asleep.

I sighed and said, "Yes, I was sleeping."

"Oh, I just wanted to talk about the article"

"What?"

"You know, the article I was writing."

"What about it?"

"I wanted you to read and review it. It is being published today. Front page!"

"Your article? Now?"

"Yes, if it is not too much of a bother. I have been a nervous wreck since last night. Couldn't sleep. I thought I should discuss it with you."

"Lady, the only articles I want to review now are *a*, *an*, and *the*. *A* good sleep is *an* extremely important ingredient for *the* sanity of a man."

"Ha ha. I see you are up. Please! I know you are interested in the case. I want to see your expression when you read it."

I stifled a yawn.

"It is being published today?"

"Yes, in our mid-morning edition. It should hit the news-stands soon."

"Do you want to read it to me on the phone?"

"No. I was hoping we could meet at the Orchid. They have a twenty-four-hour coffee shop that serves the most amazing English breakfast. My treat."

I could use a hot cup of coffee. "Sure."

I woke Pranay up, and told him to keep vigil until I returned. Abhijit had stayed indoors the entire night and received no visitors. It had been dark in the parking lot of the club, but the bag Abhijit had tossed into Reena's car, looked very similar to the one I had found in Leo's apartment. If someone was trying to hide thirty crores in cash, they would've probably bought a new set of bags, from the same shop, at the same time, and probably the same kind. It was a long shot, but worth twenty-five lakhs if I hit the target.

Half an hour later I was entering the lobby of the Orchid. The doorman gave me a cold stare, and opened the door. I caught my reflection in the mirror – a crumpled T-shirt, shorts, floaters, dishevelled hair, messy stubble, and bloodshot eyes from too much booze and too little sleep. The immaculately dressed lady at the reception stared at me nervously, as though she expected me to take out an AK-47 any moment, and start shooting in the lobby.

I walked on the shiny marble floor, across sophisticated rooms with natural lighting, dark wood, and white sofas that invited me to take a nap. Anjali was waiting in the cafe, looking quite pretty in some shade of pink.

"Thanks for coming. You are a kind man."

"I know."

She took my hand and led me to a table in the corner.

A waiter showed up, and she ordered promptly on my behalf. "Two English breakfasts." She smiled at me and added, "You will love it."

"What would be your choice of beverage, ma'am? Coffee, tea, or juice?"

"We will have tea. Earl Grey," she commanded.

I signalled to the waiter to cancel the order. "Careful," I said to her with a smile. "I think you are very close to being dominating, as your dad says."

I looked at the waiter. "Make that one English breakfast for the lady, and one tea. I will have only coffee. Black."

She said disapprovingly, "You don't have breakfast, huh? Do you know it is the most important meal of the day?"

"Oh, I do have breakfast. I just like to keep a two-hour gap between dinner and breakfast. Now are we going to discuss my dietary habits, or are we going to discuss your article?"

She immediately cheered up, and took out two neatly folded printouts from her handbag. She pushed the sheets towards me.

"Give me your frank opinion."

I glanced through the sheets. Screaming out at me was the headline, *Anil Kapoor Murder: The Real Story!*

And below that, looking smug, the byline, *By Anjali Singh*. A picture of her smiling stood right beside the byline. She waited for me to finish reading the article, and nibbled at a fingernail. She had managed to get the data right. The article started with describing the suspicious circumstances in which the corpse was found. It mentioned a police officer, who wished to remain anonymous, but acknowledged that the main suspect was a member of the Kapoor family. The article then covered the financial problems plaguing the Kapoors, and the possibility of the government reclaiming the land originally allotted for their flagship mall, due to delays in starting the construction. Towards the end, the article subtly mentioned that in all such crimes inheritance was a major motivation. The article ended by promising a sensational breakthrough in the subsequent article.

I looked at her and nodded in approval. "It is cheap, sensational, fictitious, and devoid of any character – very well suited for your target segment. It will sell very well."

She looked crestfallen and asked me earnestly, "What about the writing style? Is it good?"

I laughed out loud, appreciating her sense of humour and self-deprecation. The article was written in Hemingway's style, with the vocabulary of a teenage rock 'n' roll artist.

Her expression looked pained, and I realised that it had not been a rhetorical question. I made a futile attempt to disguise my laugh as an unexpected cough. It was too late. She looked devastated.

"It's terrible, isn't it?" Sadness loomed up in her eyes.

"No, no, please don't take my feedback seriously. I have always been a careless reader."

She blushed. "Oh, is that true? Yes, you were in fact reading it too quickly. You couldn't possibly have paid attention to the finer nuances."

"Yes, I was always too fast. My English teacher used to call me a premature ejaculator when it came to reading comprehension."

She threw her head back and laughed freely, once again her cheerful self.

I asked nonchalantly, "So, what is this sensational article that will follow?"

She leaned forward. "Remember I told you about ... uh ... how do I put it...about some sexual issue concerning someone from the Kapoor family?"

I nodded.

"My informant has given me some mind-blowing dope! It will shock the public."

It struck me then that she was overreacting to Anil's homosexuality. The public would probably be amused, rather than be shocked about this facet of the deceased's life —unless I was wrong in my assumption, and it had never been about Anil at all.

"So who is this source of yours?" I enquired.

She brought a finger to her lip. "Oh no, Mister! That is strictly private stuff. Reporter-source confidentiality. I can't tell you his name."

I noted that she had addressed the source using the masculine-gender pronoun.

"And I came here at five in the morning for you," I said in a complaining voice.

The more I thought about it, the more sense it made. I could have been a victim of my own presumptions. If Leo was the informant, he was not likely to speak about Anil's sexual life, as it would embroil him in the entire scandal too.

She misread my silence and pleaded, "Oh ho, don't be moody now."

She leaned forward.

"All right. A small titbit, and then you are not supposed to ask me anything. My source is going to give me some visual evidence tonight. A CD. At a party. Once I get the proof tonight, oh boy, what a story!" Her eyes were gleaming and she continued, "The story I am covering tonight is going to make to the front page on Sunday. I will reveal my source's identity to you on Saturday. Okay? Please!"

The waiter laid out an elaborate English breakfast before her, and poured out some coffee for me.

"How well do you know Leo?"

She swallowed a partially masticated toast in one gulp. Shock was evident on her face. She laughed nervously, and tried to camouflage her surprise by reaching for the teapot. She upset the teapot, which upset the cup in front of me. The cup of coffee tumbled and fell off the table. Molten lava permeated my shorts, scathing the sleepy and unsuspecting Junior.

"Hell!" I screamed involuntarily, jumping up and trying to get the hot liquid off my shorts.

"Oh my God!" she screamed even louder, and rushed towards me.

She picked up some tissues, and started wiping the coffee off my crotch. With the initial shock wearing off, I became aware of her attempts to cool Junior by blowing air, and gently caressing him with the tissues. Junior immediately identified her as an ally and declared peace.

The waiter was staring at us in amusement. I lifted her chin, smiled, and gestured with my hands signalling that everything was fine. She suddenly realised her position and turned red.

"Dog," she whispered as she sat on her chair. In her own way, she was adorable.

I started laughing.

"Listen, you have made me give you classified information about my boss, woke me up at five in the morning, and almost castrated me. I think I am entitled to know if my guess is correct."

She looked at me guiltily.

"I promised him that I would preserve the client-informant confidentiality. How did you know it was Leo?"

"Not important. How do you know him?"

"I can get into serious trouble if you tell anyone. Leo keeps reminding me that he is a dangerous man. You won't tell anyone, will you?"

"Cross my heart and hope to die. See, I am still alive. I want to know everything that he has told you till now."

She sighed. "He called the office two days ago. The call was transferred to me. He demanded to talk to the person in charge of the Kapoor story. I took the call, posing as my boss."

"This was on Monday evening, after six?"

"Yes! How did you know?"

"Because I was in his apartment with the police till around six on Monday. He must have called you after we left his flat."

"Oh! Does that tell you anything?"

"Yes. He had resisted divulging any information when we confronted him. Yet, when we left, he chose to call the press. He must have realised something in that short time."

"What?"

"I think I can guess. How much were you supposed to pay Leo?"

"He demanded five lakhs for the information."

"Five lakhs? That's it?"

"Hello! Five lakhs! It's more money than I can dream of!"

"Not for Leo, it's not. Anyway, what did you do?"

"I told him to go to hell. I get one of these calls every week. I told him not to waste my time, and was going to disconnect, when he mentioned that he had evidence that the murderer was from the family. That stumped me! Anil Kapoor being murdered on the farmhouse was a hell of a story. If the murderer happened to be an insider, it would have rocked the nation. I requested him for a meeting. He disconnected saying that he would call back. I tried tracing the number, but he had called from a public booth."

"Then?"

"I decided to give it a day before telling my boss. The bastard would have done the story himself, to score brownie points with the promoters. The next day I was going to inform my boss about the lead, when Leo called again."

"That was yesterday?"

"Yes. I asked him for some proof to support what he claimed. He said that that the police had found some clues, and he directed me to Inspector Babu to confirm this."

"Okay. Then?"

"I met Leo yesterday morning, before I met you. I took all my savings, borrowed from my roommate, and was able to come up with fifty thousand. I offered the money to Leo when we met. He was furious."

"Hmm ..."

"Then I started crying, telling him how difficult it was to survive, and how much this story meant to me. An amazing thing happened. He agreed! He took the fifty thousand, and hinted at...uh...certain things. It was mind-blowing information. I could see us selling ten lakh copies in a day! He is supposed to show me the proof tonight – the CD."

"Hmm...so this mind-blowing stuff that Leo will give you proof for, doesn't have anything to with Anil's homosexuality, does it?"

"Of course not! The entire town knows about that. How old fashioned are you?" She winked at me.

"Leo agreed to fifty thousand after demanding five lakhs? In one meeting?"

"Yes! My boss was proud of my negotiation skills."

I asked her incredulously, "You didn't find anything strange in that?"

"No. Why?"

"Anjali, the guy lives in a one-crore apartment. He returned jewellery to Anil that would probably be priced at a figure double our combined assets. Don't you find it remotely strange that a measly amount like fifty thousand excited him?"

She looked confused. "What are you trying to say?"

"He doesn't give two hoots about your money. He is using you as bait for something else. He wants someone to know that he has access to the press."

"Don't be silly. What kind of bait could I be?" she asked me in disbelief.

"Has he given you any evidence about this mind-blowing stuff he has been telling you about?"

"Well, he has offered to give me the CD tonight." She remembered something and said nervously, "Although there was one request that I found strange. He insisted that our publication print the first article today, but that the information he would give us today should not feature on or before Thursday. That is why we are doing the story on Saturday. Any guesses why he wants the story after Thursday?"

"Yes. Because he plans to leave the country on Thursday. He wants time, to be safely far away, when the story is published."

"But why on earth would he want to use me, or the publication, as bait?"

I realised that there was only one explanation possible. Leo was obviously using Anjali as the bait to get someone's attention. Yet, he wanted her to hold back publishing whatever he was about to tell her, until he had exited the country. He was blackmailing someone!

"I am coming with you to the party tonight."

"I can't take you! He will freak out if he sees you with me."

"This is non-negotiable. I will hide somewhere. It is too dangerous for you to go alone."

"Well ... you can come if you promise to hide, but only if you bring your car. The party is at Kandhari hills. It's a private farmhouse, and it's a long drive. My laptop will get wet if it rains."

"Laptop?"

"Yes. He asked me to bring one. He will not hand the CD to me; only let me see the files."

Anjali seemed to have lost her appetite. She signalled to the waiter to clear the table.

"So you really think I am bait?" She looked dejected.

"Yeah. I should have seen it earlier. If Leo is the source, he would not speak about his sex life with Anil."

"Whoa! Leo and Anil's sex life?"

"Yeah. I thought you knew."

"I knew that Anil was gay! I didn't know that Leo was one too. Well, that explains a lot of things." She smiled smugly.

"What does it explain?"

"He hardly flirted with me. I started suffering from low self-esteem."

"Wait a minute. Any man who doesn't flirt with you is gay? What about me? I don't flirt with you."

"Yes, you do. You think you don't, but a woman can tell."

"Is that right?"

"Yes. So, will you get your boss's car? Because if you confirm it, then I can wear this new, hot dress I have been dying to wear."

"New hot dress, eh? Does it allow you to flaunt your lovely limbs?"

She blushed. "That's not what I meant. I can't wear it if I am on a two-wheeler."

"Okay. I am just flirting with you. Don't want you to think I am gay."

She smiled.

She opened her handbag and took out a black envelope with the imprint of a rose. She pulled out a small card from the envelope and gave it to me. "This is the invite. It says Kandhari Hills at nine in the night. You know the place?"

I shook my head.

"But I will find out before I pick you up."

The only text the card had was in golden italics, *Entry for two only.*

"And what about – "I was interrupted by the ringing of my mobile. It was Pranay. "What's up?" I asked him.

"Abhijit has just left the apartment. He was driving."

"How was he dressed?"

"What?"

"Was he in sports wear or formals?"

"Formals."

"Okay. This may be our chance. I am on my way."

I returned the invite to Anjali, paid the bill, and told her I would touch base with her later that day.

It was a small four-storey apartment block. Two ladies dressed in track suits came out of the building for a jog. There was no sign of a watchman. I waited for a few minutes to ensure that there was no activity in the vicinity, and walked into the building, followed by Pranay. We entered the lift and punched the button for the fourth floor. Within seconds the doors of the lift opened into a vacant passage.

There were four flats on this floor, and all of them looked occupied. We walked to number 402. I looked down at the cylinder lock. Then I looked around the passage, straining my ears for the sound of footsteps, or doors being opened. It was quiet. I took out my toolkit from my jacket. All the stuff about detectives and thieves picking locks as easily as they pick their noses is crap. Picking a lock is a time-consuming and tedious process. The method is simple, but the skill is difficult to master.

I took a wrench and a thin, flat screwdriver from the toolkit. Pranay's obese build was a screen between me and the elevator. I inserted the wrench into the keyhole and pushed slowly, until the pin shafts started moving. The wrench was still inside, when the elevator hummed to life and stopped at our floor. Pranay muttered something incomprehensible under his breath. An eight- or nine year-old boy walked into the corridor. He was carrying newspapers in his hands. He stopped when he saw us, staring at us with a confused expression.

I leaned my body on the wrench, trying to hide it from his view, rang the bell, and said exasperatedly to Pranay, "What the hell is the bugger doing?"

Pranay stood transfixed, his face a guilty red. I rang the bell again and said encouragingly, "You told him we were coming, right?"

This time he replied, "Yes, I did. Bugger must be drunk."

The boy relaxed, and started dropping the newspapers in front of each door. He extended one to Pranay, who took it. I debated for a minute about proceeding or retreating. The lock had surrendered, and it would be a royal shame to back off now. I pushed the door open, stepped in, and locked the door from inside.

It opened into a hall that was sparsely furnished, with three bean bags, a single sofa, and a flat screen TV. The hall was adjacent to a dining room that led to the kitchen. I walked into the kitchen, and opened the refrigerator. It was filled with cartons of low-calorie fruit juice, protein shakes, tofu, and cans of tuna fish. There was a big bottle labelled "Whey Powder" on top of the fridge. A health freak. There was no liquor in the kitchen or the hall. I walked to the dustbin, and glanced through the garbage. Empty cartons of protein shakes were strewn over. Still no sign of liquor. A health freak and a teetotaller. The worst kind.

"What are we looking for?" asked Pranay.

"A black leather bag. The kind that he gave Reena in the parking lot yesterday. And his CD collection."

I walked into the bedroom. A huge bed covered most of the room. The room had a serene touch to it – white walls, white bed cover, and a two-inch thick white carpeting on the floor. A five-foot high table was on one side of the bed. A small round stage light was placed upon it, turned towards the bed. The room already had a tube light and two bulbs. I wondered why he needed additional lighting. I walked to the table and switched on the light. It was battery-operated. The bed was illuminated with fluorescent light.

"Whoa, the guy likes brightness!" exclaimed Pranay.

I walked to the middle of the room, so that I was standing at the foot of the bed. There were three slight indentations on the carpet. I bent forward and observed the marks. They formed a triangle. I didn't see any tables or folding chairs in the room. I walked to the corner of the bed and peeked under it. There was a folded tripod with aluminium legs. I picked it up. It was surprisingly light. I placed it on the three indentations on the carpet. It fitted beautifully. I looked at Pranay.

"The tripod was placed over here. It looks like a digital camera tripod to me. Try to find a camera."

We searched the room for the next five minutes, but found neither the camera nor any CDs.

I sat on the bed and looked at Pranay searching the cupboard again. It was a wooden cupboard. There was a box partition at its foot. Probably a shoe rack. Someone had taken the trouble of putting in a chain and locking it up. I took out the wrench and broke the lock. Abhijit would know that someone had been here. And that that someone knew exactly what he wanted to find.

I opened the small cabinet. It was dark inside, so I used my hands to grope around all the corners. My fingers touched something plastic. I pulled it out. It was a green plastic bag. I looked inside. There were at least ten CDs, and a small digital camera.

"Bingo."

We went to the hall and switched on the TV. I inserted a CD titled *S* in the disc player. Characters in a familiar room appeared on the screen. Abhijit was standing in his bedroom, laughing, clucking his tongue, and mocking the camera. A woman could be heard laughing in the background. The sound quality was bad and the light was dim. Abhijit adjusted the camera on the tripod, moved back, and flopped on to the bed, in the classic dead man posture.

The woman entered the frame. She was wearing a blouse and a petticoat. A diamond necklace with a shiny green stone dangled from her neck. Her saree and Abhijit's shirt lay in a heap at a corner of the bed. It looked like they had returned from a party. The woman took a sip from a glass of wine, and shifted to the centre of the bed. She spread her legs apart and beckoned to Abhijit. He removed his trousers and crawled playfully towards her. Abhijit took the glass of wine from her hand, and went out of the frame.

Suddenly, a fluorescent light illuminated the bed. I could see the face of the woman clearly now. She had a wheatish complexion and pleasant features. I guessed she was in her late twenties. Abhijit returned to the frame; he had deposited the glass somewhere. He stood on the bed, so that only his lower body was captured by the camera. He said something to the woman and she smiled. She expertly sat on her knees, rolled down his underpants, and took him in her mouth. Abhijit moaned. His hands held her hair and pushed her head forward.

This continued for five minutes. At one point, Abhijit made the woman stop, and asked her to smile at the camera. I forwarded the tape until he had come. She looked at the camera and smiled again. The video ended there.

"What the hell is this, man!" exclaimed Pranay. "Yesterday it was Reena, and now it's this? Some kind of fuck fest?"

I emptied the contents of the plastic bag on the floor. I took a CD marked *R*, and inserted it into the DVD player.

Reena was sitting on the bed with Abhijit. Both were naked, and laughing at the camera. Reena lifted her breasts, and laughed at the camera. The camera zoomed in on her nipples, and panned down to get a close shot of her privates.

"Did you see that?" I asked Pranay

Pranay whispered hoarsely, "Yes! They are perfect! I wouldn't have imagined them to be so big."

"Not that! The camera is moving, unlike the last film. It's not kept on the tripod. Someone is filming them."

"Yeah! You are right!"

The camera zoomed out, and the entire bed and its occupants slid into the frame. Abhijit lowered his mouth on Reena's nipples, and slid his fingers between her legs. Reena moaned, and stared right at the camera. She threw her legs over his shoulders, as if locking him in place. This continued for a few minutes.

I forwarded the tape and then stopped. Both of them were looking at the camera and grinning. Reena went down on all fours, her hips moving gently. Abhijit entered her from behind. The sex continued for a few minutes, until Abhijit shuddered and came. The camera managed to capture a close-up of the wetness between Reena's legs, and then panned up to her breasts. The movie then came to an end. The mysterious person behind the camera had made no appearance.

I took the CD out, and stuffed it inside my jacket. I glanced through the other CDs. There were four more *S*s, two *A*s, one *B*, one *P*, but no other *R*.

"Are you taking the CD with you?"

"Go through the rooms, and look for a bag, a trunk, or a suitcase that can hide a substantial amount of cash."

We spent the next fifteen minutes turning over everything in the apartment, but there was no sign of any cash.

"Let's go," I said to Pranay, and we walked towards the door.

He hesitated, looking at the mess we had created. "Shouldn't we tidy it up a bit?"

"Don't bother about it."

"Can't that get us into trouble?"

"What will he report? A missing CD? The police would want to know what was there on the CD. Let's go."

We walked out of the building and got into the car. My head was whirling; I felt exhausted, and my back hurt. I thought of the exotic spas and the relaxing massages I had seen in glossy magazines. Then I thought of the twenty-five lakhs that could help me afford those massages. The thought of money energised me, and I started the engine. I took a big sip from the flask, and pushed the accelerator hard.

Pranay looked at me disapprovingly. "Drinking and driving?"

"Thinking and driving," I replied as we drove.

He pouted. "So, what are we working on now? Anil's murder, or the missing money?"

"The missing money."

"And the murderer? Shalini did it with Rajesh?"

"Yeah. They have practically confessed."

"And if we find the money, the old man gives us twenty-five lakhs?"

"Yeah."

"That is a lot of money." He rubbed his hands in glee. "Tell me what I can do to help."

I made a brief stop at home, shaved, showered, changed, had two cups of black coffee, dumped Pranay, and was at the Kapoor residence in an hour.

Ram opened the door and folded his hands in greeting. "Good morning, sir."

"Hi. Is Mr Kapoor up?"

"Oh yes! He is up at six every morning."

I followed Ram to the dining hall. Paras was sitting at the dining table, and scowling at the newspaper. He flung the paper away when he saw me. It landed in the porridge. Ram hurriedly lifted the paper, and took the dish away.

"Have you read what crap they have printed? I will kill this girl, Anjali Singh."

I found myself defending her. "She is doing what any journalist would do."

Paras muttered something under his breath, and signalled for me to sit down. The table was covered with plates of toast, omelettes, sandwiches, fruits, and orange juice. Not to forget the porridge that had been taken away. And Paras was the only one having breakfast.

"Thanks for your tip about the article. I appreciate it. Can't do much about the filth that they will print, but at least we know what to expect. It ended saying that the next article would contain something sensational. I guess they will be talking about Anil's homosexuality."

"No, it's not about that."

"How can you be sure?"

"I spoke to the journalist, Anjali Singh."

"You spoke to the bitch? Regarding the case?"

"Yeah."

He said appreciatively, "You do go in deep, don't you? Especially after the case is solved. You spoke to Reena last evening?"

"Yes, I did. She told me she had seen Shalini throw the locket out of the window. And that Shalini denied this when you confronted her."

"Yes, and Reena didn't pursue it further. Reena is soft. She said she would not testify against Shalini unless the police obtained proof. Well, I guess we now have all the proof we needed. You will testify, of course. Let her and her lover rot in prison together."

I nodded.

"I am going to speak to Mr Arsani today. I hope that is okay."

Paras took a sip of orange juice and pondered. "Is that necessary?"

"Yes. I think I may be able to locate the cash if I can get some answers."

A renewed interest twinkled in his eyes.

"The cash, huh? We have given up hope. We checked everywhere. If you find it for us before the cops, it would be really helpful. Do you have any leads?"

"Yes. I want to speak to Mr Asrani, to investigate further. Just wanted to keep you in the loop."

He sighed. "Okay. We haven't told Mr Arsani about Anil's forgery, although he may suspect something is wrong; we have been probing him about the deal. Anyway, the deal is done. The shrewd bastard made a killing on this property. Find the money, and you can take a cut."

"Yes. You graciously keep reminding me of that! The fight between Anil and Sunil on Saturday ... it was because the forgery had been discovered, right?"

He buttered a toast.

"Please help yourself. Ram, get some breakfast for Vishal."

I turned around and saw Ram standing behind us, eavesdropping.

"No, thanks. I will just have some coffee. Black. Thanks."

When Ram left, Paras continued, "Yes. The fight happened because Sunil discovered Anil's forgery. I would rather not speak about it, unless you think it can help you locate the money."

"It will, I am sure."

"Well, Sunil had borrowed money at extremely high interests. We were delaying our payments to our lenders. The market was bad, and they all trusted me, so we got an extension.

"Anil closed the deal with Asrani without informing any of us. News was leaked in the market that we had disposed of one of our assets. Lenders started calling me on Friday night. I was amused at the rumours, and reassured the lenders. It didn't occur to me that Anil could have forged Sunil's signature and pulled this off. One of the lenders, not a very nice gentleman, saw the deed in Asrani's office. He was sure we were trying to dupe him, and sent the goons on Saturday evening."

"And when did you know that Anil had forged the signature?"

"As soon as the goons left. They had a copy of the deed from Asrani's office. It was signed by Anil and Sunil. Both were required to sign the deed. The property was sold at half the market price. I had refused double the price only the week before."

"So how did you know it was Anil who had forged it?"

"Well, he had tried to pull off a stunt like that in the past."

"Did he confess?"

"Confess? No confession. It was my birthday. We were under a lot of pressure. After the fight, I told Sunil to let it go...during the weekend. But of course it was Anil. I know my sons."

"Did you confirm that with Asrani?"

"No. As I said, the deal is done, and I don't want to drag this any further. But twenty-five crores are missing. And it's important that we find them before the cops."

"Were you there when the fight started?"

"No. Only Shalini, Mayank, and the servants were at home when the fight broke out. I was returning from office with Vimal, and Aditi and Reena had gone to the club to play tennis. When I reached home, Sunil was banging on the bathroom door, and had a knife in his hand. I calmed both of them down. I told them to enjoy the weekend, and that we would sort it out on Monday."

"Hmm..."

"What?"

"Nothing."

"You look as though you just realised something."

"Nothing. I swear."

I finished my coffee.

"I will go and visit Mr Arsani in his office today. You may have to bail me out if he doesn't co-operate." I got up. "Before I leave, I wanted to talk to Shalini's father. I hope that is okay?"

"Mayank? Why?"

"Haven't interacted with him at all. I thought I would just say hello. Is there a problem?"

"Okay. We'd better tell Ram to inform Shalini, so that she can prepare him. She is very protective about her father."

He called Ram and instructed him to tell Shalini that I would be speaking to her father. Mayank's room was on the second floor. The door was shut, so I knocked. Shalini opened the door, did not return my greeting, and turned away. It was a small room, sparingly furnished: a bed, a cupboard, a dressing table, and a television.

Mayank was asleep on his bed. Shalini went to him and shook him gently. Mayank opened his eyes and sat up. He folded his hands and greeted Shalini. There was no trace of recognition on his face when he saw me. She switched on the television. That grabbed his attention. She offered him some tablets and a glass of water.

Mayank looked disgusted. "I have already taken them."

"That was yesterday," she said.

He reluctantly allowed her to put the tablets in his mouth. He took the glass of water from her and, as soon as Shalini had turned away, spat the tablets into his hand and threw them under the bed. Shalini spooked him by reprimanding him without even turning around.

"I saw that! You will not get any chocolate if you behave like this."

She looked at him angrily as she gave him a new set of tablets. This time he swallowed the tablets and clucked his tongue mockingly. Shalini smiled and rewarded him with a piece of chocolate. He gulped the chocolate and extended his hand again. She playfully patted his hand away. "I just gave it to you."

"That was yesterday." She gave him another piece of chocolate, which he gobbled with pleasure.

I approached him and said, "Hello, sir. We met at the farmhouse. Do you remember me?"

He stood up, folded his hands and asked, "How is your father?"

"He is fine. Sends you his regards." He pointed to the dolphin on my T-shirt.

"I used to be a faster swimmer than you. Remember the time when I caught the fish in the pond with my bare hands?"

"Yes, long time. We all were very proud of you that day."

"Did you have your medicine? Did she give you the medicine?" he asked, pointing at Shalini. Shalini was sitting on a chair, watching me like a hawk.

I shook my head. "Yes. She made me have it, but I spat it out when she was not looking."

That thrilled the old man. He smiled and rubbed his hands together in glee. He leaned forward and whispered, "Did she give you sweets?"

I shook my head again. "No, she didn't."

He looked at me in disbelief. Then he remarked thoughtfully, "She has some now. Hidden. If you ask her, we could share them."

He extended his hand towards her, as though asking for something. She didn't respond. He retreated, looking hurt. He yawned at me, got back into bed, and closed his eyes.

"Do you remember Anil?" I asked him.

He remained motionless and, within seconds, had started snoring. I looked at Shalini and shrugged.

She said, "His medicines induce sleep. You can talk to him later."

If she knew that the tablets induced sleep, she could have given them to him after I had talked to him. Unless, she didn't want me to speak to him. I bade her farewell and walked out of the room.

I left the house, got into the car armed with a copy of the agreement Anil had forged, and proceeded to Asrani's office.

It was ten o'clock when I walked out of the house. Asrani's office was at the other side of town. I was reading the copy of the agreement, while cruising on an empty road at no more than thirty, when I heard a loud thud on the bonnet. Abhijit was running alongside the car, pounding his fists on the bonnet quite violently. I braked and locked the windows from inside. He was already at the passenger side. He quickly took out a gun, and broke the window with its butt. He opened the door and got in before I could react.

He thrust the gun against my ribs. "Motherfucker! Where's the CD?"

His eyes were bloodshot and he was gritting his teeth, looking as if it required great effort for him to not pull the trigger.

I said in my most cooperative voice, "Easy! It is in my office."

The CD was in the dashboard, but I didn't think he would be sharp enough to look. I was right. He pushed the gun further into my intestines and said menacingly, "Call someone to your office, tell them to pick up the CD and meet us in Coult Park. Now!"

"Okay."

I dialled Aarti's number. The battery had almost run out. I disconnected before I could get through. I spoke on the phone, pretending that Aarti was on the line, and asked her to get the CD from my desk and meet me in Coult Park in half an hour.

I pretended to disconnect.

"You want to take the pistol out of my guts? It is distracting me from driving."

He placed the gun under my chin, right at my food pipe.

"You pesky bastard! You think you are smart, eh? I am gonna fuckin' kill you. Kill you!"

"Relax, man. I just took it for some harmless fun. No big deal. You can have it back."

I looked in the rearview mirror. Where was all the traffic when you wanted it?

"Listen good, you motherfucker. I want the CD. And there had better not be any copies made. I am gonna fuck so you bad that you are gonna curse the day you were born."

His spittle flew all over my face.

I knew he planned to use the gun. He could have walked into my office and taken the CD, instead of planning the rendezvous in a secluded park. A car appeared from the opposite direction and he lowered the gun, jamming it into my groin.

"No funny stuff, man." I groaned in pain, and evaluated the possibility of making a grab for the gun. I gave up the idea. Junior would never forgive me if something happened to him.

"Enjoyed what you saw, motherfucker?"

It seemed like a trick question, since either acknowledgment or denial could give him an excuse to pull the trigger. I maintained my silence.

He continued, "I hope you did. Guess where I am going to shoot you."

I saw some veins pulsating on his forehead, and I made a few guesses about where he planned to shoot me.

I took a detour on a thirty-foot wide road. He barked, "Why are you getting off the main road?"

"It's a shortcut."

He didn't argue, but reiterated his intentions by jamming the gun further into my groin. It hurt a lot. I slowed the car considerably and looked around me.

"Go fast!" he shouted.

"Can't! Relax, man. You have the gun on a sensitive spot. What if a speed breaker jolts us and the trigger goes off? "

He leaned back, and repositioned the gun over my abdomen. I nodded and accelerated the car.

With any danger to Junior thwarted, I decided to give a fight to the son of a bastard. There was always the chance of the gun going off in my ribs, but I was too pissed to care. You are born to die anyway. A curve came up too fast on the left, and I drove off the road. The car tumbled on to a green patch that ended in a five-foot wide drain. I saw terror in Abhijit's eyes.

"What the fuck are you doing?" he screamed.

I slammed the brakes, let go of the steering wheel, and went for the gun pointing towards the roof of the car. The car skidded to a halt a foot away from the open drain, distracting Abhijit. I twisted his wrist to knock the gun down. I bent to pick it up, but he held my collar and banged my head against the steering wheel.

I realised that even without the gun, he was just as dangerous as before. I dived again, trying to find the gun. He used his knee to kick my face. I tasted blood ... my blood. I groped the floor with my left hand, and threw a right-hand punch upon his face. Twice. He didn't flinch. That petrified me. This was not the look of a man who had taken my best punch.

He held my neck in a vice-like grip, choking me. I tried to push him off. My vision was blurring. I was already out of breath. All that stuff you see in the movies about Rajnikanth beating up twenty people, and then breaking into a song and dance, is strictly for the squirrels. Any man, who has been in a fight, knows that two minutes of wrestling exhausts you beyond belief.

I poked his right eye, and his grip loosened. I pushed him towards the edge of passenger seat, opened the door, and jumped out, my hands on his throat. We rolled on the grass till we hit the granite next to the drain. I saw him get on to his feet in less than a second. My neck and shoulders erupted in pain as I tried to get up.

He was approaching me with an expression that read crazy. He kicked my abdomen. I started seeing two of him. I knew that the next kick would be fatal. He drew his foot back and aimed it at my face. I caught his ankle and pulled him down. I lifted myself up using his body as a support, and punched him in the face thrice. He groaned, covering his nose with his hands.

I had a million broken bones, but my legs were still working. I began to stagger towards the car, but heard a sound behind me. I turned, and watched in disbelief as Abhijit sprinted past me to the vehicle. I promised myself that I would quit drinking and go on a protein-shake diet if I made it through this ordeal. I dived at his feet just as he was entering the car. I missed him by a few inches and fell down, staring at the open sky.

Abhijit pushed the door open and stuck his head out. The white sky was replaced by his bloody face. He had the gun in his hand. Everything unfolded in slow motion. He pointed the gun at my face. A few drops of his blood fell into my eye, blinding me. I felt the passenger door, and swung it shut with all my strength. I heard a scream as it slammed against him. The door swung back and, once again, I banged it hard. I continued the operation till he stopped screaming. Finally, I got up and picked up the gun he had dropped.

He was groaning miserably.

"Here, let me have a look," I said, helping him up.

As soon as he stood up, I rammed the butt of the gun against his knee. He screamed like a madman. His pupils dilated, and he slumped against me. I dragged him to the edge of the ditch and looked down. There was water and slime that ran at least six feet deep. I dumped him there with his gun.

Fifteen minutes and half a flask of whisky later, I walked into a department store. The lady at the counter opened her mouth wider than a crocodile's yawn when she saw me. I smiled and told her I had been in an accident. I went to the restroom and took stock of the damage. My stomach had developed blue welts that burnt each time I breathed. A deep gash on my chin was bleeding profusely.

I cleaned myself as well as I could, bought some new clothes, and changed. I dumped the old clothes in a bin and walked out. I continued with my original itinerary, and proceeded to the office of Asrani Infrastructure. I looked at the address of the buyer on the agreement. The signatory was Akshay Asrani, MD, Asrani Infrastructure. On the seller' side, Anil and Sunil had signed. The witness was a Mr Thapa.

Twenty minutes later I was parked in front of a thirty-storey swanky building. I walked in and took the elevator to the second floor. I entered the lobby of Asrani Infrasructure. The receptionist was on a phone call. She saw me walking towards her, hung up, and stood up flashing an inviting smile. She was the voluptuous kind, wearing a tight white top that must have fitted her perfectly when she was in the third grade. I felt claustrophobic just looking at her breasts.

"Good morning," she said, widening her already exaggerated smile. Whatever they paid her was too little. She was the kind of receptionist that made men aspire to become her boss.

"Morning. I am here to meet Mr Asrani."

"Do you have an appointment?"

"No."

Her condescending eyes looked me over. She asked with cold politeness, "What is this regarding?"

"Official."

"Oh my! Your face! Your chin is bleeding."

"Excuse me." I took out a handkerchief and clamped it under my chin.

I saw a copy of *Crime Busters* on her desk.

"Have you read the article on the Anil Kapoor case?"

She looked confused. "Yes, I have. Why?"

"I am the detective working on it. I am here to meet Mr Asrani, regarding a transaction between him and Anil a few weeks ago. A building sale."

She looked down at the paper and her eyes gauged me anew. "Detective?"

"Yes."

The interest was replaced with respect. Maybe she was the kind of girl I could lay after a few drinks, just by telling her that I was a detective. I made a note to get her number later.

"Please wait."

She dialled a number and whispered something softly. There was a pause, and she whispered again.

"Mr Asrani would like to speak to you," she said handing over the receiver.

I took the phone and heard the muffled voices of two men. One of them was very angry.

"Hello?" I spoke into the receiver.

"Yes, this is Akshay. You are—?"

"I am Vishal, a private detective hired by Mr Paras Kapoor to investigate his son's murder. I wanted to meet you regarding the last transaction between Anil and you – a building sale. Anil was the signatory."

"What about it?"

"I think Anil Kapoor forged the other signature to expedite the deal. Wanted to see if I could get some leads about that."

His voice was muffled again, as if he had kept his hand over the mouthpiece, and was conferring with someone else.

"What the fuck have you got me into, Thapa? The private dick says that Anil Kapoor bloody forged the signature! What do you know about it?"

Thapa said something I couldn't hear. Akshay said gruffly, "Bullshit. Get it over with." He came back on the phone.

"Our CEO, Mr Thapa, will meet you. He takes care of our real-estate investments. Ask the receptionist to seat you in Conference Room number one. Thapa will join you shortly. Please make it your first and last visit."

I gave the receiver back to the receptionist. "Your boss says you should lead me to Conference Room number one."

"Please follow me, sir."

"Call me Vishal."

"Okay, Vishal."

"What's your name?"

"Rita. How did you cut your chin, if you don't mind me asking?"

"I don't mind anything cute girls ask me. I got into a scuffle with a man with a gun."

She laughed nervously, and then saw I was serious.

"Is that common?"

"All the time," I lied.

"Wow. That is exciting and dangerous. I have never met a detective in real life. Is it just like in the movies? Action and adventure?"

To me they sounded like synonyms for dysentery, and trying to make ends meet.

I nodded. "You said it."

She dumped me in the conference room and left. A five foot four baby face walked in. He was wearing a white suit and white shoes. He gave me a phony smile, and walked towards me with his arms open wide, as if we were old friends.

He patted my shoulder and said, "Hi, I am Manoj Thapa."

I shook his hand. It was soft, pudgy, and sweaty.

"I am Vishal Bajaj."

"What will you have? Tea or coffee?" he asked in a too-eager-to-please voice.

"Coffee. Black. Thanks."

He called for the coffee.

"So, how is the investigation going on? I read in a daily today that a family member may be involved. Shocking!"

I shrugged, "Still investigating."

He made an apologetic face. "I must apologise on behalf of my MD. He must have seemed rude."

This guy was too sweet. His smile read bullshit, and he had his palms open in a friendly gesture.

"Oh, that's okay. Given this short notice, I thought he was exceedingly warm on the phone."

His smile drooped a bit, and he eyed me with caution now. "How can I help you?"

"Mr Asrani mentioned that you take care of real estate investments."

"Yes, I head that division."

I gave him the copy of the agreement. "So you were dealing with Anil Kapoor?"

"Yes, I was. I was part of this deal. The MD is only the signatory. I decide whether we should go ahead with the deal or not."

"Are you aware that Anil forged the signature?"

His hand flew to his mouth. He looked away from me and focused on the ceiling instead.

"Not until you told us right now," he replied. "Well, we were suspicious when Paras Kapoor called Mr Asrani, and took down lots of details about the transaction. However, he acknowledged the transaction, and that's all that matters."

"So what happens now?"

"Nothing. We have already paid a certain amount of money. The property has been transferred in our name. And the Kapoors have acknowledged it."

"The money you paid Anil was to the tune of thirty crores?"

"I cannot divulge that. It is, in a layman's terms, called goodwill."

"That's very nice. I have already been told that you got a good discount, and gave a huge component as cash."

"Yes, that is common practice. Only, in this case, it has been a very attractive deal for us; plus we save on the stamp duty, if the registered value of the actual transaction is less. So we don't mind."

"What do you mean by *attractive*?"

"One of the best investments we have made this year! Or, for that matter, so far in any of our real-estate transactions. We bought the property at half the valuation in the market."

"I am sure Mr Asrani is happy."

He replied coldly, "The entire board is very happy."

"Who was in touch with you during this deal?"

"Anil Kapoor."

"So you met him. And Sunil was never in the picture?"

"No. I only interacted with Anil Kapoor during the transaction. For us, there was no reason to get suspicious. It was, after all, in the family." He pulled at his collar for some air. I wondered what was making Thapa nervous.

"Okay. So Anil Kapoor met you and concluded the deal?"

The coffee came. I noticed he was sweating in the cold room.

"Uh ... yes. In a manner of speaking, yes."

"In a manner of speaking?"

"Yes. Actually, I spoke to Anil on the phone."

"On the phone? What about in person? Face-to-face?"

"Uh ... unfortunately, I couldn't meet him."

I pushed the agreement towards him. "While handing over the cash? While getting his signature?"

More beads of perspiration appeared on his forehead. He fiddled with his tie.

"You never met him face to face?"

He nodded. "We planned to meet during the actual signing of the agreement, but Anil and Sunil were busy on the days when Mr Asrani was free, and vice versa. I didn't want to postpone the deal. The draft had been approved by both the lawyers. The signed agreement was sent to me by their CFO. In fact, he was the one who collected the cash. But it was okay. I was on the phone with Anil the whole time."

"So Mr Asrani never met Anil Kapoor?"

Thapa fiddled with his collar again.

"Mr Asrani is a busy man. I collected the agreement on his behalf."

"But does Mr Asrani know that none of the signatories ever met you?"

"I assure you that I have my MD's complete confidence, and he would not like to be bothered with such trivial details."

"I think he might, especially after he's been told that the signature was forged."

"But the family is going ahead with the deal," he said in a matter-of-fact tone.

"Hmm ... but even then I would want to inform Mr Asrani that while the deal was being processed, the man he had trusted with the deal did not meet any of the signatories, which is strange, especially since you signed as the witness."

He leaned forward and pleaded, "Listen, this can get me into some trouble. Why don't you forget this, and collect a little reward for whatever you have done so far?"

"What sort of reward?"

He whispered, "Money. Fifty thousand? A lakh? I am a reasonable man."

I took my time to answer. "You would give me that kind of cash just to walk away?"

"Yes. My MD is paranoid. No sense in spoiling the good deal that has been done. As of now, it is a lucrative deal. Let it remain that way. Even if Anil did forge the signature, he is dead, and the family doesn't want to press charges. How would it benefit either of us if you spill the beans now?"

In five minutes he had offered me a bribe. And it had all started when I threatened to speak to his MD.

"I don't want your money. Just answer my questions truthfully, and you will never see me again. Okay?"

"Uh ... okay."

"Who contacted you? How did the deal start?"

"We had sent mailers, a month ago, to all prominent builders and brokers, inviting offers for tenanted buildings at a yield of thirteen per cent or more. Some of the brokers got back with a yield of ten per cent or so. I was surprised to receive a mail from Anil Kapoor, offering their prominent buildings at half the valuation. I still have the email if you want to see it. It came from his official email ID. I thought there had to be a typo, or some other error, so I called him. He reiterated the offer on the phone. I was excited. It was the mother of all distress sales!"

"And you never interacted with Sunil during this deal?"

"No. Everything happened so fast."

"On the phone? Never face-to-face?"

"Well, the main exchange was via official email. He was not very eager to meet with me. In a week, we had formalised the draft, and agreed on the numbers."

"When was that?"

"About two weeks ago."

"And when did you pay the money?"

"Last week. Five days before Anil was murdered."

"Hmm ... to the CFO?"

"Yes."

"How did he look?"

"Tall. Goatee. Grey eyes. What? You know him?"

"Yeah. Can you identify him?"

"Yes, I can."

"Okay. You gave him the cash, and collected the agreement. Then you signed as the witness, went back to Asrani, and told him that you had personally met him."

"Well, yes," he said nervously. "But Anil had been on the phone all the time. Moreover, we hadn't made the entire payment. The white component was pending, and they had already transferred the asset in our name. So you see, we had the upper hand."

"When were you supposed to make the white component of the payment?"

"Well, that is the funny part. Anil insisted that his family was travelling abroad, and we would complete the rest of the proceedings on or after Thursday. That would have been tomorrow."

Thursday was the day Anil had planned to elope with Leo. So he wanted the white component to be transferred after his departure. It made sense. He wouldn't want people to become aware of the forgery until he had left the country with the cash. What didn't make sense was why Thapa had been so eager to close the deal.

"All right, Thapa. One last question, that has no bearing on my investigations, but I will not sleep easy unless you answer it truthfully. And if you do, I never walk into Asrani's office again."

"What?" he asked nervously.

"Anil was in a hurry to close the deal. And you helped him expedite a deal of around seventy crores. It took me more than a week to finalise the rental agreement for my apartment. And that deal was worth fifteen thousand. Without your help, Anil's plan would have failed. So, tell me, did he offer you a cut?"

"What? Are you insane? I never—"

I picked up the phone, and started dialling a random number.

"What ... what are you doing?"

"Trying to reach Mr Asrani."

"No!"

He snatched the phone from my hands and threw it on the table.

"Listen, I didn't do anything wrong. It was a good deal for my company. I am proud of it. If anything was given to me, it was because Anil was happy that I had helped him. So don't try scaring me."

"Wouldn't dream of it. I just wanted to place a piece in this jigsaw puzzle. So your motivation for expediting the transaction for Anil was partly some money."

"Never. I received something as a token of his gratitude," He softened. "Listen, I am willing to give you five lakhs. Let everyone be happy."

"No, that's okay. You have been very cooperative. Thanks."

I got up to leave.

"Wait. I insist. Meet me this evening for a drink."

"Thanks again. Not needed. Enjoy yourself."

"You ... won't tell Asrani?"

"Nope. None of my business."

"Really, I would like to share some of this good fortune with you. I like you."

That made me laugh. I turned around and said, "Just one more question. How much did you make?"

He brightened. "Oh, so that's it! Well, I made half of what the broker would have charged. See, I am a reasonable—"

"So you made one and a half crores in cash?"

"One point three. Name your price, but be reasonable. You know you can't prove anything."

I shook my head and walked out. He made one point three crores, cash, for a week of paperwork, and here I was thinking that twenty-five lakhs was all the money in the world. I was so depressed that I didn't even ask the smiling receptionist for her number.

I sat in the car and decided to call Anjali. The battery had gone kaput. I tilted the flask into my mouth. The flask had gone dry. I picked up last night's packet of wafers, and put my hand into it. It was empty. This was going to one of those days. I drove to office.

I walked in after forty-five minutes. Aarti looked at me.

"What happened to your face?"

"Long story. Any calls?"

"Yes. But I can't reach you, can I? Because guess what? Your phone, as you know, is always unreachable."

"Later. I am in pain now, lady."

She softened. "Can I get you something?"

"Call Pranay and tell him to get his ass over here."

I walked into my cabin, and took a few swigs of whisky before filling the flask. The pain in my neck receded. I decided I was fine for a couple of more hours without sleep. I connected the phone to the charger, and removed my shirt. Blue and black bruises covered my abdomen where Abhijit had kicked me. I washed my face, wiped away the blood from my chin, and sat down on the chair shutting my eyes for a few seconds.

Once the phone was charged, I heard multiple beeps signalling the arrival of SMSs. I walked to my desk and picked up the mobile. There were two messages, both from Anjali. The first one read:

Hi. Your phone is not reachable. Recd a call from a lady. Has info on Kapoor case. Going to meet her. Call me back.

This had come at eleven in the morning. I must have left the Kapoor residence, and been on my way to Asrani's office then.

The second one was sent at eleven-forty:

At the old zoo. Ghat Road. Ur phone still not rchble. Going inside. Spooky place. Scared. Wish you were here.

I dialled her phone. It was switched off. I waited for five minutes, and tried her number again. It was still switched off. I had a bad feeling about this. The only women associated with the case were Aditi, Shalini, and Reena. Anjali had never mentioned any of them. I called Paras on his mobile. He picked up at the first ring.

"Yes, Vishal?"

"Hi, sir. I was just wondering where all the ladies of your household were."

"What?"

"At this precise moment, where are Shalini, Reena, and Aditi?"

"Why?"

"Please this is an emergency."

"Okay. Reena is right beside me. Aditi has gone to the mall to pick up something, and Shalini has taken her father to the hospital for his check-up."

"Which hospital would that be?"

"Nayantara. What is this about?"

I disconnected without exchanging pleasantries. Nayantara was a prominent hospital located on Ghat Road. I dialled Babu's number.

"Hi, buddy!" he said cheerfully.

"I need you to send some men to the old zoo at Ghat Road. Emergency! We are looking for a female."

"The old zoo? That is abandoned. They shifted the animals to—"

"I know that. Anjali Singh, the journalist, was called to the old zoo, at the pretext of giving her some information regarding Anil's murder. I have a bad feeling about this. Her phone is switched off."

"I remember Anjali Singh. Who called her?"

"Some female. Anjali was trying to reach me, but my phone was off."

"Oh, okay. I will call the Ghat Police Station, and tell them to send some men there."

"Good. Where are you?"

"I am at the city station."

"Why don't you make it there too? Whoever called her is related to the Kapoor case."

"Okay. I am starting now. Should be there in half an hour. What about you?"

"I am at the other side of town. Should be there in an hour."

"You said a lady called? Who?"

"I don't know. But Shalini is right now at Nayantara hospital. With her dad."

"Isn't that the one on Ghat road?"

"Yeah."

"Oh! I am leaving right now."

Paras had tried my number twice while I was on the phone with Babu. I dialled his number and informed him about the developments, so that he would get off my back. I rushed out of my cabin, grabbed Aarti's mobile, and transferred my SIM card while running down the flight of stairs. The old zoo had been shut two years ago. It was out of city limits. One had to take a detour of at least a kilometre from the main road to reach the zoo. I drove the car through the irritatingly slow city traffic, and jumped a few signals to make up for lost time. Babu called me after about half an hour.

"Yeah?"

"We found her body!"

I slowed down and parked at the side of the road, hoping that I had not heard him right. "What?" I felt the panic in his voice.

"We found her body. In the fountain. Murdered. And we arrested the murderer too. He was fleeing the crime scene."

"Who?"

"Rajesh. Shalini's ex."

"Hold him in custody. I should take another twenty minutes to reach you."

"One more thing!" Babu said. "We have proof! Shalini did it with Rajesh. We have them now!"

"What's the proof?"

"We found an earring in Anjali's fist. It has been identified. They have confirmed that it belongs to Shalini."

"Who are *they*?"

"Well, Paras sir and his family. They arrived here shortly after I reached. You called them, right?"

"Not exactly. Never mind. So what are you going to do now?"

"I am going to talk to Rajesh. I am sending some men to Nayantara to escort Shalini and her father here. You should get here fast."

"Shalini was not on the site?"

"No. Only Rajesh."

It took me fifteen minutes to reach the turning for the zoo. I got off the main road, and drove the odd kilometre, till I saw the rusted iron gates and a dilapidated sign that read *City Zoo*. I drove in.

Dense foliage comprising wild grass and weeds covered the land. The sound of crickets was deafening. I followed the fresh tyre marks until I came to a fork on the muddy road. Anjali's pink Scooty was parked there. Her small footsteps were visible near the two-wheeler. She had parked the vehicle here and walked towards the right. Someone must have been directing her on the phone. There was a hedge running parallel to the road. I took a right from the fork, and drove another fifty metres until I came across a police jeep and two cars that I recognised as the Kapoors'.

The driver of the jeep pointed to an opening in the hedge. It was imperceptible. One couldn't find it unless he was aware of its existence, or was being guided towards it. I walked through it, and found myself in a small square-shaped lawn, with a fountain in the centre, and four cemented benches at each corner. The area had been created as a resting spot for visitors. The people surrounding the fountain stopped squabbling as soon as they became aware of my existence. I glanced at everyone. All the Kapoors were present. Ram was also there. Babu quickly walked towards me, looking visibly relieved.

"What took you so long? And what happened to your face? You are bleeding!"

I wiped the blood from the wound on my chin.

"Where is Rajesh?"

"He is in the jeep. Handcuffed. Shalini and Mayank should be here any minute."

Babu pointed towards the fountain, motioning that I should step forward and take a look. All of a sudden I felt nervous. My feet felt heavy. I stood rooted to the spot and stared at Reena. She didn't register any emotion when her gaze met mine. If she was aware of my confrontation with Abhijit, her expressions did not give her away. Paras coughed slightly. He was the only one standing at the foot of the fountain, near the body.

Babu came closer to me and whispered, "They will come and take the body. Don't you want to...um...look for clues?"

I nodded, and started walking towards the fountain. My senses were still trying to come to terms with the fact that Anjali was lying there – dead. The grass covering the lawn was eight inches high, erect, and the blades had sharp tips. They reached my calves, cutting the ankles through the socks.

Anjali's body was immersed in the fountain. I avoided looking at it directly, staring at the fountain for some time. It was an old, rusty fountain, filled with approximately four feet of water. Probably just rainwater over the last couple of days. Some gushed out from a crack at the bottom of the fountain, forming a stream around my shoes. I could feel the intense gaze of many eyes at my back, urging me to act. I took a deep breath and looked at the body. Anjali's left foot rested on the edge of the fountain, while the rest of the body was partially immersed in the water. She was wearing a pink top and a long white skirt that came down to her ankles.

I used my handkerchief to lift her face out of the water. Her face was bloated, and her complexion had turned white. Her eyes were partly open, protruding, and swollen. I felt nauseous, and gently released her head back into the water. A sharp pang ran through me, as I remembered that just hours earlier I had had breakfast with her. I felt disgusted. I silently cursed this unnecessary waste of a life. I felt a weary kind of anger that comes when you have been pushed too far. I wanted to break some bones. I wanted to drown someone. I wanted to stab someone.

"Here's the earring," said Babu.

He handed me a lone earring. It was gold-plated, and a blue stone was embedded in it.

"It was clenched in Anjali's fist. It belongs to Shalini. Reena and Aditi have identified it."

Paras exploded, "Damn her! I told you she was crazy. Crazy!"

"Can we get all the civilians out on the road?" I asked Babu.

Babu nodded and ordered one of his men to escort the Kapoors outside. All of them looked relieved to leave the scene. Even Paras walked away eagerly.

I asked Babu, "Where did you find Rajesh?"

"I dispatched men from the Ghat Road police station right after your call. They caught Rajesh near the entrance. He was fleeing on his bike."

Anjali had messaged me last after arriving at the zoo at eleven-forty. She must have parked her bike and then typed the SMS. I had seen her last message after reaching my office, around twelve-thirty. The police would have taken an additional twenty to thirty minutes to reach the scene. What was Rajesh doing at the crime scene for over an hour? Anger consumed me as a thought crossed my mind.

"Any signs of sexual assault?"

"No. She was drowned."

"And your men found him at the gate, on the bike, at around twelve-thirty?"

"Twelve forty-five. They reached here within half an hour of your call."

"That's strange. It means he was at the scene till at least an hour after Anjali had arrived."

Babu pondered this over and asked, "Why?"

"Maybe he was waiting for someone."

"Oh, you mean Shalini?"

"I don't know. Has he confessed?"

"Not yet. The bastard is pretending to be shocked. He has admitted nothing. But I haven't given him the special Babu treatment till now. I should have arrested him yesterday at the Kapoor residence."

I leaned forward. The water surrounding the body was a tinge of red and brown. The brown was from the mud. The red was blood.

"There is some red sedimentation in the water. I don't see any wound. Do you?"

"That is normal, said Babu authoritatively. "Nosebleed occurs underwater."

"There is too much blood for a nosebleed." I lifted her head out of the water for a second time, and felt her scalp with my fingers. I felt a cut below her head. It was a deep, asymmetrical wound, probably inflicted by a blunt instrument. It had been a powerful blow.

"There is a wound on her head. That explains the blood."

Babu observed the wound. "Yes! She must have banged her head on the ground while struggling with Shalini. And that's how she got Shalini's earring in her fist. A murderer cannot be lucky twice."

"You know what bothers me?" I said more to myself than to Babu.

"What?"

"What was Rajesh doing at the crime scene? Why didn't he just leave with Shalini?"

Babu stared at me incredulously.

"Not again! Maybe they left together. Shalini realised that she had left her earring behind. She sent Rajesh back. Clear?"

I nodded.

"Yeah. That would make sense, I guess."

"You guess? We have a dead journalist. Two murders in three days. Our chief suspect's earring was found in the victim's hand. Don't guess now. It is over. The case is closed! I have already informed the commissioner that we are arresting the murderers."

Babu had lifted Anjali's head to examine the wound on her head. A blade of grass caught my eye. It was stuck in the wound. I plucked it out. It was soggy and blunt, and almost eight inches high. There was no grass floating in the water, or in the fountain bed.

"Where did you find the earring?"

"It was clenched in her left fist."

I lifted Anjali's hands and observed her nails, and then her wrists. Her nails were clean, and there were no apparent cuts or bruises on her wrists that suggested a struggle. The right leg was immersed in the water, while the left one was above the water, resting on the perimeter of the fountain. Both her sandals were intact. I took off her footwear and examined her feet and ankles. They were unblemished, and her toes had no blood or loose skin.

If Anjali had been conscious, she would have fought back. She would have gone for the eyes, torn an earlobe as well as the earring, and kicked the perpetrator till her feet bled. The only reason why she would not resist would be that she was unconscious or semi-conscious due to the blow on her head. There had been no struggle underwater. But then, how did the earring get into her fist?

"What are you thinking?" Babu asked me.

I ignored him and observed the gap in the hedge that led to the lawn. I imagined Anjali parking her two wheeler at the fork on the road, and walking towards the opening. The murderer must have instructed her to park her vehicle and then directed her here. He would have most probably been on the phone. She would have entered and seen a lawn filled with wild grass, weeds, and a dirty fountain. She would have stopped at the opening— scared, and ready to run. There was no way she would have come towards the fountain, unless there was coercion involved.

I walked towards the hedge and examined the grass. There was a trampled patch of grass some six feet from the opening. It looked as if something heavy had fallen there. But that was it. There was no sign that someone had been dragged across the lawn to the fountain. I observed the ground for two or three minutes before one of the policemen informed Babu that an ambulance had arrived. Two hospital workers walked through the hedge, carrying a stretcher. They were there to collect the body.

"Can you ask them to wait until Shalini arrives?" I requested Babu. I wanted to see Shalini's reaction when she saw the body.

Babu nodded, and signalled to the hospital staff to wait.

A policeman was holding a pink handbag. I recognised it as Anjali's. I took the bag and went through the contents.

"Did you find a mobile phone in the bag?" I asked Babu.

"No, not in the bag...or in the vicinity. Looks like either Shalini or Rajesh got rid of it."

"Can you track all the calls and messages she received today? We are interested in the calls today, between eleven and one."

I saw a black envelope with a red rose at the centre. It was the invitation card for the rendezvous with Leo tonight. I dropped the bag on the ground, as I held the envelope, and sneaked it into my pocket while picking up the bag.

"Did you find something on the ground?" asked Babu.

"I think I know how he did it."

I handed the bag back to the sub-inspector and walked towards the hedge. It was at least ten feet high. There were some gaps between the leaves and twigs through which the road was visible. The murderer had been waiting for Anjali, armed with a blunt weapon. He must have guided Anjali to the opening, and then hidden himself as she walked in. And then he had hit her head.

I walked along the hedge until I could see the fork where Anjali had parked her bike. There was a wide and irregular gap, the twigs had been bent, and anyone standing there could clearly see the pink scooter. He must have waited here. I looked at the ground. It was moist, covered with more wood than grass, and had no visible footprints.

I knelt down and the examined the ground. I noticed a heap of grass and twigs at one spot. They had been uprooted very carefully from the surrounding area. I scattered the heap, and uncovered a footprint. Someone had stamped a foot so hard that a depression had been formed in the moist earth. I scooped it up and let it run through my fingers. I felt a small roll of soggy paper. It was a cigarette stub. I found four more stubs. All of them were dirty, barring one which was surprisingly clean. It appeared that the smoker had stamped the stubs to extinguish them, covered them with grass, and then carelessly thrown away the last cigarette. I handed over the clean stub to Babu. He observed it for a few seconds and said, "The filter is long. Imported cigarettes."

"Does Rajesh smoke?"

"Probably. Else, how would the stubs be here?"

"Hmm...I think I have seen Sunil smoke imported cigarettes."

"What's that supposed to mean?" Babu asked, caution evident in his voice.

"Nothing. Just an observation. How many minutes does it take to smoke six cigarettes, one after the other? Say, in nervousness."

"I don't know...maybe three to four minutes per cigarette."

"So he must have waited for almost half an hour before Anjali showed up."

"Not he. They. You forgot Shalini's earring," Babu reminded me.

"Let's go and talk to Rajesh."

We made our exit and found all of them there, waiting for us. Sunil was smoking an imported cigarette. I walked up to him and asked him if he could lend me one. He looked surprised, and extended the packet towards me.

"Sure! I didn't know you smoked."

I tilted the packet towards myself and counted only three cigarettes in it. I took one out and thanked him.

I walked to the jeep and opened the door. Rajesh was sitting inside, his head in his handcuffed hands. Our presence fell like a thunderbolt on him. He trembled and moaned, "Is she here?"

"Shalini? No, she is on her way."

That seemed to reassure him, for he relaxed a little and said something inaudible.

"I beg your pardon?"

His lowered his head again and looked at his feet, as if in a trance. Babu spoke in a sharp tone, "You speak now, you don't suffer. You speak at the station, you suffer."

That seemed to do the trick. Rajesh stared at Babu in fear. I extended the cigarette towards him, and he clutched it eagerly. Babu's face lit up and he immediately signalled that I should light it for him. I lit a match and moved towards Rajesh. His hands were shaking. A few seconds later, he let the cigarette fall to the floor. His shivering increased and he mumbled, "I want to speak to my mother."

Babu pounced on him. "And what will you tell her? That you murdered a young woman? You are doomed. Whether you confess or not, we know you did it. Have you seen the inside of a jail? Do you know what kind of people are taken there? Don't make it hard for yourself. Confess, and I will take care of you inside the jail."

Rajesh looked at Babu and then stared at the floor, maintaining an obstinate silence.

I said, "Listen, Rajesh, you need to talk. You were found fleeing from the site of a murder. Who called you here? Shalini?"

He gave me a melancholic look. "I want to speak to my mother."

I climbed into the jeep, sat next to him, patted his shoulders, and said encouragingly, "You have to speak. Babu means business. Nothing will to happen to you if you tell us the truth. Trust me. Did someone call you here?"

Suddenly, big tears fell out of his swollen eyes and rolled down his cheeks. I tried to reassure him, but his sobbing increased. He covered his head with his hands, and started shuddering violently. I hoped it was not an anxiety attack.

Babu said angrily. "Cry. Cry, you bastard! Crocodile tears. Where were your tears when you were killing the girl?"

I looked at Babu to signal the futility of any further questioning. I was just getting out of the jeep, when Rajesh put his left hand on my shoulder. He was shaking violently. He pleaded in a hoarse voice, "I am innocent! Please!"

Babu moved threateningly towards him. I stepped in between them. There was a distant roar of an approaching vehicle, and a police jeep appeared around the bend.

"Shalini and Mayank are here," said Babu.

"Don't tell her we have Rajesh. I want to see her reaction when she sees the body."

"Okay. I will instruct the others too."

"Good. Did you note that he didn't smoke the cigarette?"

"Yes, because he knew that we found the cigarettes! But he did take it, right?"

"No. He took it because he was dazed. But he held it awkwardly. I don't think he smokes."

Babu gave me a *not again* expression, and was going to say something when Paras approached us and said angrily, "She's here! Keep me away from her. I don't know what I will do to her."

Shalini got out of the jeep, followed by her father. She looked around and shrieked in panic, "For God's sake, what's going on?"

She was already on the verge of tears. The Kapoors stared at her with fear and loathing. Confusion replaced panic on her face, and she asked, "Is everything okay?"

Mayank was standing behind her, looking amused at his surroundings. He tapped Shalini's shoulder, and wrinkled his nose in disgust. "It stinks here."

Paras interrupted them. "No need to act. We found your earring."

"What?" Shalini was shaking with nervousness, but tried to maintain a brave front.

I quickly stepped in. "Shalini, there has been a murder. The victim was a journalist working on Anil's murder case. She received a call from a woman who called her here."

She stared at me in disbelief. "Oh no!"

Babu held the earring above his head, so that she could see it.

"We found this at the crime scene."

Shalini stared at the earring, walked a few steps forward, touched her ears, and looked bewildered.

"This is mine! I removed them after ... after Anil's death. Where did you find it?"

Paras came forward, took her hand, and started dragging her towards the gap in the hedge. He said in anger, "Come, I will show you where we found the earring."

I obstructed his path. "Just a minute. There is something I want to see."

I walked up to Shalini and said, "May I inspect the soles of your sandals?"

"What?" she looked even more confused than before.

"Just a quick glance. Your footwear."

I led her to a car, made her sit, and lift both her feet up one by one, so that I could examine her shoe soles. I knelt down and the scrutinised her white salwar kameez, from her knees to her ankles. I made her stand up, and walked round, trying to spot any dried droplets of water or mud on her clothes. I examined both her earlobes. I thanked her, made Mayank sit in the car, and inspected him similarly.

"What is going on?" Paras enquired.

I turned towards Aditi and Reena. "Can any one of you confirm if these were the same clothes they were wearing when they left for the hospital?"

"Yes," replied Aditi. Reena nodded in affirmation. Even Ram mumbled an acknowledgement.

"And this earring belongs to her?"

Again, all three of them nodded. I turned to Shalini, who was still shaking nervously.

"Shalini, were you wearing your earrings today?"

"No, I couldn't. I am not supposed to wear any jewellery till all the rituals are over."

"What's the point of this?" Babu barked from behind.

"I don't think she has been here at all."

There was silence for a few seconds and then Babu asked, "How can you say that? Because her shoes are clean?"

"Dirt on the shoes can be wiped off. Look at her dress. It is spotlessly clean."

"So?"

"Look at everyone else who has been on the lawn."

I pointed at Babu's khaki trousers. They were a mixture of brown and green right down to the ankles. I pointed at Sunil's trousers. They were muddy all the way down to his shoes. I pointed to the jeans Vimal and Aditi were wearing. Mud and green grass were stuck all over their jeans, right up to their knees. My own trousers were drenched with mud and water

I pointed to the unblemished white fabric of Shalini's salwar. Not a molecule of mud, water, or grass on it.

Babu lifted his leg and tried to scratch some mud off his khaki trousers. He came closer to Shalini and observed her salwar. He looked quizzically at Paras and shrugged.

"He is right. Doesn't look like she has been here."

Paras exploded, "Well, then maybe she stood on the road while he murdered her. You are unbelievable!"

"If she hasn't been on the lawn, what was her earring doing in Anjali's fist?" I said.

Paras thundered, "Her earring! Are you crazy? Her earring proves her guilt!"

He looked around at the others, as if wondering at my imbecility.

"Actually, it is the earring that makes me doubt her involvement in this murder," I said locking eyes with Paras.

"Damn the earring. What about Rajesh?" Paras challenged me.

Shalini asked in a jittery voice, "Raj? What happened to him?"

"We have him!" replied Paras. "We have him, and he has confessed."

Shalini turned white and whispered, "Confessed? Confessed to *what*?"

"Confessed to murder. Confessed that he helped you murder her."

Shalin swooned, and I held her so that she could lean on me.

Paras was merciless.

"She's acting. Just like she did while she planted the locket. We have your boyfriend's SMS. Vishal taped your conversation."

Some spittle dribbled down his lips, and he shook violently with rage. I made Shalini sit in a jeep, and waited for her to get herself together.

"Where's Raj? Where is he?"

I didn't want both of them to meet, so I lied. "He is at the police station. Right now I want you to see the body, and confirm if you knew the victim."

I waited for a few minutes until she was steady on her feet. I led her to the edge of the fountain and then pushed her forward, observing her reactions from a distance. She walked hesitantly until she was near the body. She took one glance at Anjali's puffed face, tottered away, fell on the ground, and threw up. Either she was genuinely appalled, or she was one fine actress. I gave her the benefit of the doubt for the time being. I turned to see the Kapoors standing behind Paras, watching Shalini with disgust and pity. I walked towards Shalini, helped her to her feet, cleaned her up, and escorted her to a nearby bench. She looked very sick now. They made quite a pair – Rajesh and her. I asked Aditi and Reena to sit with her.

After a little while, I returned to her. "I know you were not at this scene, but it would help if you could remember where you were between eleven and one today."

"I was with Dad," she said in a trembling voice. "The doctors were conducting tests. We were in the hospital all the time."

"Did anyone see you?"

"Yes. Of course. Dr Khanna and the lab attendant. They were with us all the time."

"Good. A lady called Rajesh to the zoo. The call was made from your mobile. Are you carrying your phone?"

"No. My father-in-law borrowed it. He said that his phone had broken, and he was expecting some urgent calls."

I knew Paras had confiscated her phone to preserve the SMS from Rajesh.

Suddenly, Paras spoke up. "Why don't you arrest them, Inspector, and end this? This has gone on long enough!"

Babu looked at me and said hesitantly, "Maybe Shalini was standing at a distance, like Paras sir said. Or maybe she was instructing him on phone from the hospital."

I shook my head. "That is not my point. I am wondering how her earring got here. Especially, since I am sure Anjali was attacked by a man and not a woman."

"How can you be sure that Anjali was attacked by a man?" asked Babu.

I signalled to them to follow me. I walked towards the hedge and knelt near the trampled patch of grass. I looked up at them.

"Anjali entered through the hedge and stood here. The man came from behind, struck her with a blunt object. It was a single blow, inflicted swiftly and powerfully. From the angle of the wound, it was someone much taller than her. She was probably unconscious after that. From here, the attacker picked her up and carried her to the fountain. Not dragged, but carried. Shalini couldn't have carried her. She weighs less than Anjali."

Babu came closer to me and asked, "Carried her from here?"

"Yes, there is at least a distance of twenty feet to the fountain. Anjali was about two inches taller than Shalini, and weighed more. She was carried by a man."

Babu knelt down beside me. "How do you know all this?"

I pointed to a few red stains that were a contrast on the green grass.

"This is blood from her wound when she fell to the ground."

Babu looked down, noticed the blood stains, and said excitedly, "Oh, it is blood!" He checked himself, and raised his eyebrows questioningly. "But it could be a stray animal's or even a bird's."

"There is a fistful of grass pulled out of this spot. The murderer pulled out those strands while picking Anjali up. There were strands of grass stuck in the wound. It must have come from here. Watch."

I stamped my right foot on the grass with great force. When I lifted my foot, the grass remained stamped. I pointed to the bloodstained trampled patch.

"You can make out the outline of her body. This is where she fell. If the murderer had dragged the body across the fountain, the grass wouldn't have remained erect, and the blood would have trickled down. So he lifted her and took her to the fountain. She was still unconscious. He must have held her under the water effortlessly until she drowned. That is why there is no evidence of any struggle."

I got up and walked towards the fountain with an imaginary body in my hand.

"He lifted her and placed her gently in the fountain. He positioned the body correctly and then applied force, taking his time. She was unconscious and hence, didn't fight him. The earring was placed conveniently in her fist. Why? That is what I am trying to figure out. Rajesh would not want to put the earring there because if Shalini was caught, he would be caught."

I picked up a rock and hurled it into the fountain. Water and mud splashed out, with droplets falling on everyone who was within four feet of the fountain. I repeated, "There was no struggle. If a woman is being drowned, she gets wild and kicks. She kicks her sandals off. The only reason Anjali did not do so was because she was unconscious. That blood you see in the water trickled from her head."

Babu walked over and observed Anjali's wrists and feet. He took a bigger rock than the one I had picked up, and threw it into the fountain. Water splashed in all directions again, wetting everyone within six feet of it.

Paras had been watching me like a hawk. "Great!" he said immediately. "Now we know how Rajesh murdered the poor lady. Right, Inspector?"

Beads of perspiration appeared on Babu's forehead.

"I have a feeling that the doctor and the lab attendant will confirm Shalini's alibi. And, sir, you confiscated her mobile yesterday. Where did you keep the mobile?" I asked Paras.

Paras looked surprised.

"It's kept on the mantle in the ... wait a minute. Are you now implying that someone made that call to frame Shalini? How can you be so sharp one moment, and infinitely dumb the next? She could have used the hospital phone to direct him here. Maybe she made the call on the sly. How does it matter, for God's sake?"

Babu looked at me and said uncertainly, "Maybe Shalini stood at a distance, like Paras sir said. Or maybe she gave instructions over the phone."

I pressed my forehead to comfort the migraine.

"That doesn't explain her earring. There can only be one explanation, if Shalini hasn't been at the murder scene. Shalini and Rajesh planned the murder in advance. Rajesh murdered Anjali, and then, for some reason – maybe he panicked – he tried to frame Shalini by planting the earring. That is the only theory that seems logical to me. Then Shalini wouldn't have to be near the fountain, and her jewellery would be accounted for."

Paras said excitedly, "That's a perfectly valid explanation. Her boyfriend panicked after the second murder, and tried to frame her."

Babu nodded appreciatively and said, "Very probable. It will be easier to make him confess now."

Paras agreed. "Damn right. Arrest them, and let's get on with our lives."

Babu hesitated again. "I can't get a warrant for Shalini's arrest right now. But I am arresting Rajesh because he was found at the scene of the crime."

Paras called his sons to him, and announced, "Vishal has just figured out how they did it."

Something didn't feel right. I had one of those feelings that keep gnawing at your gut, telling you that something is wrong. I walked away from the crowd, and sat down on a bench. I opened the flask and took a generous sip of whisky. The drink hit me hard. I gulped down some more and closed my eyes.

The humming of insects receded, and my senses gradually became numb. And suddenly I knew what was bothering me. Neither Shalini nor Rajesh fitted the profile of the murderer I had in mind. We were dealing with a sharp and incisive mind that planned everything meticulously.

Both the murders were planned and executed with cold detachment. Shalini and Rajesh seemed too impulsive, too transparent, to be able to execute the murders in such a manner. The murderer had calculated each step, and minimised the risk of getting caught. Something didn't add up. And yet, Shailni's behaviour made her culpable. Shalini did plant Leo's locket outside the gate, and then made sure Babu found it the next day. She had almost confessed when I interrogated her in her room. And then there was the SMS from Rajesh I had found in her phone.

On the other hand, the very facts that the murder happened so close to the hospital; that Rajesh was found loitering at the scene an hour after Anjali had arrived; and that Shalini did not enter the zoo, and yet found her earring clenched in Anjali's fist, added up to a frame-up.

One thing I was sure of was that Anil and Anjali had been murdered by the same person. The patterns were similar. Both the murders were planned in detail. In both cases, there was reason to believe that there was a third party involved. In Anil's case, it was made to appear as if a villager had committed the murder; and in Anjali's case, it seemed as if Rajesh had committed the murder. In both cases, Shalini was a suspect, and her behaviour intensified suspicion. In both the cases there were clues that pointed towards Sunil's involvement: first the knife, and now the cigarettes.

I felt the headache invade my head deeper, and opened my eyes in frustration, to find Aditi staring at me. Her eyes showed intense torture that reflected my own state of mind. It was as if she could read my mind. I stared at her, finding her more attractive than ever. I diverted my eyes.

It was the whisky that acted as the catalyst. It came suddenly and completely, making me sit upright, propelled by sudden buoyancy that came from within. The feeling of impatience that had been gnawing at me came to rest. A faint recollection of a remark made by Malti yesterday, and seconded by Paras that morning, came to my mind. It was all so evident that I was surprised I had missed it.

I turned the theory over in my mind, and all the loose ends were taken care of. Everything I had learnt while working on this case fell into place. I remembered the first and most crucial question I had asked the Kapoors at the farmhouse. And I remembered the answer Paras had given. The last piece fitted into my theory as the final piece of the jigsaw puzzle. I was conscious of a warm feeling of elation, and the knowledge that I had solved the mystery at last. The money and the murders had to be connected, and now I knew how.

I looked up and saw the murderer observing me with speculative interest. I smiled, realising how beautifully he had played with everyone, including me. He seemed confused by my smile. I pointed two fingers towards him, and shot him with an invisible bullet. I saw the awareness and terror in his eyes. He knew that I knew.

The hospital staff were lifting Anjali's body from the fountain. Now that I knew who did it, I knew what I was looking for. I could feel his gaze fixed on me, as I requested the staff to put the body down and let me take one last look. I knelt down and observed the wound on her head once again. Babu walked towards me, looking uncomfortable.

"What happened?" he asked me.

I felt silly for having missed it all along.

"This is how the blow would have been inflicted," I said, casually swinging an imaginary blow at Babu's head. Only one pair of eyes understood the import of my actions; everyone else seemed amused.

Babu was not pleased.

"Now, do you want to carry me to the fountain to drown me?"

"You are a mind-reader."

"What?"

"Can you get one of your men into the fountain for me?"

"Are you serious?"

"Yes."

He thought for a moment, made a decision, and called a junior cop. The cop took off his belt and shoes, and got into the fountain.

Then I said to Babu, "Imagine you are the murderer. Anjali is semi-conscious in the fountain, and you want to drown her. Remember, you don't want her to move or struggle, or else you will get water and mud on your clothes."

Babu tilted forward, put his right hand on the head of the cop, and pretended to exert force. He looked at me and asked, "What now?"

"There were some marks on her neck. I think he held her by the neck. That would give you more force too."

He removed his hand from the cop's head and put it around his neck.

"You don't want to get wet. Her legs are free. She may kick you. You would want to hold those too."

He brought his free hand on the cop's right knee, and stood there, pretending to exert pressure to drown him.

"Thank you. That's enough."

"Now, I insist that you tell me what you've been thinking."

"Come here. Check this out."

On Anjali's skirt, near her left knee, there was a small tear, a circle no more than half a centimetre in radius, probably made by the finger that tore the fabric in the process.

"So?"

"So we know who did it."

"How?"

"You just showed me."

"What?"

Everyone had surrounded us, so I whispered to Babu, "I know who did it and why. It's not Rajesh or Shalini."

"What!" he exclaimed loudly.

"Shh...listen to me. I should be able to get the proof tonight. Anjali had some information from Leo. Those facts could have linked the real murderer to Anil."

I thought for a moment and continued, "If Anjali has been murdered, Leo is next."

"He is? But we don't know where he is. He's disappeared."

"He's in hiding until he gets what he wants – tonight. And then he'll leave the country tomorrow."

"How do you know all this?"

"I will tell you later. You got to do me a favour."

"What?"

"Just for tonight, you need to post two of your men outside the Kapoor residence, and ensure no one leaves the house. Can you do that?"

"Uh ... I can, actually but only if you tell me what it's all about."

"Listen, Babu, I have a hunch. I need solid proof. If I am right, I will hand over the proof to you, and you can make the arrest. That way, you are protected from brickbats in case I am wrong, and will get the bouquets if I am correct. Deal?"

He thought about it.

I said, "But I assure you this is big."

"Okay. I trust you. None of them will leave their house tonight."

"Great."

We walked towards the group. I announced for everyone to hear, "I am going to a party tonight at Kandhari Hills. Anjali was supposed to pick up something from someone there."

I locked eyes with the murderer, and he paled.

The sky was dark. The rain was playing drums on the roof of my car. The trees on either side of the road blurred past as I sped along the lonely highway. It had been more than half an hour since I had seen the lights of another car.

"Are you sure about the route?" I asked Pranay.

He looked at the map on his lap and nodded.

"Yes. Got it from the Net. We are near the place."

He looked thoroughly confused. I peeped at the map on his lap, and saw a handmade diagram that showed sloppy lines representing roads, marked with arrows that went everywhere.

"What's that? The diagram of the impaired blood circulation to your brain?"

He said excitedly, "Look, I see a car in front of us. Finally."

I saw a blue Sonata drifting ahead of us. I had a hunch that it was heading to the same place. We rounded a sharp bend, and saw the bright lights at a lonely bungalow just off the main road. The Sonata followed the road that led to a big iron gate. I moved in closer. The headlights of the Sonata flashed on the gate.

The driver sounded the horn three or four times. A man dressed in a raincoat ran towards the car. He seemed to be a security guard. He looked inside the window, flashed his torch, nodded to someone, and let the Sonata pass.

He jogged towards my car and knocked on the window. I rolled it down and he barked, "Invitation?"

I took out the card I had found in Anjali's bag, and showed it to him. He let us pass. I followed the Sonata into the parking lot, and counted six cars already parked next to each other. At the entrance to the parking area a man stood with a bunch of umbrellas. He handed one to the occupants of the Sonata, and one to us. I parked next to the Sonata. A couple got out of it and ran towards the house, huddled under the umbrella. We got out of the car and followed the couple into the bungalow.

I kept the umbrella at the porch, and queued up behind the couple. A huge man wearing a yellow tie over a red shirt, green trousers, and brown shoes, stood at the doorway. His hair was greased back, and a friendly grin was stuck upon his face. He checked the invitation card of the couple standing ahead of us. The porch was well-lit.

I observed the man and the woman. The man was of medium height, stocky, unshaven, and dressed in formals. The woman arrested my attention right away. She was tall and thin, built like an athlete. She was wearing a black, backless gown, with a slit that ran up to her thigh. A pair of black stilettos added to her seductive power.

The rainbow with the greased hair let them pass, and extended his hand towards us. He ran a critical eye over my clothes, and muttered a disdainful greeting. He looked over my shoulder, glanced at Pranay.

"This is a couple pass," he said, sounding confused.

"So?"

"Aha...sir...you are stags."

I looked at him with hatred, took Pranay's elbow in mine, and said angrily, "Don't be impertinent."

The guard mumbled an apology and let us pass. We entered a dimly-lit enormous living room. I stood near the doorway letting my eyes adjust to the darkness. The only sources of light in the room were some shaded lamps placed strategically in all the corners. There was some kind of Sufi music audible from invisible speakers, and the sweet smell of incense lingered in the air.

This was a room meant for relaxation. People were sitting in groups of three or four, on sofas and divans. I counted five groups. I walked around the room inconspicuously, trying to spot Leo. He was not in the room. No one paid any attention to me, and people spoke in soft voices only with members of their own group. A bar fitted with stools stood at a corner in the room. I looked at Pranay and pointed at it. We walked up to it and sat down on the stools. I had an excellent view of the door, and could see anyone entering or exiting the room.

The bartender was dressed in loose clothes that did nothing to hide his paunch. He fiddled with his ponytail.

"Hi, I am Johnny," he said. "What can I serve you?"

I ordered Scotch, and Pranay ordered rum. Johnny did a few fancy tricks, throwing the glasses up in the air and catching them. I was in no mood for entertainment, but I applauded dutifully.

Pranay whispered, "Weird party. Looks more like a conference. Did you spot Leo?"

"Haven't yet."

"What made you sure he would be here?"

"He was supposed to meet Anjali here tonight. He doesn't know she's dead. He should be here to collect some big cash. He's leaving the country tomorrow."

"Big cash, huh? So what do we do when we meet him?"

"Beat the hell out of him and snatch a CD."

"A CD?"

"Yeah."

"Similar to the one we saw at Abhijit's apartment?"

"Hopefully."

I finished my drink, and Johnny refilled my glass promptly. Pranay waited until Johnny was out of hearing range. "Why was Anajli interested in the CD?"

"Because it had the murderer in the frame."

"No kidding! Shalini is in the video?"

"No."

"Rajesh?"

"No."

"You said that it has the murderer in the frame."

"It has."

"When did you decide that Shalini is not the murderer?"

"Stop talking and start drinking. Be on the lookout for Leo."

There was some activity in the centre of the room. The biggest group in the room had six members. I narrowed my eyes to concentrate. A man was holding a glass bowl. He stood up and offered the bowl to a woman. The woman picked up what looked like a piece of paper from the bowl, unfolded it, read out something, and there was excited laughter. The woman, who had picked up the piece of paper, got up and exchanged her seat with another woman from the group, so that they were sitting with different companions.

"What kind of game is that?" Pranay sounded confused.

"Well, it is definitely not Tambola."

"That couple who was in the Sonata," said Pranay again. "Behind you. The lady in black has been eyeing us for some time."

I turned around on my stool to see her. The lady in black, and her companion were sitting near us with another couple – a short, fat man; and a shorter, petite lady. I could not see the faces of the new couple, since their backs were towards us. There was a notable difference in the body language of the two couples. The lady in black and her companion were gregarious and talkative. The other couple appeared uptight, occasionally nodding their heads.

After a few minutes, the companion of the lady in black leaned back on the sofa and stopped talking. The lady in black continued talking animatedly, definitely the centre of attention in the group. She nudged her companion in the stomach playfully, attempting to draw him into the conversation, but he ignored her. After a few minutes, she stopped talking. I sensed inactivity in the group. She glanced at the bar casually, and our eyes met. I lifted my glass to my lips and took a sip, staring at her all the time. She broke eye contact and leaned back to her companion.

Then there was silence in the group again. She looked up and found me still looking at her. I pretended to be captivated by her. She broke eye contact again, and started swaying to the music. She was aware of being watched. I smiled at her. She smiled back. She got up and said something to her group, pointing to the bar. Her companion made a half-hearted effort to get up, but she pushed him down again. She walked towards the bar slowly.

She stood beside me, leaned on the counter, and said in a husky voice, "Johnny, some wine, please. White. Where are Sangeeta and Vinod tonight?"

"Oh, you know how they are, ma'am! They throw the party, but are terrible hosts. Late as usual."

She smiled and shook her head in amusement. Johnny poured her a glass of wine. She took a sip, standing at the bar.

I sniffed the air, tilted my head in her direction and said, "Nice fragrance."

She looked up, gave me a predatory smile, and said huskily, "Thanks. You like it?"

I pretended to be nonplussed. "Pardon? I was referring to Johnny's cologne."

She gave me a nervous smile. I offered her my hand. She was an attractive lady, but her beauty was cold, not warm. She shook my hand, turning towards me on the stool, so that her gown slipped a couple of inches further up a supple thigh.

"You guys look lost. New on the circuit?"

I didn't know what circuit she was referring to, but I blabbered confidently, "Yeah. Just came back to India. Vinod invited us over to...you know, test the circuit."

She leaned towards me with some sarcasm.

"Yeah, right! We have been frequenting the circuit for three months now. No luck."

"We?"

"Me and my husband. He's sitting over there." She pointed to the driver of the Sonata. "Where are you guys from?"

"Oh, we were travelling. Returned from Europe recently."

"Nice! I keep travelling to eastern Europe all the time. You been there?"

My knowledge of geography did not permit me to distinguish Eastern Europe from eastern India, so I gave her a cryptic reply, "Yeah. Been there, done that."

She glanced towards Pranay, took a sip, and asked, "You guys a couple?"

"What do you think?" I let my eyes rest on her bare thigh for a few seconds.

She smiled and said, "I think you were being cute with the bouncer."

"Yes, I was."

She spoke with excitement. "I knew it. You bulls?"

I thought of all the possible permutations of the word *bull* that came to mind. Bull-shitters? Chicago Bulls? The animal known for its virility?

I looked at Pranay, and smiled at her. "As bull as they come."

She leaned forward, put her hand on my knee, and said in a seductive voice, "Hmm, I thought so. Never wrong with my men."

She finished her remaining wine in a single gulp and asked Johnny for a refill, "Don't get authentic bulls in India. The imported ones are always the best."

I did not know what she meant, but I laughed aloud. She laughed with me. I kicked Pranay, and he laughed too.

Her eyes seemed impatient and urgent. "Listen, I don't have much time. I am Dia. What's your name?"

"I am Paras, and he is Babu" I said, pointing at Pranay.

"Okay. As I said, my husband and I have been frequenting the circuit for the past three months. Not happening at all. We are bored out of our wits. That couple sitting with us was referred to us by Vinod. Nice people, but not my kind. You know what I mean?"

It dawned on me what this entire set-up was all about. I asked her, trying to sound casual, "Your husband a bull too?"

"No. At least not by preference. He is more the watching type. But it's not like abroad. All the single men we have met here are perverts, ugly, or uncultured. So we stick to couples." She paused and looked doubtful. "You okay with that? Being watched?"

"Was always an exhibitionist."

She grew even more excited, and slid her hand further up my thigh. "Great! Let me think of a way to make those people scram. Will have to be polite. They were referred to us by Vinod, after all."

"I would hate to see them hurt. Vinod is a great guy."

She offered me a cigarette. "Do you smoke?"

"Only passively."

She tapped my crotch, looking naughty. "Good for your virility. I hope you will not be a disappointment, and finish your charge in six seconds like the last so-called bull."

"We won't know until we try, will we?"

"What about your friend?"

"Well, he prefers drinking, and will not mind."

"Oh! I meant ... you guys have never done it together? One woman?"

It was my turn to finish my drink in one gulp and said, "Oh yes. We prefer no holes-barred sex. All puns intended."

She looked at Pranay, whose face had turned a deep shade of red.

"Well, the more the better. But my hubby will be watching all the time. You guys are okay with that, right?"

She stared at me wickedly, and I could smell her arousal. I squeezed her hand. "Not a problem. What about the shorty and his wife?"

She gulped down her wine and got up from the stool.

"I will think of something."

"Great! My friend and I were just discussing that it would have to be a sixty six in case he decided to go down on you."

"What?"

"Well, with his height he will always be a couple of inches shorter. So it must be sixty six instead of sixty nine."

She stared for a moment, and then started laughing in her deep, resonant, husky voice. "Oh my god! That is so wicked. Come as soon as you see them leaving."

It sounded like a terrible cliché, but I said it anyway, "The bulls are roaring to go."

She got off the stool, blew me a kiss, and left.

Pranay said as soon as she left, "Charming, aren't you?"

"Have you seen Leo yet?" I asked hoping he hadn't come when I was conversing with Dia.

"Nope," Pranay said. "What was the woman talking about?"

"It's a swinging party."

"Swinging, eh?"

"Yeah. The couples are here for swinging."

Pranay looked around, then stared at me defiantly and asked, "Oh yeah? Where are the swings then?"

He repeated, "Well, where are the swings, wise guy?"

I placed my hand on my forehead and replied calmly, "Swinging as in couple swinging. Couple swapping?"

Realisation dawned in his eyes. He looked around and asked,

"You mean ... they trade partners for sex?"

"Yes."

"Fuck!"

I finished the contents of my glass, and was just about to request Johnny for a refill when I saw Leo. He had just entered and was scanning the room. I realised a bit too late that the area near the bar was illuminated. He spotted me before I could duck, and walked in a hurry towards the corner of the hall.

I got off the stool and followed him. Leo had entered a passage and taken a right that led to another room. I entered the room, just to see him open a door to the porch that led to a garden at the back, where he vanished in the darkness. I looked around for a light-switch, but found none. It was raining cats and dogs.

It was dark as a tomb outside. The rain had doubled in intensity since I had entered the bungalow. I couldn't see a thing, and ran with my arms outstretched to avoid bumping into a tree. After a few seconds I stopped. I stopped because I could no longer hear the shuffling of Leo's feet on twigs and broken branches. I stared in all directions, letting my eyes get accustomed to the darkness. I stared so hard that my eyes felt sore in a few seconds. I spotted a stationary shadow standing less than five feet away from me.

Suddenly, a spot of light hit the ground and then rose to my face. I covered my eyes instantly, but I had already seen Leo. He was smiling. I grasped the import of that smile, groaned, and tried to turn around, but it was too late. There was a thud, and my world came crashing around me.

I woke up surrounded by a wet darkness, conscious of a throbbing pain at the back of my head. I wondered if I was dead. I decided I couldn't be dead. Death wouldn't be so painful. I lay there for a few seconds, waiting for the pain in my head to recede. I shook all my body parts. Everything seemed intact, yet I was aware that something in my clothing had been tampered with. I realized something was wrong with my posture. My right arm was stretched out, and the fist was wrapped around a solid object. I released the object, counted all five fingers, and used the other hand to bring out the mobile phone from my pocket.

I punched the keys arbitrarily, and used the light from the display screen to illuminate the ground. A body was impaled in a knife. I turned the light towards the face of the victim. Leo's expression was frozen in terror. He was not breathing, and his heartbeat had ceased. His body still felt warm, so I couldn't have been out for a long time. My body started shivering uncontrollably as I lifted myself off the ground. I had taken a few steps towards the porch when the lights were switched on. Pranay was standing there with a couple. I waved my hands to draw their attention. Pranay saw me wobbling and ran towards me. I leaned on him for support, and then sat down on the cold floor.

"What happened?" he asked.

My teeth chattered like a sewing machine needle and I stammered, "Wh ... wh ... were ... we ... were ... you? Di ... didn't ... fo ... foll ... follow me?"

"You didn't tell me! I thought you were rushing off to the loo. When you didn't return for five minutes, I decided to follow you. Johnny told me that the loo was in the other direction. So I ran here and saw the door open."

"Mo ... mor ... mor ... moron."

The woman screamed, "Is that blood?"

The man standing next to her bent forward, scrutinised my damp T-shirt, and encored, "My god! Is that blood?"

Pranay gasped audibly as he inspected my T-shirt. "That is blood! You hurt? What happened?"

"Whi ... whis ... whisky."

Pranay ran inside the room and returned with a bottle of whisky in two minutes. Jack Daniels. Sealed. I nodded my head in appreciation and broke the seal open. I took two sips, letting the alcohol warm my body. My teeth stopped chattering.

"Who are they?" I asked Pranay.

"Uh, they are the hosts. They own this place. Sangeeta and Vinod."

I looked at them. "A torch. And an umbrella. Fast. Please."

The man nodded to the woman, who ran inside the house. I turned to Pranay, "Call Babu. Tell him to come over." Sangeeta came back with the umbrella and the torch.

Vinod passed them to me and asked, "Were you involved an accident?"

I took the umbrella and the torch from the man, and gave him the bottle. He would need some reassurance. I stood up with some difficulty and said, "You may want to stay here. There's a dead body in the garden. My friend has just called the police."

They appeared shocked for a few seconds, and then attacked me with a deluge of questions. I ignored them, and leaning on Pranay, opened the umbrella, and stepped out in the rain again. The ground was slippery and my steps were unsteady. I bent to examine Leo's body, while Pranay positioned the umbrella over us.

I switched on the torch and ran it along the outline of Leo's body. He was lying on his back. His intestines were all over the place. The killer had stabbed him multiple times in the stomach and the chest, piercing the knife one last time near the heart. Immediately, I knew that this was a different murderer from the one who had stabbed Anil, or drowned Anjali. While Anil and Anjali had been murdered with minimal force, planned in detail beforehand, Leo had been stabbed with frenzied ferocity. Since the Kapoors were under house arrest, there could be only one man who would commit a murder like this.

We walked back to the porch, where the couple had lost their colour.

"Whose body is it? Is someone dead?" asked Sangeeta.

"Okay, Sangeeta and Vinod, I am Vishal. There has been a murder on the lawn."

"Oh my god!" The woman swooned, falling into her husband's arms.

The man snatched the torch from my hand, and pointed it in every direction, trying to spot the body. He was paralysed with panic.

"Murder! Whose murder?"

"The body is behind that tree," I said pointing towards the direction of the corpse. "The victim is a man called Leo. You know him?"

He replied by turning away, dragging his wife inside, and shutting the door on my face. The lights of the porch were switched off in a few seconds, plunging us into darkness again.

"Shit," I muttered.

"What happened to them?" asked Pranay.

"I think he thinks I murdered Leo."

"What! Did you murder Leo?"

"No, but I'll murder you if you don't shut up. Let me think."

They wouldn't just leave us here. There were multiple exits from the garden. They would probably get help and come back.

The lights were switched on as abruptly as they had been switched off, and the door opened. Vinod was standing there with a gun pointed at my face. Sangeeta crouched behind him looking terrified.

"Hands up!"

This was the second time I had had a gun pulled to my face in one day. I groaned. "Relax, I need to clean up and get into some clean clothes. The police are on their way."

"Hands up! I mean business." He extended the gun forward by two inches, to show that he meant business.

I negotiated, "No one does hands up any more, man. Can't I just freeze?"

"Over your head, you bastard!"

I was shivering due to the cold. He was also shivering, due to fear.

I walked towards the door and said, “Look Rambo, either pull the trigger, or let me clean up. I would rather die of a bullet than of pneumonia.”

The man took three steps back for every step I took forward, tripped over his wife, and both of them fell down to the floor. I waited until he had got up and pointed the gun towards me, and then turned to his wife.

“Can you guide me to a bathroom? I need to get out of these clothes.”

She was transfixed with fear. Pranay butted in, “It’s okay. We are private detectives. We have informed the police, and they are on their way.”

The man still looked at us in confusion.

“I hate to drip all over your marble floor. The bathroom?”

The couple exchanged looks, nodded at each other, and guided me to the bathroom. I could see that Johnny and the bouncer were busy escorting all the guests outside.

I entered the bathroom, and was overwhelmed by what I saw before me. The bathtub was bigger than my apartment – large mirrors, tiled floors, a television, a music system, gold faucets, and a sauna in the corner. I grabbed a towel from the neatly stacked pile of towels, and asked Sangeeta to get me some dry clothes.

I looked at my reflection in the mirror and grimaced.. All I needed was a pink snout, and I would fit right into a pigsty. I used the towel to wipe the dirt around my eyes, face, and shoulders. I opened the cabinet above the washbasin, took out some antiseptic, and dabbed it generously on my head where Abhijit had struck me. He could have done more damage, but our confrontation in the morning must have impaired his strength. Not to forget he must have been in a hurry. After hitting me, he would have stabbed Leo, dragged me towards the body, taken the CD, and rushed to the parking lot. I was out for ten to fifteen minutes, so he didn't have much of a lead on me.

The woman returned with some clothes, probably Vinod's. I smiled and said, "Thanks. I will replace these."

"Someone should call the police," said the woman to her husband.

"My friend has already done that. They should be here in half an hour or forty minutes."

Vinod asked me, "Who are you? How did you get in?"

I sneezed several times, and requested them for some privacy while I changed. Vinod lifted his gun again and said, "We are not budging till the police arrives."

"Suit yourself."

There is something about having a gallon of water in your underwear that makes you do away with modesty. I stripped to my underpants, and looked up at the woman, who turned a shade of beetroot. I raised my left eyebrow to show that I meant business. Neither of them made any movement to turn around. I stepped out of my underpants, making the woman blush, and leisurely put on the new clothes.

Pranay came back with the bottle of whisky just as I had finished changing. I was still shivering, and felt feverish. I took a few sips, and checked my wet trousers that I had just removed. My wallet was in the back pocket. I always kept it in the side pocket. I remembered the strange feeling I had had when I regained consciousness – that something had been tampered with. Abhijit must have taken my wallet out of the side pocket and planted it there? I opened the wallet and went through the contents. A few wet notes, debit cards, and a driving licence. Everything looked intact.

I drank some more whisky and asked my hosts, "Did you know Leo, the man who was murdered?"

"No!" said the man promptly.

I looked at the woman, and she immediately averted her eyes.

"Okay. He had an invite, so he was definitely expected at the party. And I know what kind of party this is."

The man lowered the gun and negotiated with better manners, "We don't know half of the people in this room, okay? People get invites through friends. Every couple, who has been a member for more than six months, can take extra cards to invite new people. We don't know any Leo."

"All right. Do you know a man called Abhijit?"

The man paused, as if thinking about the name.

"No. Never heard of him."

"What about you, ma'am?" I asked his wife.

"No. Never." Her trembling lips belied her words.

"You must be an amnesiac. I remember seeing you in a CD, playing naked-naked with him. Your necklace gave you away. Green emerald. The CD was titled *S. S* for Sangeeta?"

The lady stared at me in disbelief, her jaw dropping open. The husband mopped his forehead.

"You have been very good hosts. I will make a deal. Okay?"

"What?"

"The cops will be here shortly. I see all your guests have left. They would want to know what I saw here. I am not interested in your promiscuous misadventures. I will not mention anything to them. All I want to do is ask some questions."

The man said defensively, "It's not promiscuous. It's progressive."

"I am sure it is. What about the deal?"

Vinod looked at Sangeeta and nodded his approval. "What do you want to know?"

"For starters, cut the bullshit and acknowledge that you knew Leo and Abhijit."

He thought about it. "We don't know any Leo. Suppose I say I knew Abhijit, as a fleeting acquaintance ..."

"That's very progressive indeed. You are okay with your wife banging a fleeting acquaintance of yours. I must be obsolete. Anyway, how did you get acquainted with Abhijit?"

"He was part of the circuit. We met him last year at a party, but it has been more than six months since when we saw him last. What's this about? Is he in trouble?"

"What about Reena Kapoor? I am sure you know her."

"Uh, I know a couple of Reenas, but no Reena Kapoor. I swear."

The *I swear* confirmed his lie.

I was going to interrogate him further, when the bouncer showed Babu and Paras through the door.

I looked at them, surprised. The fever made me sluggish. I realised there was no way they could have reached this place in twenty minutes after Pranay had made the phone call.

"You reached here quite early!" I said to Babu. "And why is Mr Kapoor with you?"

Paras stepped forward and said, "You bastard! You bastard!"

Babu was cold and asked me, "We were already on our way here when Pranay called me. Leo is *dead*?"

"Yeah. In the garden. But why were you on your way here?"

Babu called two junior cops standing outside to stay with me, and went to examine the body with Paras and Vinod. A few bewildering moments passed before they returned. Babu observed my discarded clothes and remarked, "You were found with blood on your clothes."

"Yeah. And with my fingers around the knife. What is going on?"

"You are under arrest for the murders of Anjali and Leo, and on suspicion of involvement in Anil's murder too."

"What!" Pranay was nonplussed.

I looked into Babu's eyes and realised he was serious. I groaned and took some sips from the bottle, while everyone stood around silently.

I collected my thoughts and asked him, "You obviously have some proof?"

Paras interrupted, "We know you did it along with her. I will make you rot in hell for the rest of your life... bastard."

He was trembling with rage.

"You have a driving licence?" said Babu.

"Yes."

"Can I see it?"

I handed him my wallet. He took out my licence, glanced at it, and handed me a piece of paper from his pocket. It was a photocopy of my licence, with my signature on it.

He said, "We tracked the last calls Anjali received at the zoo. Between eleven and one. There were only two numbers she had called, and received calls from. One was your original number, and the other was the one that you activated last night.

"The SIM for the second one was bought from a shop near your house. The shopkeeper told me that he checked the original licence before taking the photocopy. The license is with you. That means you had that SIM on you. I wonder why you didn't tell us you had two numbers."

"Because I don't. The license was flicked from me earlier, and and planted in my wallet this evening. What else have you got?"

"You were right. There were no signs of struggle on Shalini at the site of Anjali's murder. The only person who showed signs of struggle was you. Your face was scratched, and your trousers were torn," added Paras.

"That was because I got into a fight with a man named Abhijit this morning. What else have you got?"

"That's why you knew exactly what happened!" Paras exploded. "Aditi called you to the farmhouse. You must have reached early and broken the lock yourself. You wanted to disgrace my family. That's why you befriended Anjali and murdered her. That is why you told Babu to place us under house arrest tonight, so that you could come here and murder Leo. You were destroying my family."

He was a man possessed with rage.

"Motive?" I asked.

"You couldn't stand it. Aditi with Sunil. You wanted to take revenge on her family because she ditched you three years ago."

I laughed loudly. "So I murdered three people, and tried to frame your son, because I resented someone's happiness?"

Paras motioned to Babu, who came forward with a pair of handcuffs. He looked at me with distrust.

"Aditi is a very beautiful woman. We have the SIM registered in your name, with the original document in your wallet. And Mr Kapoor has reason to believe that you found the missing twenty-five crores. That is why you wanted to meet Leo alone. You are under arrest."

In spite of the circumstances, I admired the murderer's master stroke. I panicked as I suddenly realised how easily he had incriminated me. And, if I didn't do something fast, he would get away with it. Babu put the handcuffs on me and Pranay.

"Why are you arresting him?"

"Accessory to murder."

My head felt heavy, and the fever was making me drowsy. This was no time to play sick. I tried to concentrate. I needed to get Abhijit. He had the CD. If it was destroyed, I was screwed. I knew that the murderer would personally collect the CD from Abhijit, and then murder him. With Abhijit gone, there was no way I could prove my innocence. It was his sweet revenge. I had jeopardised his original plan to frame Shalini. I was amazed at his foresight and his moves. This was check mate.

I tried anyway.

"Babu, you can arrest us and keep us in custody, but I request you to send someone to intercept Abhijit. The murderer is at the Kapoor residence. Abhijit has a CD with him that—"

"Shut up!" Paras thundered. "Inspector, enough is enough. I am going to have you transferred to the saddest place in the state if you don't stop listening to him and put him away."

Babu motioned that I should be silent. I remembered the CD that showed Reena with Abhijit.

I said to Pranay, "Where's the CD that has Reena and Abhijit?"

He realised what was on my mind and said excitedly, "It is still in the car."

I turned around and said with conviction, "Babu, I have a CD in the car. It has Reena with that man, Abhijit. I would like to show it to you. It will take two minutes."

Paras interrupted again, "Reena? You stay away from my family, you bastard. Enough is enough. Babu, I demand—"

Babu interrupted Paras, "It will take only two minutes, sir. I think he is entitled to that much."

Minutes later we stood in the rain, looking at the broken glass of the car window. Abhijit had taken the CD with him.

Paras said accusingly to Babu, "Have you wasted enough time? Should I call the commissioner and tell him you are biased towards a murderer?"

Babu shook his head. "No, sir. We are going non-stop to the police station now."

I sighed, aware that in half an hour Abhijit would be dead, the CD lost, and I would rot in prison. He had committed a perfect murder, or rather murders. He would collect the CD from Abhijit, and after murdering him, plant part of the money in my apartment. I needed a miracle to get out of this one.

Pranay and I were ushered into the back of a jeep by the two cops escorting us. The driver started the jeep and drove towards the gate. Paras and Babu followed us in another jeep.

I felt a surge of panic when I saw Pranay in cuffs. The jeep moved out of the gate. I closed my eyes, giving in to the demands of the fever, trying to blank out and worry later. Then I heard a shout. The jeep stopped suddenly. I opened my eyes to see an ashen Pranay looking terrified. Babu was running towards our jeep. He came nearer, and instructed one of the cops to get out and take his place in the other jeep. He took off our cuffs and ordered the driver to go to Apollo Hospital.

Before I could ask him what was going on, he said, "Mr Kapoor got a call. Shalini is in hospital. She tried to commit suicide. She left a note saying she murdered Anil and Anjali. To hell with Paras sir. I want to hear your theory now."

I smiled. Not even the murderer could have predicted this one.

"Finally," I said to Babu. "Before I tell you what happened, I want your men to pick up Abhijit, along with this guy called Thapa. Here's his card. Tell your men to bring both of them to Apollo right away."

We reached the hospital half an hour later. We were in the lift, on our way to the ICU, when Babu received a call on his mobile phone. The police had caught Abhijit fifteen kilometres away from Kandhari Hills. He had two CDs, and two crores cash, in his possession. His clothes had been covered with blood, and he had fought like a wild dog resisting his arrest.

Sunil's expression froze when he saw us get out of the lift. He looked concerned and ran towards Paras, who could barely walk. He held the visibly shocked Paras in his arms and said consolingly, "She will be okay, Dad. She will be okay."

Dad gave a vacant, disoriented look to Sunil, and that worried Sunil further.

"She's okay, Dad! The doctors were able to make her vomit up the pills. She will live."

Dad still didn't register any emotion, and walked towards the bench next to the coffee machine. Sunil looked at Babu and asked, "What's happened to him? Is he all right? And why haven't you arrested Vishal yet?"

Babu stepped forward and said, "You said you found a suicide note. Can we see it?"

"Sure. It's with Vimal."

Vimal was walking across the corridor, with two cups of coffee in his hand. He looked at Paras approaching the bench, gauged that something was wrong, grew concerned, and walked towards him.

"The inspector wants to see the suicide note," Sunil told Vimal.

Vimal took it out from his pocket and handed it to Babu, who glanced at it and handed it to me.

It read, *I murdered Anil and Anjali. Both of them are free. Please let them go*. It was signed by Shalini.

Sunil said angrily to Babu, "Why did you hand the note to him? Are you crazy? Why hasn't he been arrested yet?

"I never believed for once that he was guilty," Babu responded with conviction. "I got...carried away. And what do you want me to arrest him for? This note proves his innocence. And, as usual, he has a theory that explains everything."

Aditi and Reena had escorted Mayank towards us. Ram was standing in a corner.

I asked Sunil, "What do you think Shalini means by *both of them are free*, in the note?"

"What?" He sounded confused.

"What do you think she means by *both of them are free*?" I repeated.

"Well, she means Rajesh and ... you, of course. It was a conspiracy." He looked around for support. "That's it, isn't it? He had taken a new phone connection and...and he did it for the missing twenty-five crores. What's going on? Dad?"

I asked Vimal, "What do you think she means when she says *both of them are free*?"

He thought for a moment, and replied slowly, "I think Shalini could be referring to Mayank and Rajesh. It couldn't be you. For starters, you haven't spent enough time with her. And obviously, since you are standing here, you have managed to convince Babu that you are innocent."

I looked at Sunil and said, "Your brother is absolutely correct. That is why Shalini has been acting guilty. At some level, she believes that she is actually guilty of both the murders."

"What's going on?" Sunil repeated.

"Shalini believes that Mayank murdered Anil. She believes it, I guess, because, the actual murderer created circumstances that made Mayank appear guilty...maybe spilt some blood on his clothes the next morning, after murdering Anil. That would explain her nervousness at the farmhouse.

"She planted Leo's locket at the back gate to throw suspicions off her father. But Reena saw her throwing the locket outside the window. Shalini panicked, and confided in Rajesh, and that explains his SMS to her. He was trying to help her.

"After Reena confronted Shalini about the locket, Shalini became paranoid, convinced that we were laying a trap for Mayank. That is why she made sure I couldn't talk to Mayank this morning, by giving him sleep-inducing tablets.

"Here comes the interesting part. After Anil's murder, Shalini was in a highly vulnerable state. That is what the murderer was counting on, to make her believe that Rajesh had murdered Anjali. In her distress, she believed that both the men who loved her were sacrificing their happiness to protect her.

She believed that Mayank had murdered Anil to bring an end to the daily torture inflicted upon her; and Rajesh had murdered Anjali to protect Mayank, for her sake. And that,

Sunil, explains the note. Shalini was referring to Mayank and Rajesh. She really believes that Mayank murdered Anil, and Rajesh murdered Anjali."

They were looking at me. I took the cup of coffee Vimal was holding, had a sip, and continued, "The murderer planned the entire thing on Saturday evening. I knew that the call from Anil to Leo referring to a jackpot, and his murder the same night had to be connected. I never believe in coincidences. But Shalini's culpable behaviour distracted me.

"The murderer planned a flawless murder. He broke the lock at the back gate, to make it look like a villager's job. If I hadn't arrived at the scene, the police would have gone on a wild goose chase in the village. But the murderer was a compulsive planner. He doubtless realized that something was amiss, and decided to keep a backup, in case the police found clues.

"Mayank was the perfect person for a frame-up. He took sleeping pills, and would not remember a thing in the morning. The murderer's foresight was rewarded, as we were able to prove that there was no villager involved at all. Not that he had much to worry about. He had a second backup in case Mayank was proved innocent, or Shalini did not play as per his plan. The second back-up was Sunil."

"What!" Sunil and Aditi cried in unison.

"The knife used to murder Anil was the same one Sunil had chased Anil with; and the cigarettes found at the scene of Anjali's murder, the same brand that Sunil smokes. They were deliberately planted. He must have been furious when I proved that Shalini couldn't have been at the zoo when Anjali was murdered. And, he knew I didn't suspect Sunil. I let him know I had found him out.

"I got complacent, assuming that there was not much he could do, since Babu had instructed his men to restrict your family's movements tonight. He knew where I would be; I had mentioned that at the zoo. He planned quickly and instructed Abhijit, probably over the phone, to murder Leo and frame me by planting some money in my apartment. He would have later murdered Abhijit too.

"The plan was perfect. With the CD in his custody, Abhijit out of the way, and the money planted in my apartment, he would have got away with the crime.

"Everything went as per his plan and I got arrested, but Shalini ruined it for him by trying to commit suicide and leaving behind a suicide note. One can't predict everything, can they Vimal?"

The accusation hung in the air, and the people around me expressed their astonishment and indignation. Vimal's only reply was raised eyebrows. He was a cool customer, as I had expected him to be.

Paras stared at his son. "Vimal, Vishal has a theory that you murdered Anil, because you were being blackmailed by Anil."

"That's absurd, Dad!" said Vimal calmly.

"What!" Reena appeared appalled.

"Dad!" exclaimed Vimal. "How can you say such a thing? Especially after the copy of his license was found?"

"That was flicked by you," I said, "when you handed me the wallet at Leo's apartment."

"Is this a joke? Dad, what's going on?" said Sunil.

I continued, "Anil was blackmailing Vimal. Vimal and Reena were part of a couple-swapping circuit. Anil and Leo came to know about it. They had some proof – most probably a CD, and they started blackmailing them. Anil must have asked for five crores to withhold the secret from Mr Kapoor and the rest of the family.

"Vimal paid Anil the money, and Anil promised the leave the country with Leo on Thursday. That accounts for the five crores found in his apartment. What Anil didn't know was where the five crores came from. It was Vimal who had forged the signatures. He had posed as Anil, facilitated the entire deal, and made the payment to Anil from the thirty crores paid to him by Thapa, on behalf of Asrani.

"Vimal knew that Anil was leaving the country for good on Thursday. He insisted that Asrani transfer the white component directly to the company's account on or after Thursday. Anil would have left the country by then, and everyone would have assumed that Anil had committed forgery just like he had done in the past, and then eloped with Leo, taking the cash with him.

"Everything was going as per Vimal's plan, but some of the investors came to know about the Asrani deal, and sent goons to the house to recover their money on Saturday evening. Sunil reacted instantly, accusing Anil of the forgery. Anil was smart enough to put two and two together, and realised how Vimal had managed to arrange five crores. Anil didn't expose Vimal; instead, he started blackmailing Vimal on two counts.

"My guess is that Anil demanded a substantial amount of the money, if not the entire amount, from the remaining twenty-five crores. He threatened Vimal that not only would he blow the lid off his and Reena's sexual adventures, but also inform Mr Kapoor of the forgery."

Everyone was looking at Vimal and Reena. Reena's face was exceedingly vulnerable, but Vimal showed no signs of panic or alarm. His naturalness was in itself unnatural.

I addressed Vimal. "The police are on their way, with Abhijit. They found the CDs, and two crores in his car. I believe you instructed him to plant the money in my apartment. Mr Thapa is on his way here to identify him. It's over, Vimal and Reena. You better own up."

Vimal's face looked disconcerted for the first time upon hearing Thapa's name. Reena had paled, her lower lip trembling.

Paras spoke up. "It's true, isn't it, Vimal?"

Vimal's expression changed from smooth and urbane to something very ugly. He launched forward and said to me, "That's an interesting fairly tale. Do you have any proof?"

He tried to smile, trying to hide his panic and get back in control. The doors of the lift opened, as if on cue. The police escorted a terrified Thapa, and a defeated Abhijit, towards us.

"No, this isn't a fairy tale. Fairy tales have happy endings. This one won't."

A cop handed two CDs to Babu, along with a bag. Babu opened the zip, and showed the money to everyone.

I put my arm around Thapa's shoulder reassuringly. "Thanks for coming, Thapa. We need you to identify this man."

"What's this about? I don"t know about any black money. It"s between Asrani and Kapoor. I am just an employee. I want my lawyer."

"Relax. I am sure Mr Asrani would be touched by your loyalty. However, we are not interested in the cash. We are investigating a murder. All we want you to do is identity this man. His name is Abhijit. Do you know him?"

Abhijit stared threateningly at Thapa and, for a moment, Thapa seemed nervous. Babu stepped forward and slapped Abhijit so hard that blood started trickling down his lips.

Thapa shrieked, "Yes, I know him! The one with the goatee and grey eyes! He was the CFO who met me on behalf of Anil Kapoor. He handed the agreement to me and collected the cash."

I held the CDs before Vimal and Reena.

"I have already seen the one titled *R*, so I know who's starring in it. I bet the second one was taken from Leo this evening, and has Vimal in the cast too. That's what it was all about, wasn't it? Anil was blackmailing both of you because he had a CD that showed one or both of you indulging in sex with different partners. But you wouldn't have murdered him just for that. After he found out about the forgery, you couldn't risk him exposing you in front of Mr Kapoor. Ever. Not to forget, twenty-five crores is a huge amount."

Paras's voice quivered, "Is it true?"

Vimal muttered a weak no.

I continued, "When Anil told Leo to postpone their tickets, and demanded more money, you realised that he would be a perennial risk. That's why you decided to murder Anil on Saturday. When Leo heard that the police suspected one of the family members, he realised what must have happened. He started blackmailing you, but unlike Anil he was smart enough to use Anjali as insurance.

"You were supposed to pay him the money tonight, or he would have exposed you to the press. Leo would never have imagined that you would murder Anjali too. With Anjali dead, you decided to close the chapter by having Abhijit murder Leo, framing me, and then murdering Abhijit himself."

Abhijit looked at Vimal and Reena, and shouted, "What! What is he talking about?"

Vimal tried to pacify him. "Relax. He is just—"

"Fuck you. Is that why you wanted to meet me alone at the farmhouse?" He looked at me and shouted, "I have nothing to do with any murder! I am innocent! Fuck them! I will testify. I will—"

"Shut up," hissed Vimal.

"Oh, I don't think you are innocent," I intervened. "The blood on your T-shirt would match Leo's. You murdered Leo this evening. Also, I saw you handing the bag to Reena at the parking lot. You are Leo's murderer, and an accessory to the murders of Anil and Anjali."

He broke down.

"Shit, shit, shit! Both of them used me. I didn't want ... I am not a murderer. They promised me money ..."

"I think we should play the CD now," I said to Babu.

"I will ask someone from the administration to get a laptop. Or we could—" began Babu.

"That will not be necessary," said Vimal, interrupting him. "Please don't play it in front of Dad. It's not suitable."

Paras broke down upon hearing these words from Vimal. Reena had tears of mortification in her eyes. She mumbled something to him.

He replied calmly, "It's okay, baby. I take full responsibility for the murders of Anil and Anjali. Abhijit murdered Leo. Reena was not directly involved in any of the murders."

Abhijit charged at him. 'You bastard!'

Two cops held him back, while he shouted vile abuses at Vimal and Reena. Babu looked at Paras, and signalled to a cop to arrest Vimal and Reena. Vimal put his hands behind his back, stared at me, and asked, "How did you know?"

"I knew that only one thing could have gone wrong for Anil's murder at the farmhouse. If the party extended outdoors to the lawn, or to the beach, there was always the risk of someone walking towards the back gate and finding the lock already broken. You couldn't risk that happening. If the lock had been found broken, Anil would have immediately become suspicious of you. So, being the meticulous planner that you are, I was sure you would have found a way of ensuring that the party stayed indoors.

"When I got to the farmhouse, my first question was whether the party had extended outdoors. Mr Kapoor replied that it hadn't, since Reena had been running a high fever the previous evening. She seemed perfectly fine to me the next day. Later I came to know, from Malti and Mr Kapoor, that Reena and Aditi had gone to play tennis at the club the evening Anil was found murdered. That means the fever came and vanished in an evening. That was too much of a coincidence.

"When I saw her collecting a bag from Abhijit at the club, I knew she was involved. You made your mistake, Vimal."

"What was that?"

"Anil was stabbed in the heart with a single, powerful blow. The murderer had to be a man. If Reena was involved with the missing cash, you were my suspect; naturally. But then today, I became sure. Anjali was struck from behind, on the left side of her head. Again, it was a single blow."

I walked up to Babu, stood behind him, and swung my left hand pretending to hit him on his head.

"You see, I am right-handed, and I had to use my left hand to get a proper arc and enough force to hit him on the left side of his head, as Anjali had been struck. I would have to criss-cross my shoulder if I tried to do it with my right hand. So the murderer had a powerful left hand – someone who could bring Leo to his knees with a single, left-handed punch. You should have let Leo pass that day, Vimal. You are left handed, aren't you?"

Babu said, "Oh... is that why you used your left hand when you pretended to strike me at the zoo?

"Yes. And that is the same reason I made you pretend to drown the cop. A right-handed person would hold the neck with his strong arm, and use his left arm to hold the right leg of the victim. A more impactful posture for drowning someone. But the tear in Anjali's skirt was on her left leg. That meant the murderer had used his left hand to hold her neck, while immersing her under the water. And that was a fatal flaw."

A nurse appeared and stammered, "You... you ... are with Shalini Kapoor?"

No one seemed to be in a right state of mind to respond to her query, so I said, "Yes."

"The patient is conscious now."

Across the horizon, the day was coming to an end. I jerked to a stop as Bruno stopped abruptly, and sat down on the ground for the umpteenth time. He hated walking. He looked back longingly towards the apartment. I tugged at his leash, but he stayed put. We had covered exactly four hundred metres from my apartment. I pointed to the boundary of the park that was visible from his position, and encouraged him in canine language.

"Good boy. There. Only ten more steps. Then food time."

His ears perked up on hearing the word *food*, and his resolve weakened momentarily. I took the opportunity to tug at his leash to get him back on his feet.

The park was buzzing with the idiosyncratic activity of a Sunday evening. A toddler jumped in front of me from behind a pile of discarded leaves. He pointed at my head and started speaking gibberish. Happy gibberish. It took me a few seconds to comprehend that he was fascinated by the bandages on my head. I think he wanted to touch the bandages. I was just bending my head forward to oblige him, when his mother appeared and dragged him away, eyeing me suspiciously.

I looked around the park, and saw her sitting alone on a bench near the far end. I started walking towards her. She was looking at some kids playing. She seemed engrossed in their antics, and didn't notice when a small wayward leaf landed on her head. A few strands of her hair were blown aside softly by the breeze, and her eyes were lost in thought. With her timeless beauty and aura of mystery, she could have been a statue placed on the bench. It was exactly a week since I had got her call and started working on the case. It seemed like an eternity.

She did not notice me until I was standing next to her.

"Hi. Did I keep you waiting?" I interrupted her trance.

"No. Thanks for coming on such short notice."

"No sweat. I live just around the corner, and a little walk is good for the dog."

She looked down at Bruno. He exhibited a surge of activity, anomalous to his nature, and charged forward excitedly, jumping all over Aditi.

She laughed. "Oh my! He's a friendly dog! I thought you didn't like pets."

"I still don't. He was incidental."

"Incidental?"

"I had no choice. Had to keep him."

Aditi stood up. Bruno put his paws on her midriff, licking her with his tongue.

"What's his name?"

"Bruno."

"Sit, Bruno!" she ordered, and then said to me, "Funny, he reminds me of the Bruno we picked up from the dhaba on the highway. He was the same colour. Such a long time ago."

She stopped patting him suddenly, looked up; and said half-amused, half-serious, "I just had a crazy thought. It can't be the same Bruno, can it?"

"Why can't it be the same Bruno?"

She stood up again and looked at me attentively. "You are joking, right?"

"Don't have a sense of humour when it comes to dogs."

"How is that possible? I thought he was ..."

"Dead? Well, he is not dead. But as you see, he is *as fit as a piddle*, if that counts."

She looked at Bruno and ran her hand over his coat. "It is him! How did you make him change cities?"

"He flew. Cost a bomb at that time. But I couldn't let him be there all alone. It was ... a promise. Your promise to him."

She looked at me, then at Bruno, then misty-eyed she said, "Thank you."

"For?"

"I don't know. He was my responsibility and I ... I just feel guilty about it. I can breathe easy now that I know he is safe and sound."

Bruno was acting crazy jumping all over her.

"Do you think he recognises me?"

"You can bet on it. This is the first time I have seen him use his hind legs. I think he wants to play with you."

She smiled, interfering with my breathing, as she followed Bruno to the grass. She kicked off her sandals and dodged him as he chased her. The sun was setting. Men in the park looked at her in amazement, mesmerised by her beauty. They would not forget this moment for a long time. Neither would I. The case was solved, the murderer was in jail, and I had twenty-five lakhs in cash, lying in my apartment. Yet, I felt strangely unfulfilled.

She was a quagmire that would never let me go. Would I stop loving her? Probably not. Would I love anyone else like

I loved her? Probably not. Did I hate her because she had dumped me? Definitely not.

A woman as beautiful as her had a right to be selfish: getting unsolicited attention and approval from males all her life, being admired for her looks everywhere she went. How could she turn out any different? Among the scores of men, who had been affected and haunted by her beauty, I was a more fortunate one. At least, I had been able to chase an impossible dream. I had always known in my heart that she was not destined to be an ordinary spouse; to run a household, juggle a career and children. She was cut out for the finer things in life – bungalows, travel, gowns, imported cars, diamonds, and a life of luxury. Our lives could have never converged. She would go back to her affluence, and I would get back to my ordinary existence, living each day as it came.

She called out to me to join her. Bruno was running all around her, with no trace of past hurt. I guess both of us couldn't learn to hate her.

The sun had set. People were returning home. The case was closed. There was no need of maintaining further contact with her.

She shouted delightedly, "Vishal, come here."

She was sitting on the grass, laughing like a kid, while Bruno still ran around her in circles. I could think of a thousand reasons to decline her invitation, put Bruno on a leash, and bid her farewell. And never see her again. Instead, I got up and started walking towards her ... towards the perpetual emotional ambush called Aditi. What the heck, you are born to die anyway.